FEARFUL CITIES

Emily McCombs

Martin Sisters Publishing

Published by
Martin Sisters Publishing, LLC
www. martinsisterspublishing. com
Copyright © 2012 Emily McCombs
Martin Sisters Publishing, LLC, Kentucky.
ISBN: 978-1-62553-024-0
Editor: Brittani Wolanin
Fantasy
Printed in the United States of America
Martin Sisters Publishing, LLC

~ For my grandfather,
because without him this novel
wouldn't be in your hands.

Chapter 1

Dimitri trailed behind Cynric, purposefully scooting his feet as to make more noise than necessary. "So, what's the plan all mighty one." His voice dripped with sarcasm.

"Right now, the plan is to get you back to the apartment before we are all exposed due to your carelessness. Honestly brother, do you not hold an ounce of decency in your bones? Surely all of the demon characteristics did not fall on me."

He smiled, knowing he'd fooled his brother again. Every night, around eight or nine o'clock, Dimitri would leave the apartment and say he was going to Razor's--a local bar where demons could hang out and mix casually with humans. Truth be told, he would either go to one of the city's art museums or a bookstore. Although his brother thought he was just a stupid drunk, Dimitri would rather he think badly of him, than destroy him for being too human. Something he was quite capable of doing.

Cynric didn't understand his actions, which were based on emotions rather than vengeance. To him, humanity was something they both lost a long time ago, something they couldn't get back. He had everything he could possibly want and more; fast cars, flashy houses, tons of money, and power. Every creature was insignificant

5

in comparison and was only associated with when deemed useful in his eyes. Cynric had lost more than his humanity, he'd lost his soul.

His brother stopped, spinning around to face him. "Are you going to stop doing that," He pointed at his feet, "Or am I going to be forced to chop off your feet?" Cynric's eyes looked fierce in the dim light cast by the clouded moon.

Dimitri thought for a moment, trying to think of a good excuse to go back the way they'd came. He settled for the semi-truth. "I told you I wasn't ready to leave yet. The bartender was getting ready to give me her number and I haven't eaten today." He swallowed hard, trying to forget the sound of beating hearts. It was torture going an entire day without eating, but he didn't want to hunt innocent people. Most of his traits portrayed him as a very mundane creature, but the hunger transformed him into the monster he wished to destroy. Emotions meant nothing while in hunting mode. He would have to kill someone soon, even though it would cost him a bit of humanity. He felt the ice form over his heart when he made the decision to go back. He stopped thinking about it.

"In that case, feel free to go back at any time." Cynric lowered his voice slightly, although it still held a hint of anger. His hand waved into the air around them as if to say 'go on.'

Dimitri turned, letting his hands fall lightly to his sides as he walked toward the ever-hungry beast that beckoned him to accept his true nature.

Cynric sighed after his brother was out of sight, "I do not understand why I even bother trying with him." Suddenly realizing the late hour, he opened the door and proceeded up the stairs to the apartment. Once inside, Cynric headed straight for the hidden office and threw himself into the chair behind his large oak desk.

The room wasn't large, there was barely enough room to breathe. Dark, wood paneled walls incased the green carpet, and the onyx demon lamp cast an eerie glow over every surface. It may not have been the comfiest place, but it had been home for the last seven months.

Knowing he must wait a little longer before setting his plan in motion, Cynric decided to iron out a few last minute details. As he filed through some papers on his desk, he came across an old picture of him and his father-- rather the demon that turned him and Dimitri into demons. His mind went back to the day it was taken. Modric had just bought him a new truck. The two stood in front of it, while Dimitri snapped the photo. It was one of the happiest memories he had with him, and one of the few times he saw his father smile. Cynric laid the picture in a drawer, knowing if he stared at it for too long he would get emotional, which he desperately tried to avoid. In his eyes, emotions led to being helpless, and he needed to be stronger than that. Besides, his brother was emotional enough for the entire demonic race.

It was disgusting to see his own brother living like a mortal. Modric had tried everything to get Dimitri to change. He put him in hell for fifty years, hoping it would drive him into fighting for the demons of earth. When that didn't work, he began sending him out on missions in order to boost his powers and let him get out all his love for humanity. Needless to say, that didn't work either. Now Modric was dead and Dimitri used his death as an excuse to drink.

"UGHH..." Cynric yelled, throwing his fists down on the desk. It shuddered from the blow, placing another dent in the wood. *Humph...cheap piece of junk.* He made a mental note to get a new one before returning to their castle in Moliston, which sat in the heart of the Bermuda Triangle. Covered in geysers, molten lava, and active volcanoes, the island made a great home for the Akassa brothers. Their inherited castle was quite large, seeming to protrude straight from the black rock below. Cynric missed it desperately. There, they could at least eat a more balanced diet. In the mortal world, they were forced to be inconspicuous, which drove him crazy. Demons weren't meant to be caged up in tacky apartment buildings, only eating under the cover of darkness. January wouldn't come fast enough.

The clock struck eleven, signaling the night was half over. His friends would be returning to Camp Demon--the abandoned warehouse where he housed all his soldiers-- and he needed to speak with them. With no time to waste, Cynric grabbed the passports and called for his house goblin, Gemedes- a short creature with little hair, tan colored skin, and wrinkles showing his age. He was the only one who could slip into the warehouse and retrieve the two without being noticed by humans. Jamik and Arriann were Cynric's best and tonight they would be rewarded. These two made up one of the keys to his entire plan. The other would arrive shortly.

Gemedes heard his name being called from the other side of the apartment. *This is it;* he thought with a grin, *the time has come for my months of work to pay off. Tonight I will finally find out the plan.* He walked down the hall, trying not to show enthusiasm and opened the hidden door to the youngest Akassa brother's office.

Cynric was seated in his wing backed chair. His smile contrasted with the soft green velvet, and his enticing emerald eyes mirrored the gems lining the entire seat. He looked eager, triumphant.

"You called me your majesty." Gemedes hated calling him that, he was a monster, not a prince, and definitely not his king.

"Ahh, there you are. Please come in, I need you to do something for me Gomez." Cynric smiled.

Gemedes flared with anger, *how could he still get my name wrong?* He had worked for this thing for six months now. His real king requested he become a spy for the council and offer his services to the Akassa brothers. Although it caused him misery to work for these abominations, he agreed and arrived here in April, one month after Cynric and Dimitri moved to Chicago.

Cynric still smiled but not quite as nicely, he was waiting for a reply. Gemedes had a tendency to get distracted easily.

"Er. Yes anything you ask sire." He kneeled.

"Go and retrieve Arriann and Jamik. I have matters to discuss with them."

"Yes, sire. I will." He glanced around quickly, trying to find an excuse to stay in the room when he got back from his quest. Spotting the dusty bookshelf he added, "And if I may, I will return and clean those bookshelves behind your desk, they look filthy."

He knew Cynric would never let him stay in the room, not when they were discussing his plans, but it was worth a shot. Either way, he had a strategy to catch the majority of the plans. If this didn't work, he would hide in the fake plant outside the door and listen with a cup.

Cynric answered, cutting into his thoughts, "Oh, I was meaning to ask you to do that yesterday but tonight is good too." He returned his gaze to the piles of papers and blueprints on his desk after shooing Gemedes away with the wave of his hand.

Hurrying out of the room and grabbing his thick, black cape from the hook on the wall, Gemedes stepped out onto the silent city street. He mentally formulated a checklist. First, retrieve the boneheads for Cynric, then, return and complete his second, although more important, job. Frankly, he couldn't figure out why Cynric would let him clean while he discussed his plans, just maybe he had played his part better than expected.

*

"Where do you think you're going?" A small voice pierced Dimitri's ears as he walked toward 5th Avenue. *What was she thinking coming up on a strange man in the middle of the night? Perhaps she thought he was someone else.*

He stopped and glared at her, "Look, I don't know who you…"

His words were suddenly cut off by the growling animal inside of him, it raged to be let loose. Be able to feed on this innocent woman's flesh. Quickly, Dimitri forced himself to finish. "Who you are, but I'm just trying to get home so if you would be so kind?" He pushed past her, trying to make a run for it, or rather trying to run away from what he was about to do.

Soft, delicate hands grabbed his arm, twisting him around so he was facing her again. "I don't think so, you see I saw you talking to that man and I heard you say you were hungry." She smiled seductively, "I can give you what you want."

The monster rattled the cage within, trying to find an opening. Dimitri looked away, "No. I am going home and you are going to go back to wherever it is you came from alright? I need nothing from you and I require nothing from you. Now move!" He shoved her down, which was a really bad idea, because as soon as her body

9

smacked the pavement, tiny drops of crimson seeped from the scratches the asphalt had made. The monster wailed in excitement and overpowering lust. He had to run away or eat.

Moments passed and she never moved, he could hear her heartbeat, see her eyes staring up into his, but she wouldn't dare make a sound. Taking careful precautions not to breath in, Dimitri found a few bandages in the woman's bag. He quietly tended to her wounds, helped her up, and pointed for her to go. But, she never moved. Her eyes stayed trained on his and soundless words passed between them.

She said, 'I'm not going anywhere until you tell me why.'

Then he said, 'It's complicated and you wouldn't believe me.'

'Try me.'

"Fine. I'm a demon. You heard me talking to my brother earlier about being hungry and wanting to feed, well the food I eat isn't human food. Alright, technically it is, because I eat humans, but…"

Her scream pierced the night, making his gut twist with the uncomfortable urge to silence his meal. He grabbed her throat, forcing her to swallow against the inside of his hand. "I don't want to kill you. God knows I don't want to, but don't you see, it won't let me win." Her body struggled against his, making the beast writhe with anticipation. Dimitri's voice slipped into his seductive tone, making him irresistible to humans. "Shhh…don't be afraid, I won't let him hurt you my sweet." His hands caressed the side of her face, she whimpered in protest, tears welling up in her eyes.

This was it, the monster had broken loose and now another innocent life would suffer. It was his fault, all his fault. Demon teeth replaced his human teeth as he tore into her fragile flesh, blood swimming down his relieved throat. It was like pouring battery acid into an unhealed wound for him. His humanity screamed for him to stop, but it was too late, the girl was dead. Her body was lifeless in his arms and the night was silent once again.

After gathering her valuables, Dimitri threw the girl into Lake Michigan, cleaned his hands and face, and walked silently back to the apartment. His midnight snack already just another haunting memory.

*

Arriann entered the room, followed by Jamik. Gemedes came in last, heading straight for the bookshelves and beginning to clean immediately. He knew he'd be kicked out if he didn't stay busy.

Cynric turned and looked straight at them, "Both of you come in and sit down." He gestured toward the empty chairs, which were fire proofed after an accident in the later part of June; demons like Jamik flamed up easily.

That night, the two appeared as humans. Arriann sported her usual grunge look, complete with blonde dreadlocks, black tights, and long black boots. Jamik dressed more chic; contrasting his spiky blue hair with a pair of designer boots, grey denim jeans, a black leather jacket, and a white button down shirt. Of course neither ensemble came close to their original demon forms. As a Dybbuk demon-- meaning half-werewolf, half-dragon--Jamik could breathe fire, run extremely fast, and fly. His partner on the other hand was what historians considered a transfer demon. She could take form as any living creature, even ones she imagined. Together, they produced one unstoppable team, though they weren't the only monsters within the city limits.

Gemedes wondered how the humans didn't get suspicious. He thought with the constant disappearances, at least some of them would get caught. Then again, he had noticed many new things about his new employers; how well they hid their eating habits was the least of his worries.

"Alright, I am sure you both realize why I called you here," Cynric started, snapping the goblin back to attention. "You two are the best I have and you never let me down. With that said, please realize what I am asking of you will test your abilities and it will be equally boring as well. Are you up for it?" He paused looking them both up and down.

Arriann was the first to speak, as usual, "We are always willing to do your bidding Lord Cynric, just tell us what you need; right Jamik?" She nudged him in the rib, a little harder than necessary.

Gagging, Jamik looked at Cynric. "Yes, as Arriann said," he cast an evil glare in her direction before continuing, "We are always willing to do anything you ask, when you ask."

Cynric bowed his head slightly, then proceeded to hand them each a passport. "You are going overseas. I have arranged for a private jet to take you in exactly four hours. Gomez will take you to the airport."

Both demons grabbed their passports and looked at Cynric laughing nervously. "You can't be serious; we're going to the home of the Asparas fairies? Don't you know what they do to our kind?"

Then Jamik added, "A friend of mine went over there on a routine mission for you and I never heard from him again. Is that what you want, our death?" He stared at Cynric waiting for a reply.

Laughing, the king replied, "Yes, that is exactly what I wanted. My two best fighters to leave on a dangerous mission and never return." He paused shaking his head, "Your friend, as you call him, was killed only because he didn't stay focused on the task I gave him. Let's just say he wanted to try some international cuisine and the fairies jumped all over him. I am sending you two for this reason; I know you will do only what I ask. Correct?"

They looked at each other and nodded.

Cynric continued with his plan, "The King needed to iron out a few peace negotiations in Japan." With a roll of his deep green eyes he began laughing. "You will make sure he remains in Japan until I send word for you to release him, which won't be until after the war has started in his homeland. Hold him hostage or something; I don't care as long as he stays out of my way. Do you understand?"

"Yes sir we understand, but won't Aislinn get a message to him, asking for help?" Arriann asked.

"Don't worry about her, I have a plan-"

"You always have a plan," Jamik interrupted, "but this is the King's daughter. How could you possibly keep her in the dark? Let me send a few of the new guys I have been training, they are really something."

Arriann laughed heartily beside him, "Yeah, if you mean

something to destroy. Those two are nothing but a couple of idiots. They would get themselves killed and the entire army exposed. No way! Cynric can handle that problem himself."

"Don't underestimate my powers Jamik! I am well aware of whom she is but she is no match for my brother." Then with a nod Cynric added, "However, my plan will never work without both of your cooperation. Do I have your word?"

They all stared at each other in silence for a moment before Cynric clapped his hands together and turned toward the bookshelf, "Gonzalez?"

Gemedes, shook his head in frustration, stopped cleaning, and raced to Cynric's side instantly. "Yes, sire?"

"Call the airport and make sure the plane is ready for departure. Then return my two companions to Camp Demon and see that they have all they need for their journ-"

Before he could finish, Arriann stood and stated, "We can gather our own weapons and such, and I would like some food before I travel. Could we have something big, like a butcher, and a travel agent on the side?" Both she and Jamik licked their lips in satisfaction.

Demons loved the taste of human flesh almost as much as they loved a good fight. The butcher would make a great entrée while the travel agent would complement as a magnificent side dish. Much like humans would pair steak and potatoes, demons paired large men and tiny women.

Cynric looked at her and they all started laughing before he turned back to Gemedes, "Yes, that sounds delicious go and fetch a butcher and a travel agent. I was beginning to get a little hungry myself."

On that final note, Gemedes dashed out of the room. "Well at least they didn't add a third course to the menu," he mumbled. As he left the laughter filled room once again. The search was on.

He was heading toward the butcher's shop on East Avenue, when he caught a glimpse of something out of the corner of his eye. Waiting to cross at the crosswalk he watched a man emerge from the shadows dressed in heavy layers of dark material too thick to be a normal coat. As the man neared where Gemedes was standing it became clear who the stranger was, Harlem.

Actually a better description would be the weirdest warlock who ever existed. He was tall, with pale skin and eyes that went from a fierce orange to lime green in the center. His hair, which was white to match the falling snow, always changed color based on the environment. Nevertheless, nothing could compare to his outfits. He wore a gray pinstriped shirt that was covered in black, velvet, swirling designs, black jeans, boots, and a large coat made of black bear fur. In addition to his usual attire was the jeweled cane he carried in his right hand. Shaped like a rattle snake, with two large rubies for eyes, it smacked the pavement as he crossed the street, sending waves of earthquake-like tremors under Gemedes's feet. He had to be the creepiest man in the entire supernatural world.

The closer he got, the more Gemedes wished he was not a goblin. As a goblin, he had to remain perfectly still in the presence of warlocks. He was glad there was only one in existence. *I wish old pumpkin eyes would go on by, every time I see him I want to carve him into a jack-o-lantern and dance in circles around his head,* he thought, then mumbled, "Then we'll see who's standing still."

Sooner than he expected, Harlem stood in front of him. "Good evening my young Gemedes. I trust you are keeping the Akassa brothers happy?" His Russian accent seeped through his words, making them all the more horrifying.

Gemedes regretted mumbling, he had a tendency to just say what was on his mind. Harlem didn't look unhappy, actually he looked quite funny. Most of the goblins on Roanke Island, thought he looked like a Halloween costume gone wrong. No matter how odd he looked, Gemedes was glad Harlem didn't hate him. His cousin Vex told him how Harlem had slaughtered a whole family of goblins once, making them stand still while he set each of them on fire. He was one man you didn't want to mess with.

"Well, are you going to just stand there and look at me? I know I am gorgeous," he flipped his head, "but stop wasting time and do what Cynric requested? You know he hates to wait." He looked at

Gemedes intensely before abruptly turning on his heels and sauntering toward the brother's apartment.

For a second Gemedes thought about what that could mean. Why would Harlem be going into the wicked brother of the east's apartment? He didn't let the thought of them working together enter his thoughts, because the war would be over before it began.

Quickly and as quietly as possible, Gemedes began running again, only to be distracted by a strange glow on one of the outside walls of the butcher shop. He slowed his pace and was standing in front of what looked like a black hole in the center of the brick, but he knew that if that were the case it would have just went straight into the shop. This hole looked like it lead to nowhere. Gemedes turned and was preparing to brush it off as his imagination-he did have a wild imagination- when a voice spoke to him.

"Gemedes, my friend," The voice sounded. "Please don't leave, it is me."

He knew that voice, but before he could say anything King Galiron soared a near six feet in the air beside him, wearing a look of deep appreciation with a hint of sternness. He looked Gemedes in the eyes and began speaking, "My old friend, how are things around Cynric's way?" There was a smirk on his face.

Gemedes was certain it was the first time he had ever seen him crack even a hint of a smile. "He is sending Arriann and Jamik to hold you hostage until the war starts, like you expected. Why must we go along with him sire, if you knew this is what he would do? I don't understand."

The King only nodded as if this news troubled him but didn't shock him. Actually, he seemed too calm about the entire ordeal. "I need to know Aislinn is ready to make decisions. You are doing exceptionally well at hiding our plans. Please know I am proud and honored to have you on our side. But wait before you warn the island of Cynric's plans. Try to find out as much as possible first." With that he disappeared along with the black hole. The butcher shop wall returned to normal as if nothing had happened.

Sighing, he rounded the corner to finish his task. Cynric was probably already in the process of hiring a new house goblin to kick around since most of them died within the first year of service anyway. With demons in and out all the time it was hard to keep some of them from killing his pets- perhaps that was why Cynric had no business trying to remember his name, it didn't matter because he would end up dead. For the sake of not becoming dinner or worse fired, he quickened his pace and caught the butcher just in the nick of time. He didn't even make a sound.

It was the coldest night in Chicago yet and he longed to be back in the forests of his homeland even if he had to put up with Justahl- the protection knight who always made fun of him- every day for the rest of his life. He cast the thought out of his mind before it could distract him. The role he had to play right now was far more important and he still hadn't picked up the side dish yet. Cynric would set him on fire for sure this time.

After the feast was complete, Gemedes was instructed to take Jamik and Arriann straight to Chicago O'Hare Airport. Once in the car however, those instructions were thrown out the window entirely.

"We need to return to Camp Demon Arriann. I don't trust his judgment on this, my guys are going in." Jamik and Arriann were arguing in the back seat of Cynric's black Camaro.

The car was exactly what Gemedes expected, especially when it came to Cynric. He loved to showcase how rich he was. All immortals had money, the Akassa brothers just had a little more. The black exterior of the 2012 Camaro was sleek, without a single scratch and it matched the black, leather interior.

"Jamik, we are going to the airport and getting on that plane. Cynric will handle Aislinn Celthric, I will bet my life on that." Arriann rebuked.

Jamik's voice turned persuasive, "It would only take a second. Gemedes turn around."

Gemedes gunned the gas pedal down, making a U-turn back toward the western outskirts of downtown- Camp Demon was located about five miles outside of the city. He wasn't about to disobey Jamik, plus this worked out to his advantage. Jamik would do

16

what he wanted either way, this way Gemedes could be there.

"NO!" Arriann screamed. "We are not going back. TURN AROUND!" She began punching the back of his seat, both fists pounding into him.

Bringing the car to a screeching halt, Gemedes turned around in the driver's seat, "You two be quiet, I agree with Jamik. I mean, Cynric is smart but Aislinn is smarter and wiser; all fairies are. So, why not send in a couple of spies, you know scan the area and figure out what's going on. Cynric might even thank you all for thinking of something he didn't." His argument was really convincing, in other circumstances, meaning if he wasn't a spy, he would have believed those wise words. Inwardly laughing at their stupidity for not catching on he added, "So, are we going or not? Face it Arriann, he would do it anyway, even without your permission. This way you can say you helped if the plan is successful."

Jamik and Arriann looked at each other for a moment before Arriann sighed, "Let's get back to the camp, it seems we have a second mission tonight. Why do I suddenly feel like a secret agent?"

"That's because we're like secret agents, only our boss doesn't even know our secret. We're like double-secret agents; James Bond would be proud." Jamik began humming the 007 theme song.

Arriann looked confused, "Who is James Bond?"

"Ughh...only the coolest guy in the history of television. Well, next to John Wayne and that one guy who use to be on 'American Idol;' Simon Cow or something."

Ignoring the new argument over who would be the next 'American Idol,' Gemedes drove off down West Main. He had won over the two best demons Cynric owned. Now, if only he could get them out of the car long enough to warn the knights. He hoped Peitar would answer his call this late, he couldn't afford for the demons to survive.

Chapter 2

Council Issues

"You could be a little more reasonable than that Aislinn. He died protecting your father." Seth yelled as he stomped across the floor of the council room. His father was the late King of Elventrale, the elf city covering the entire southern border of Roanke Island. Ellyis had wanted nothing more than his two sons to follow in his footsteps. Something his younger brother, Quid, wanted, and something he feared most. He never wanted to rule, especially now since his father wasn't here to help him.

Aislinn, the friend he'd had since birth, looked at him lovingly. She always said he was like a brother to her. Right now, if they were blood related, he'd have treated her like he did Quid when they argued. Instead he just stood there, waiting for her rebuttal, and admiring her beauty. She wore a long blue dress, which signified the council meeting, and her curly, golden hair was twisted into a neat bun on top of her head. Her eyes matched her iridescent purple wings, and her pale skin gave off a hint of the sparkle most fairies possessed. Although she was just a friend, he still hoped to find someone just like her someday. Someone who cared for the creatures of this world as much as he did and someone just as selfless.

Finally, she spoke, her voice ringing through the room like a song. "I understand that Seth, but he was the first elf brought onto the council. Before him, elves were just citizens of the land but, your father changed everything. My father considered him a friend and one of the best protection knights this island has ever known. Maybe Quid could be-"

He was tired of discussing this with her. They had been arguing for hours and the council meeting would begin soon. He could also sense someone nearby--that was his natural elven talent, tracking and sensing the presence of others, his entire family could sense emotions-- so, before she could finish he held up his hand in defiance, "I don't want to argue about this Aislinn, he is too young. I know we are ultimately immortal since we age only one year for every fifteen human years, but we aren't invincible. Maybe he can train in a year or two." Knowing she would add something he changed the subject entirely, "So, have you heard from your father?"

"No, I tried reaching him earlier through one of the communication devices but it was just a buzz. I am beginning to worry about him." She looked away and wouldn't meet his eyes. He'd distracted her, at least for now.

"There's no need to worry, after all he is the most powerful ruler who has ever lived. I would bet my best bow on that fact and you know how I feel about bets."

She laughed, "I know, you hate bets. Typical elven nature I guess, huh?" Grabbing his hand she pulled him into a hug before taking her seat on the left side of the stage. "I still can't believe I'm in here. Did you know this is the first time I've ever set foot in this room? Father told me it was nothing special, but just look at it." Her hands gestured to the council room.

Seth glanced around, following her gaze. The room was pretty vast, and everything was carved from pure marble. There were several floor-to-ceiling pillars along the perimeter of the room and twelve golden chairs seated in the middle of the floor, which was an original work from an ancient. It was a picture of a garden, but instead of paint the entire piece was made of individual precious stones; emerald, quartz, and rubies, to pieces of gold, pearls, and even a few diamonds. Each of the twelve chairs sat on a crest, also engraved in the floor. The crests symbolized each family represented in the Mazikeen City council. King Galiron designed this room, over three hundred years ago when the first members of the council were initiated. He handpicked one member from each fairy family and appointed them as an official delegate. Eventually there were exactly twelve members, most of which still held their original seat--fairies don't die unless they're killed in battle, they age one year to every ten human years--and their sole purpose was discussing issues that faced the island. The leader of the council was King Galiron himself, who always sat at the head in a golden chair, engraved with the official Mazikeen City coat of arms. It wasn't until about fifteen years ago that Seth's father had been chosen to join the council, giving the elves a seat for all of eternity. This seat was on the right hand side of Galiron's.

As Seth stared out across the room he wondered how long it would be before more seats would be added to the room, he could almost see the image of a seat for each family of his kind. His first rule of business as king would be to discuss this option with Galiron; he would listen to anything his people said with no questions. Today would be the start of a new era, he would be initiated into the council and in just three months he would be king of the elves. He sighed and let the hint of a smile linger on his lips for a moment before regaining his normal facial expressions; stern and poised just like his father.

The large gold doors opened on the far end of the room as Amara, Aislinn's sister, and Quid, Seth's only brother and last living relative, entered the council room. They both approached the stage and began talking.

"Hey guys what's up?" Amara began, "We were just wandering the halls of the castle and heard voices."

Seth realized that it was them he could sense earlier. He looked at Amara and then glared at Quid. "You two shouldn't be wandering the castle without supervision, you could break something."

Quid shrugged. "Sorry Seth. We were just going for a walk, that room is boring."

"Boring, I thought they installed a XBOX in there last week?" His voice rose in volume but he couldn't help it, his brother's constant need to be involved in anything dangerous was on his last nerve. If Seth told him to stay somewhere or do something, he found a way to do the opposite. It was annoying.

"They did but we have been playing for over four hours, we needed a break. Plus we're hungry. Where is Chef Perdy?" Quid questioned.

Aislinn cut in before Seth could make a smart remark, "He is on vacation with his family and won't return until tomorrow. I'm sure Thomas will be more than happy to cook you something. Want me to summon him?"

"Nah, I'll go make myself a moonstone smoothie." Moonstone smoothies were Quid's favorite dessert, they tasted like a cross between a peach and a pomegranate.

Amara started dragging Quid away, but he turned and came back. "Seth, when can I start my knight training? I've been practicing like dad showed me, and I overheard you all talking." He looked at Aislinn, "Do you really think I could be as great as my da-"

Seth rose out of his chair, enough was enough, and screamed; silencing him before he could finish. "NO QUID! YOU ARE NOT STARTING TRAINING NOW SO JUST GO!" He pointed to the door, his face blood red.

Amara stared at the man in front of her, *had he always been so hot?* She wondered. When he was through talking, rather violently yelling, she could have sworn she saw fire flame up in his eyes. That was the angriest she had ever seen him, especially toward his brother. She grabbed Quid, who was stunned, his mouth gaping in horror, and wheeled him toward the doors. They slammed as the two made their escape.

Once they were gone Seth sat down and buried his head in his hands. His entire body shook in anger and hot tears threatened his tired eyes. He hated yelling at Quid but his brother didn't realize the danger a protection knight could get into. There was no way he would ever allow his only brother to be slaughtered by a demon or any other creature who decided to test the borders of the island. Still, there was no reason for his behavior, he would find Quid after the meeting and apologize.

Aislinn looked at him with questions raging behind her eyes, he could tell. "Go ahead and tell me what a fool I made of myself. I know you want to." But Seth wasn't sure if hearing her say it was what he needed, to be honest what he needed she wouldn't even consider giving him. He really needed a good punch in the stomach and only Justahl was willing to lend a hand in that case. If someone wanted a fight, Justahl was the fairy to challenge; he could literally have you pinned before you said 'hey you want to fight?' Needless to say, he was the best protection knight left on the island, but his younger brother, Peitar, wasn't far behind. Seth made a mental note to find one of them before apologizing to Quid.

"You didn't have to be so harsh on him you know. He would come more near understanding the truth than just a big fat no. Why did you scream at him like that? Are you ok?"

He could only stare at her. No, he was not ok, he was devastated and what was worse is that he felt out of control. A true king never lost control like that, ever, and he was about to lose it again.

Seth knew he had already hurt his brother but what's one more person. He got up without another word and stalked out of the room, no backward glances, leaving Aislinn alone in the large room. Shock and hurt were the only emotions he could pick up from her thoughts but for once he didn't care. *Justahl or Peitar better be close by*, he thought as he left the castle walls and his friend behind, heading toward the edge of the island.

Aislinn glanced around at the now empty room. She was trying not to think of the ancients warning to her. The ancients are the spirits of old warriors who can see the future, provide guidance during wars, and maintain peace within the supernatural world. Each fairy receives an ancient prophecy so to speak, on his or her eighteenth birthday. However, the prophecies they tell are limited

23

and cannot be discussed with anyone, if they are discussed with someone else it must be approved by an ancient first. After explaining the prophecy briefly, they return to the spirit garden in the City of Death. The City of Death is a place for dead warriors and soldiers to rest while their homes are being built in the Heavens. Every fallen soldier goes there no matter what they did in life, the ancients are the most respected and honored spirits in the entire afterlife.

Aislinn had received her prophecy seven months ago and had been haunted with disturbing nightmares ever since. She could recall that night with perfect clarity.

She was lying on the large iron bed in her bedroom, which was cold as ice. A tap came at the window and she jumped. It was eerie quiet in the castle that night. Grabbing her night robe she crossed to the window and slowly opened it.

Suddenly Aislinn was back on her bed and the room glowed brightly. She swore under her breath. A short man, one she didn't recognize, walked across the room to where she sat. Her body shook all over from the freezing night air that flowed through the open window. He just stared at her.

Finally she mustered up the courage to speak, "Umm...hello. Are you the ancient?"

He smiled warmly. "Yes my child, I am Prisane Syr. You know my sons Sythril and Xavor? They are knights under your father's command."

Aislinn nodded. So this was their father, she would have to tell them she saw him. How many of the knights' fathers were knights before them? She wondered.

"I am here for your prophecy young one. Would you like to know your future?" His smile radiated like the most beautiful sunshine.

"Yes."

"Ahh, this is a wise decision because soon you will have a choice to make. The fate of the entire kingdom will depend on this decision. All I can tell you is the right choice may seem like the wrong one but, always follow your heart." His voice didn't waiver only grew more dark and demented as he spoke.

She was frozen, her eyes locked on the spirit as he retreated out of sight.

Aislinn's thoughts refocused on the room in front of her shaking the awful image of that night out of her mind. She rose and began pacing the stage. How could she do anything to stop this prophecy if she didn't even know who it was referring to? She had to tell Seth, perhaps he knew something. But first she had to ask permission and give Seth time to calm down from the earlier incident. For now, all she could do is hope the ancients were wrong and her entire kingdom wasn't in jeopardy. Not likely, but it was still worth a shot.

She could hear the voices of council members outside in the hall, putting a hold on her previous thoughts. It was time to start and she had to prepare herself to lead her first council meeting. Hopefully her father wouldn't be too disappointed if she injured Seth while making him an official delegate of the council. Maybe they had forgotten to sharpen the sword.

Council members, all twelve of them, filed in and took their seats. Aislinn smiled at all of them and nodded at Justahl who came in with his arm around Seth, probably for support. The meeting was called to order and all eyes were on her.

"Hello my friends; I welcome you to the nine hundred and seventy-fifth council meeting of Roanke Island. Will Seth Arabiraheal please step forward?"

Seth took a deep breath and began walking toward the stage. He really looked awful. Once he reached her seat, Aislinn hugged him and shook his hand letting everyone in the room know she accepted him as a member. Now came the fun part.

"Anyone who objects to Seth becoming a delegate of the court please speak now." When no one said anything she grabbed the sword, to her demise it was sharp, and continued with the initiation. "Do you solemnly swear to attend all meetings, emergency or otherwise, follow all orders given by the King, and keep all business discussed in the meetings a secret?"

Facing her, Seth answered, "I solemnly swear to do just that

Princess of the council. I swear to do all that is asked of me and treat each member as my brother. I promise to honor and respect each of them until the day I lay my life down for this kingdom."

"Then with this sword," she touched each shoulder lightly three times before returning it to its spot beside her father's chair, "I officially knight you into the council of Mazikeen City. Fellow delegates please come forth and initiate him as your brother." She backed away allowing the other members to come up.

After each fairy had shaken his hand, Seth took his seat on the right hand side of the stage. He would remain there for the rest of his life and Aislinn couldn't help but let a few tears fall from her eyes. *His father would be so proud*, she thought before wiping her eyes with the back of her hand.

"Amara, why is he such a jerk?" Quid was sitting by Croak River, tossing pebbles into the dark water below. His brother didn't care anything about him or his life, maybe he should just leave. No, he couldn't do that, Amara was his best friend and he really liked her. Actually Amara was becoming more than a friend and he didn't know how to feel about that. Would Seth listen if he talked about girl problems? He decided it would be better not to tell him.

Amara came around a nearby tree trunk and leaned against it. "Of course he cares about you Quid. He is just trying to protect you. Don't you realize that?"

She wasn't really comforting him anymore. They had been out here for what seemed like days, did council meetings usually take this long?

Clearing her throat, Amara walked over and sat down beside him. Quid's heart started racing, hopefully she couldn't hear that well. "Look Quid, everyone has reasons for what they do, even us."

He loved it when she considered them as a pair instead of individuals. "I know but it is just frustrating. I would make a great protector, wouldn't I?"

She looked at him and nodded. "Of course you would, Aislinn said so and Seth knows that too, he is just protecting you. He thinks you will suffer the same fate as your father and I don't think he could

26

bear losing another family member."

Well, she had him there. It was no use arguing, he knew she was right. "I know." He sighed before rising up and tossing the rest of his pebbles into the river. "Come on I'm sure the meeting will be over soon. I want to find Seth and congratulate him on getting the seat."

Amara stood and started to follow when they heard someone calling their names.

"QUID! AMARA! ARE YOU GUYS OUT THERE?" Seth was yelling from about a hundred yards away.

Quid looked at Amara and laughed, "Well that was easy, come on."

She shook her head, "I have a better idea; we can play with his mind. Follow me." Before he could answer she was running toward his and his brother's old hangout.

Crossing over a fallen tree he was greeted by the familiar smells of the place he considered a second home. Honeysuckle bloomed all around him, tiger lilies grew in patches all over the clearing, and he could hear the sound of the river rushing nearby. Taking it all in, he noticed the old tree where their tree fort had been was gone. It had been in the middle of the clearing, standing nearly fifty feet in the air. He frowned, knowing it had been knocked down and chopped up to make weapons.

Amara appeared beside him with a large grin on her face. "Recognize it?"

"Yeah but the tree, its gone."

"Oh, sorry about that I didn't know." Seth was shouting again. She frowned, "Ok we have to make this fast. Close your eyes so he can't see what you see."

Quid closed his eyes and didn't think of anything.

Amara stood in front of him for a few minutes before whispering, "Now when I count to three get up and hide. When you reach your hiding place, close your eyes and wait for me to come to you." She backed away, "One…two…three!"

He began running towards a cave he knew about. It was nestled in another clearing about fifteen yards from the old spot. When he reached the cave, he followed instructions and waited.

Minutes later he was accompanied by Amara who laughed, "Alright. Now that we succeeded in leading him to the clearing we can start our game."

Quid laughed with her, thoughts of them kissing playing on the edge of his mind. "What game?"

"You'll see. On my mark, you will go back to the clearing and run around in the brush. It will make him mad but be hilarious for us." She started rolling with laughter. "Ready?"

"Yeah let's do this." His nerves were on end because his brother was already mad and this stunt was going to make him furious. But the girl he liked was planning this and he didn't want to seem like a chicken. So he impatiently waited for her signal.

To Seth, the entire meeting was a blur. The last thing he remembered was leaning against the golden doors, debating an exit strategy, and before he knew it he was sitting on the right hand side of the King's chair, his family crest glowing when he sat down. All he could think about was his father and how proud he would be if he could see him now. "There was no one like you father." The words stung his throat and his eyes became blurry again as more tears formed, threatening to expose his true emotions. Quickly, he blinked the tears away and focused on finding his brother. Quid had to be around here somewhere.

He reached out with his mind again and saw their old hang out spot, deep in the forest to his left. Seth darted through the trees with lighting speed but slowed as he reached the stump he had saw through Amara's eyes. Where are they? He wandered around and spotted two figures moving quickly through the brush that surrounded the clearing.

"Amara," he yelled, "Quid, you all come out of there I need to talk to you." He was getting annoyed because he could hear their laughter.

"You want to yell at us some more?" That was Quid, he was sure of it.

Seth spun and caught Quid's belt. "Stop, you're getting on my

28

nerves. I need to talk to you and want to be calm when I do." He sat him down on the stump and called out to Amara, "And Aislinn needs to see you in your father's study. We are leaving in one hour for town. Now go on back to the castle." He heard her retreating footsteps.

"Look Quid, I didn't come here to yell at you. Actually I wanted to apologize for earlier, I should not have acted so savagely and I am truly sorry. Can you forgive me?"

Quid stared at him, "Umm…yeah I guess I can. What do you want to talk to me about anyway?"

He sighed heavily at least four times maybe more he couldn't be sure. "I know you want to train to be a protection knight and I am proud of you for being so loyal to your homeland but I have reasons for not wanting you to train to be a fighter. You are the only blood relative I have left and you're my only brother. If I were to lose you it would be worse than when I lost dad because it would mean I have lost everything. Does that make sense?"

"You wouldn't lose me Seth. I love you, but just because dad died in battle doesn't mean I will. You have to let me train; otherwise I will be useless in a battle. What if we are attacked again?"

"We won't be, the demon activity is at an all-time low and has been for months now. Cynric and Dimitri are not going to do what their father did; they are too smart for that. There won't be another war."

"Yeah, smart," Quid laughed. "Those two might do something worse. Cynric is just plain evil, or so I hear."

"I know what Cynric is capable of but trust me he won't-"

"He will it's just a matter of time Seth. Please you have to let me at least know how to protect myself. I won't become a knight yet, I will wait as long as you ask just please let me train. Please."

Seth saw Ellyis in his eyes; he would be a great protector. "Alright-"

"Wahoo!" Quid yelled.

"Now, wait there are conditions."

"Awww…..what are they?" The enthusiasm had left his eyes.

"You can start training in one week with the rest of the thirteen year olds but, no knight stuff until I say so, understand? And if you get hurt, I don't want any whining."

Quid nodded in agreement then hugged him, "Really, those are the only conditions? Thanks Seth. I can't wait to tell Amara. She will be so jeal-."

Suddenly the woods around them were filled with screams. Seth grabbed Quid and shoved him down under a nearby fallen tree. "Stay there, understand, and don't move."

Seth bounded off in the direction of the scream, bow and arrow ready for battle.

Moments later he came across a battle scene straight out of a horror movie. He couldn't see how many fairies were actually fighting because everything seemed to be moving in fast-forward. The demons were gross looking with long needle tipped tails that swung from side to side, making it impossible to get too close. One was a sickly white color with strips of human flesh hanging off of its entire body and its head was gone, replaced by a large black hole. It seemed to be screaming but no sound came from it. The other creature had two large claws for hands, jagged shark teeth, and crimson red eyes; it appeared to be injured where a sword had scathed its upper arm. Faster than humanly possible, Seth pounced on its back and shot an arrow between its shoulder blades; a perfect kill shot.

The other demon noticed his dying friend and raced toward the portal. Had that been there five minutes ago? Seth didn't know, what he did know was it was getting away. He crossed the area in two seconds and latched onto its back, gagging from the smell of rotten fish that rolled off of it in layers of stench. The demon didn't even seem to notice.

Not knowing where the portal led and seeing that his plan to make it angry wasn't working, Seth dropped to the ground in one swift movement. The demon disappeared, but not before he caught a glimpse of the thousands of demons that awaited it on the other side. He quickly looked at the sign above one's head, 'Camp Demon:

Today Chicago, Tomorrow the World.' The portal disappeared and with a sharp snap, everything went black.

Chapter 3

Signs of War

Waking, Seth glanced behind him for the attacker. Whatever it was was long gone now. He rose to his feet, intent on surveying the damage, but his stance was short lived as a dizzying feeling caught in his head. Rubbing the knot on his skull he sat back down. Maybe the creature had hit him harder than he realized.

After a few moments of deep breathing and keeping his eyes closed, Seth stood up again, this time he succeeded. He finally gathered enough courage to find the fairies he had seen in the fight. Surely they weren't all dead? Honestly, he couldn't be sure. He remembered seeing them fighting the demons, but moments after he stepped in the others disappeared. It was really strange.

A movement came from behind a nearby tree. Seth hoisted his sword in the air, his bow and arrows were lying broken a few feet away. He prepared for another attack. His efforts were not needed, seconds later Xavor stepped out of the brush, he looked awful. There was a long, deep cut on his head that still gushed with blood, scratches covered his entire body, and he was limping.

Rushing to his side, Seth noticed two more bodies lying on the ground; Peitar, Justahl's brother, and Sythril, Xavor's brother. Both were covered in blood and lifeless. "Don't look Xavor. It will be alright but we need to get you to the infirmary fast."

Xavor leaned on his shoulder as he helped him back to the castle, leaving the bodies in the woods. On their way, they found Quid cowering under the fallen tree where Seth had left him. "Come on Quid, the fight is over. Help me carry Xavor back to Aislinn, he is terribly injured and needs medical attention." With Quid's help the two lifted Xavor up, "Careful of his leg, I think it is broken…Yeah that's good. Now come on it is getting dark out and who knows when the demons will come back."

Quid looked terrified but that sort of pleased him, he needed to be afraid. Being a Protection Knight was not all fame and glory, it was bloody, brutal, and always tragic.

"Hey Seth, do you think those demons were a sign? I mean what if another war is starting."

"Don't worry kid; those two weren't Cynric's. Arriann and Jamik are his best, he wouldn't send other demons to do their job. I don't know what this means, but whoever sent them, knew they were stronger than most demons." Shaking his head, as if he could pass the memories off as a horrific dream, Seth quickened his pace. "We need to let Aislinn know, did you see anything at all?" He looked at his younger brother, hoping he might have seen the person who attacked him.

Quid shook his head, "Nope, nothing at all. I was too terrified to look though. There was a weird noise once, it made my ears hurt."

"What kind of noise?" Xavor had become completely silent, not even breathing. Seth hoped he was just in a coma instead of dead; two bodies were enough for one night.

"Well, you know in the scary movies when the main character starts running through the woods screaming for his or her life?"

"Yeah."

"Imagine that scream mixed with a weird static noise. It was crazy."

"Huh, that doesn't make any sense. I didn't hear anything." Seth recalled the demon with the gaping mouth that looked like it was screaming, but it didn't make a sound. Something was terribly wrong with this entire situation.

They reached the castle's exterior walls before dusk, Xavor was still not responding. Seth knew the demons wouldn't be back for a while, giving him time to warn Aislinn of the situation in Chicago.

"What is this?" Aislinn questioned Seth with terror in her eyes. He hated causing her pain.

"Xavor was injured in the woods. Demons attacked him and two other knights; Peitar and Sythril's bodies are still out there, I couldn't carry them all. I'm sorry Aislinn, I tried to help but I was too late." Seth bowed his head. He knew Justahl would be lost; his youngest brother was gone, never coming back. How could he break the news to him?

Aislinn bowed back to Seth. "Thomas," she called for her servant using the intercom system.

Her house goblin arrived moments later. Seeing Thomas made Seth's body twist as if he were remembering an awful pain, he quickly brushed it away as paranoia.

Thomas's body had gone rigid, most likely with fear, as he stared at the three of them. But before Seth could get a sense of his true emotions he gathered himself and acted calm. "You called your majesty."

Seth really needed to regain control over his emotions, before he started accusing Aislinn's house goblin of hiding something. Thomas was nice; he had nursed Quid back to health after a horse ran over him three years ago. It nearly broke his arm but Thomas pushed him out of the way. Seth owed this creature dearly.

"Yes, please help Quid take Xavor to the infirmary; he is in need of immediate attention. I need to talk to Seth alone. Go now!" She gestured for Thomas to take his place, supporting Xavor's head, "Quickly, before I have more dead bodies to explain."

He handed Xavor's head over to Thomas before walking to take a seat beside Aislinn on one of the thrones.

The throne room mirrored the layout of the council room. Except for the difference in the number of chairs, one had three large chairs in it instead of fifteen smaller ones, people wouldn't be able to tell them apart. He felt odd on a throne, *King Seth*, he thought, that is not what he would be called. His father had told the people from day one, to call him brother; Seth would do the same.

"Seth," Aislinn placed her hand on his shoulder. "I know you feel like this is your fault, but it's not. No one knew the demons were coming, well with the exception of the knights. Wait, you said there were only two bodies in the woods. Where is Justahl? Did they take him back with them?"

Seth shook his head, "Justahl wasn't with the others. Or at least I didn't see him. To be honest, I didn't know how many were out there until I found the bodies, everything was a blur. It was like fighting blind. I do know there were two demons; I killed one and the other disappeared through a portal." He dropped his head; he was going to be a king soon and couldn't even kill two demons.

"Don't beat yourself up Seth. You did all you could but, I am confused about one thing. Where did the portal lead?"

He knew it was time to tell her everything, but he didn't know where to begin. "I guess I will start from the beginning. Alright, Quid and I were sitting in our old hangout clearing in Frost forest. I was apologizing for my outburst earlier this morning in the council room and telling him the reasons behind my hostile behavior." He fumbled with his hands nervously. "We came to a compromise on that argument by the way."

"What was that?" She giggled and the sound of it filled the room with kindness and love.

"I agreed to let him begin his training with the other thirteen year olds next week, as long as he didn't insist on being an official knight until I said so. It was the best I could come up with, he wouldn't budge."

Aislinn laughed a little louder and then gestured for him to continue with the hard part. A part he really didn't want to relive.

"As we were preparing to come back to the castle, a scream pierced through the trees, a scream of total agony. Quickly, I shoved Quid under a nearby fallen tree and rushed toward the source of the scream. When I arrived…" Seth broke off as images of the fight rushed through his mind. He could remember the feelings of every creature in the fight, even the demons' triumph as they succeeded in knocking fairies down one by one. "It was awful and the few fairies I caught glimpses of were losing terribly. I knew I had to step in but I didn't know how. One demon had a spiky tale which made it impossible to sneak up behind it so I pounced on the other one's back. I shot it between the shoulder blades. The other demon noticed me then, it started retreating back to the portal. Quicker than I thought possible I lunged on its back, but the smell was horrific and it didn't stop. So, I jumped down and tried to catch a glimpse of where the portal took him. It…it…." He couldn't finish, it was too terrible.

"What? Where did it take him Seth?" She shook his arm violently, but he was vaguely aware of anything she said.

Shutting out his surroundings, he closed his eyes and waited. He was trying to build up the strength it would take to tell Aislinn and every other creature on Roanke Island their worst nightmare had become a reality. "The portal led to an abandoned c-c-camp." He stuttered slightly. "There was a sign behind a demon's head. 'Camp Demon' was written in bright red letters and underneath it was their camp motto."

Aislinn looked ultimately terrified and shocked. She blinked three times and took countless deep breaths before asking, "What was the motto?"

"It said, 'Today Chicago, Tomorrow the World.' After that, I blacked out. Someone attacked me from behind, but don't worry I'm fine. Nothing a stiff drink won't cure." He laughed without humor.

"Oh. My. Gosh." Aislinn framed each word individually, as if saying them slower would make the entire situation disappear. No such luck. "Do you know what this means? It has to be Cynric and Dimitri; they're the only ones who could raise a demon army. They have been in Chicago for the last seven months, my father said so. I should warn him. They might try-" She didn't finish. Instead, she sighed once before rising and motioning for him to follow, "Come my friend, you have to find Justahl. He will want to help retrieve the bodies out of the woods, then, start arranging the funeral boats so we can send them out at dawn. Please send my regards to him for his loss. I would do it myself, but it I must get word to my father; perhaps he will bring back more soldiers. An emergency council meeting will be held in exactly one hour, so make it quick."

Without another word, Aislinn walked wearily from his presence; leaving him with the feat he was dreading most, telling Justahl.

*

Justahl was beginning to get worried; he had paced his small house for hours. "Where are Peitar and the others? They should be back by now." He mumbled to himself.

A knock came to the door. "Justahl, are you in there? It is Seth, Seth Arabiraheal?"

Crossing the floor in two strides he flung the door open. *What is he doing here?* He thought. "Hey Seth, what's up?" He bowed and motioned for the elf prince to come in.

Seth walked through the door with certain unwillingness to each step. "Justahl... I need your help with something. Your brother and two other knights were in a fight earlier this evening. Xavor is in the infirmary and-"

He didn't dare let Seth finish. "Where is Peitar? What do you mean a fight? Who was he fighting?"

"Peitar and Sythril are dead. They were attacked. Two demons came after the three of them, while they were out on patrol." Seth sighed in despair. "I am so sorry. I tried to save them but....but....Can you forgive me?"

Justahl couldn't shake the feeling of guilt from his mind. Somewhere, deep in his chest his heart was breaking, he could feel it ripping to shreds, tearing him apart a little at a time. Peitar is gone. His mind screamed the words over and over at him. Peitar was dead and it was his fault. If he had been there, done something, anything, it would be him who was dead, not Peitar. He wanted it to be anyone else but Peitar. His brother was so loving, kind, and loyal to his kingdom, now he was gone forever. Why did it have to be Peitar? He was so full of life and joy; everything had humor in it in some way. Peitar loved to mock sword fight, Justahl could recall the last time they had battled it out on the training grounds. It was just last week, before the annual fairy knight championship tournament, Peitar wanted to enter, but Justahl refused and told him to wait until next year. Now next year would never come for him, his life was over and he never even got to say goodbye. His brother was his best friend through and through, but Protection Knights don't cry, he told himself. He had to face facts, Peitar was gone and now it was left up to him to be the brave one. It was time to do what he could for his kingdom, even if that included carrying his brother's body to the funeral boats and setting him free.

Standing and brushing away the few tears that had fallen from his eyes he exclaimed, "Let us go and retrieve the bodies my friend." He patted Seth on the back before putting on his armor and grabbing his sword. Peitar would be proud of his loyalty.

"We can wait; it is still a good half hour before the emergency council meeting." Seth described the reasons for the council meeting, trying to leave out the parts about Peitar; Justahl was glad.

"If what you say is true Seth, we need to hurry and gather the bodies. Demons could be lurking in the shadows, waiting for the chance to feed off them."

Seth shook his head and waved his hand in the air, "No need, I put up a blocking spell around the area so nothing or no one could get through. It will be safe. But, I suppose it wouldn't hurt to get back to the castle before midnight, the sooner we get there the sooner the meeting can start. Aislinn said we will send the bodies out at dawn."

Justahl just nodded in agreement, knowing his brave act would be crushed if he spoke a word.

The two headed out of the house and into the darkness of Frost forest. Justahl looked at the clear sky above them as they walked; he noticed a slight difference in the atmosphere that night. Peitar was up there now, watching over him and keeping him safe; for the first time in his life, Justahl cried.

*

Aislinn stared out across the room, the council members were getting restless. Most of them were talking amongst themselves saying things like, "When is the King going to be back?" and "I heard he wasn't coming back at all. She's our new ruler." No matter what a few were saying, they all stared directly at her. Where was Seth? She had told him one hour and midnight grew near.

At last, Seth walked through the double doors on the far end of the room; he carried Peitar and Sythril's armor. It is customary that each knight who dies in battle is released of his earthly duties, his armor and weapons are given to the king until a new knight is appointed to the council. In tonight's case however, they would temporarily fill the fallen knight's seats with other members of the council; one war was enough.

Moments later, she noticed Justahl entering through the doors. Seth was already seated on her right-she was in her father's chair- he wore the same emotions on his face as Justahl, although Justahl's went much deeper than the surface. She knew he would never be the same.

After several calming breaths, she rose and faced the council, "Welcome to an emergency meeting of the Mazikeen City council. You may now be seated." Pausing to allow everyone the chance to get settled she continued, "I am sure most of you know the story of how Peitar and Sythril died this evening; however, I can guarantee you don't know the entire story. Seth." She waved Seth forward so he could explain today's events more thoroughly.

Seth told the story from start to finish, explaining every last detail. When he was finished speaking, he returned to his seat. Aislinn let all the information sink in before asking for suggestions. "If anyone has questions, battle strategies, or anything else to make noted at this time please feel free to voice all opinions."

Justahl stood from his seat in the middle of the room, "I have one question, when we will let the people know?"

Aislinn nodded in acknowledgement of his question, "I will announce it at dawn. Before the funeral begins, I will let every creature on this island know to prepare themselves for battle. Those wishing not to fight will be given the chance to leave. Are there any other questions?"

No one said anything else for a long time and before they knew it, dawn had arrived and the sun peaked out from behind the western mountains. It was time for the funeral. At least the council had reached a unified decision first.

Seth followed Aislinn onto the platform, the same platform he had stood on a year ago, when his father had been sent out on a funeral boat. This time wasn't much easier. Peitar and Sythril had both been great knights and no one would ever take their place in his heart. He bowed as Justahl and Xavor lowered their brother's bodies into the boats.

Each boat had been hand carved out of fallen trees in the woods, the wood bleached to turn it a bright, luminescent white. Both boats were covered in each fairy's family crest and scriptures in Gaelic-the fairy language- rimmed the entire length of them.

He knew Justahl and Xavor needed a friend so, after whispering his comforting words to Aislinn, he descended from the platform and wrapped his arms around his brothers. They were both trying not to cry; each failing miserably.

Every creature on Roanke Island was there from house goblins to Harlem. He seemed a little too chipper, considering he was at a funeral. Seth tried to ignore him but something kept him glancing over at the warlock, maybe it was his hair, it was purple after all.

"Everyone, I have an announcement to make before we continue with tonight's ceremony." Aislinn began what would be the hardest speech she had ever given. Seth nodded in support for her to continue. "Most of you are wishing it were my father telling you this instead of me, well you're not alone. I do not like this situation any more than the rest of you, but seeing as how my father is still in Japan and unreachable through speaking devices, I am all you have for the time being. Please know I am terribly sorry for the news I am about to share, it is terrifying and it is not easy for me to talk about. However, as your current ruler and your friend, it is my duty to warn you."

Seth noticed the lack of fear in her eyes as she paused, staring out at the crowd. She was stronger than he thought; she would make an excellent queen someday.

"Cynric and his brother Dimitri Akassa are building an army of demons and housing them in an abandoned campsite in downtown Chicago. The emergency meeting of the council, held earlier tonight, was not only called to appoint three temporary Protection Knights, it was also a strategic meeting. As an entire council we have decided to prepare for what will quite possibly be the worst war this island has ever seen. I know what you are thinking and yes, it will be worse than Modric's war last year. Seth saw nearly seven thousand demons through that portal and we assume there are more, a lot more. Now, before anyone panics or vows their loyalty, please know that a battle against them will mean countless deaths and possibly entire families destroyed. I wish this fate on no one. Each of you is a friend to my family, in some way or another and I know how much you love this island, but you do not have to fight if you don't want to. The rest of us will understand if you chose to leave."

Seth couldn't believe that no one in the crowd left; perhaps he had underestimated his fellow friends and neighbors. Instead, all of them raised their bows, or swords, in a sign of approval for the council's decision to fight. Justahl was the first to raise his bow, holding it higher than anyone on the shore.

"Alright, now I have warned you of what you can expect during the war but, there are other matters to discuss. First, all underage fairies will be relocated during the battle, as well as all the elders who are too weak to fight. Second, every fairy, elf, and goblin old enough to fight will report to the training grounds every day at noon; this includes today. We are unsure of the exact date the war will break out, we assume it won't be more than a couple of months so be prepared. Lastly, no one and I mean NO ONE; will be allowed to travel out into the woods alone. This includes all fairies, goblins, elves, and knights. Anyone who is found out alone will be charged and thrown in prison. Does everyone understand?" Aislinn glanced around, looking for an argument but, to her relief the entire shore was quiet, "With nothing left to say, it is time for the funeral to begin. Everyone who wishes to take part in the ceremony, please come forth and light a remembrance candle."

Fairies and other creatures on the shore, began lighting floating candles and released them into the sea, the boats were cast off shortly after. The boats seemed to be floating in a sea of light, gliding off into the sunrise. It was really spectacular. Then, as customary for all Roanke Island funerals, fireflies were released to signify that the fallen creature or creatures were free, never to be burdened by his or her worldly problems again. Seth was beginning to think the dead had it easy. This war could kill us all, he thought as the fireflies disappeared into the morning sky. He could hear birds chirping in the trees of Frost forest and waves crashing against the rocky shores of the funeral site.

Most Roanke Island funerals don't last long after the sun rises above the mountains but, this one seemed to be dragging on for a little longer. Creatures from all over had come to pay their respect and left slowly. Xavor had been wheeled back to the care unit; he was still in pretty bad shape. Now, the boats were gone. All that was left of Peitar and Sythril were the memories they left with their loved ones, who were still on earth.

Seth approached Justahl slowly, he was still sitting in the sand, "It was a beautiful ceremony Justahl. I know Peitar would have been proud of you for holding your composure. Are you sure you want to fight? I mean, you're going to be alright?" He placed a hand on his friend's shoulder. It was a small gesture but, what did you give someone when they've lost everything? He had lost his father, mother, three older brothers, and now the only brother he had left was gone too. No one should have to endure that alone. Seth wanted to help, he just didn't know how.

Justahl just stared out into the waves, "Yeah...I will be fine in a few days, I just need a little time to heal....He was the only brother I had left, how am I supposed to cope with something like that? I shouldn't have let him go out without me. It's my fault he's out there," he pointed towards the ocean, "instead of here."

"I don't know what to tell you about losing a brother but, I can tell you that if I lost Quid, I would literally die on the inside. I can see it in your eyes Justahl, you're a mess. But after a while I think I could cope with him being gone. Quid would want me to move on, just like Peitar would want the same for you. Don't blame yourself, he was a great knight and I fear for our lives more than his and Sythril's; this war is going to be brutal." Seth let his hand drop from his shoulder, "I guess we will see each other at noon for training. Do this for him Justahl, he would want you to. Plus, we need you; Aislinn said no one goes out alone. So, patrols will be trickier, we will have to send two out at a time and since there are only nine of you left, someone will have to pair with me. If you leave and don't fight, I would have no one to patrol with?" With the last question left unanswered, he turned to walk away but, Justahl caught up to him.

"Seth, I'm not going anywhere. My entire family has died protecting this land and so will I, if need be. I do have a favor to ask though. Would you say the farewell for Peitar? I would but, I just don't think I can."

Walking back to the waves, Justahl two steps behind him, Seth raised his sword in the air, "Peitar Alaheim Lerin, we set you free. May your spirit watch over us until the end of our days. Farewell to the knight of the east, to the friend of many, and to the best brother anyone will ever know. We will never forget you but remember you for all eternity. You were a brave, loyal, and kind soldier; now you will rest in peace forever. Le grá síoraí."

Justahl just smiled, letting a few more tears escape before sitting back down in the sand.

For once Seth actually felt someone else's pain without having to enter their thoughts. He hoped it would never happen again. Saying those three final words, Le grá síoraí- With everlasting love- in Gaelic, the official language of Roanke Island, made him feel all the pain from his father's funeral. With a heavy heart, Seth walked back towards the castle. Training was looking more intriguing every second, at least he understood fighting; sorrow was harder than sword fighting any day. He disappeared into the forests that surrounded the western shore, leaving Justahl behind. The forest seemed different, strange, as though someone or something was watching him. Maybe today had been harder on him than he thought.

Chapter 4

Mole on the Inside

Gemedes cleaned the living room vigorously. The apartment was rather silent, since Cynric and Dimitri spent most of their time over at the camp. For the past two days, they left before the sun came up and returned after dark. The only noise filling the apartment was the sound of honking horns and sirens from the busy streets five floors below. Gemedes liked being alone, it gave him time to think and search the apartment for clues.

A strange noise cut into his cleaning, making him jump. Laying down his duster, Gemedes rushed to the secret door of the office and opened it without thinking about what he was doing. He mentally slapped himself on the forehead. *You are so stupid*, he thought, *anything could have been making that noise. It could have killed you.* However, his fears were not necessary, the room was completely empty. That's odd, he could still here the noise. *Where is it coming from?*

Just then, a giant swirling figure stepped out of a portal beside Cynric's desk. Gemedes froze, *what is that?*

He thought about all the demons he had encountered in the last six months but, not a single one of them looked or sounded like this thing. The sound faded as the smoke cleared; a man, dressed in designer clothes, appeared in its place. So the sound did come from a demon but, not a demon he recognized?

Still standing, gawking in shock, Gemedes bowed and greeted the visitor. "Hello. Who a-a-are you?"

Suddenly the creature disappeared and reappeared right next to him. "My sweet, delicious friend," The demon scraped the side of his face lightly, then, licked his fingers in delight, "There is no need to be afraid. I am Iklin, demon of death; I come to relay a brief message to Cynric. Where is he?"

Gemedes answered, "Dimitri and Cynric have been at the camp all day but, they should be back anytime now. They always return at dark."

"Good, I will wait for-"

Iklin's words were cut off as the office door flew open. Cynric and Dimitri stormed over the threshold.

Cynric spoke, "Who the hell is this?" He pointed towards the visitor, "Iklin is that you?"

"Of course it's me you fool, who else were you expecting?" Iklin roared then smiled, "Speaking of expectations, I am not pleased with your recent activities."

"What do you mean you're not pleased with his activities?" Dimitri mocked his sultry voice with perfect clarity. "He has done nothing wrong, what is the meaning of this?"

Iklin's smile only intensified at his words, "It seems he has not told you the entire truth my young prince."

Cynric looked at Dimitri, shrugging his shoulders in confusion, "I have no earthly idea what you are referring to Iklin. Perhaps you are mistaking me with someone else. What exactly are you accusing me of anyway?"

Gemedes knew that face, anger and pride, Cynric wore it well and often. He knew what this strange new demon was referring to, Jamik's plan. Could he tell them or should he just remain quiet? He remained quiet.

"You really have no idea how awful your plan was do you?" Iklin laughed, "Well for one, your little demon army is out of the bag, so to speak. Sending in two demons to spy on the fairies of Roanke Island was immature and lacked any imagination what-so-ever. Personally, I thought you had more potential but, it seems I was wrong." He shook his head in disappointment, "I will be watching your plans more closely from this point on, and I hope your next step is more thought out than this one. Honestly, two demons in their original forms could not be more obvious. To make the situation worse, I had to deal with two dead fairies and one dead demon. Pathetic."

Stunned one of the demons survived, Gemedes asked, "Two knights were killed? Who were they?" He realized his voice sounded too caring, so he added, "Not that I care but, I am curious. Knights don't usually die easily, right?"

"SHUT-UP GEMEDES!" Cynric screeched.

Gemedes looked astounded, the first time this idiot remembered his name and it had to be in this situation. This was absolutely ridiculous.

"No, they usually don't but, in this case...well you get the picture." Iklin answered his question and then turned back towards Cynric, as if remembering something important, "That reminds me, and exactly how did the knights know of your plans?"

Cynric had had enough, "THEY WEREN'T MY PLANS!" Pausing he looked at Dimitri, "We only found out about the attack yesterday but, it seems the problem is worse than Frex let on."

"Yes, well I hope whoever was responsible for this is taken care of immediately." Iklin warned.

Dimitri stepped in again, "Wait, you said the army had been exposed," he looked at Cynric, then back to the visitor, "Flex said nothing about a survivor. What do you know?"

Iklin stared, his eyes pits of black. "There were two survivors, Seth and Xavor. Xavor was knocked unconscious by one of the demons, before the elf even showed up. I don't think Seth knew about the attack, he didn't come until the battle was nearly over."

"Alright, but that still doesn't explain how the army was exposed." Cynric was beyond furious now, his eyes glowed intensely.

"Thanks to the lack of brains possessed by the demons, the elf noticed where the portal led; I saw him mouthing the word Chicago, while I collected the souls."

As the demon of death, Iklin must gather all dying demons- this is why they seem to disappear- and return souls of other creatures to the heavens. He is also in control of wars and battles. All plans have to go through him. Cynric knew this, Jamik did not.

"Is it bad if Seth knows where the portal leads?" Gemedes asked. He was glad that some good news came out of the situation; this whole thing was beginning to get out of hand.

Iklin ignored this question, "Cynric, some advice if you will. I know you think I hate you but, I don't. Actually I am quite fond of you. However, I do find your plan to be slipping through your fingers and can't help but wonder why. You seemed so sure of yourself a year ago but, now….it seems as though you are losing your spark."

"I am well aware of how my plan is going. Now please leave. I am no longer in need of your assistance. NOW GO!" Cynric pointed at the portal Iklin had just come through.

Without another word, Iklin stepped back into the fires of the underworld. Swirling smoke engulfed his body and he returned to his true form, wicked, dark, and smoky.

Gemedes ran out of the office and hid in the plant. *Spying from here will be easier than dodging flying objects*, he thought.

"I told you that idiot would double-cross you Cynric." Dimitri yelled, "Now look at the mess he's made. Do you honestly believe tha-"

"Dimitri I don't know or care how Jamik got those demons over there but, as soon as he and Arriann return I am going to tear him limb from limb." Cynric raged, "Let's call in you know who, maybe he knows something. Do you still have that communication device?"

"Yes, but you seem to be missing the most important part of Iklin's message."

"And what exactly is that?" Cynric questioned.

"The knights knew the demons were attacking, they even knew

where the portal would appear. Doesn't it seem a little too convenient?"

"Yes, I realize your point but how? Hmmm…we must have a spy in our midst but, first, we call in Harlem. He might know who it is."

Things are getting out of control, Gemedes thought. He had to escape and he had to do it fast.

"Harlem! Harlem!" Cynric yelled into the device frantically, "Harlem, if you don't answer me right-"

All at once a portal appeared beside the brothers. Harlem stepped through, dragging Thomas-Aislinn's house goblin- behind him. He threw Thomas into one of the chairs, then, took the seat beside him. "What exactly are you doing? You know I can't speak with you while traveling." His eyes glistened as he looked at them and his hair changed from purple to orange-adjusting to his new surroundings.

Dimitri cleared his throat, "We didn't know you were coming here," he bowed, "forgive us."

"Just tell me what you need. I received an urgent message telling me to come immediately, so get on with it before I get gray hair."

It was Cynric who spoke first this time, "As I was getting ready to say, before you showed up, there is a spy here in Chicago. He or she is working with the fairies; otherwise the knights would not have known where the portal would appear that day. Seth was there as well and now, thanks to whoever the spy is, everyone on the island knows about my army."

Harlem yawned in boredom, "That is your problem. I hardly see why you needed me to go out of my way, just so you could tell me the same story I heard two days ago." He laughed, "Aislinn announced to the entire kingdom what you two were doing. I do hope that wasn't part of the original plan because, personally I think it sucks."

Fury coursed him, "It was not part of the plan but, thanks to recent events, I will need those rituals we discussed sooner than I thought, preferably tonight."

"Ah yes, well if you expect it done tonight, I suggest we go shopping." Harlem explained.

"You don't seem to understand. In order to continue with my original plan, I need to question all the creatures who knew what Jamik was doing. Did Thomas know anything?" Cynric asked.

Dimitri cut in, "Of course he didn't brother, why wouldn't he have told us?"

"Oh for heaven's sakes, yes he knew. I didn't tell you two because, I figured you knew already. Jamik told everyone at the camp it was your plan." Harlem replied.

"I am well aware of what he told everyone but, you do admit Thomas knew about the demons' attack and where the portal would appear."

"So did Arriann, Frex, and your house goblin, Gemedes." Harlem argued. "It seems the only logical spy would be one of them. Thomas was only aware of the plan after Arriann and Jamik left for Japan. I find it hard to believe he would have had time to warn the knights before the attack. Don't you?"

Cynric nodded in agreement, "Fine, I will start with Gemedes. He is the one who drove them to the airport; perhaps he knows more than he lets on. I trust you will be able to put a truth spell on him?"

"I am the most powerful warlock who has ever lived and you question my ability to cast spells on goblins? Really Cynric, I thought you knew better." Harlem's eyes glowed with fury. "Consider it done. But first, we will gather the materials needed to perform the rituals. Since I own Thomas, I say when his job is complete and I am letting you know now, he will no longer spy for you. So, unless you have other arrangements I suggest we go ahead with the first ritual before consulting your goblin."

"Let us go to Razor's, there are a few supplies we need there first." Cynric grumbled.

"What kind of supplies?" Harlem racked his brain, mentally checking off each item on his material list, none of which could be found in a bar.

"You will see when we get there. Come Dimitri it is time to go."

Gemedes was still in his plant, the voices getting closer to the door. He hid deeper into the leaves, trying to conceal every inch of his body. The door knob twisted and released the demon brothers, Harlem, and Thomas into the hallway.

Before they could exit the apartment, Dimitri spoke, "Exactly when do you plan on closing the portal...oh magic one?" He rolled with laughter.

Without humor Harlem replied, "Since when did someone die and make you king? Oh, wait I forgot, Modric chose Cynric to rule not you."

"Just close the portal. We are getting nowhere arguing about who was left in charge." Cynric's voice broke into their argument.

"Fine, but only because I have to," Harlem sulked and with a flick of his wrist the portal began to close; swirling in on itself.

Gemedes knew this was his only chance to escape. Fleeing into the office, after Harlem turned his back, he disappeared into a vortex of trees and sounds. Luckily, the portal led back home.

"Seth," Justahl called out into Frost forest, "Are you sure this is where you saw Harlem and Thomas go?" The two had been searching the woods for hours before Seth noticed Harlem and Thomas running in this direction.

Turning he answered, "Of course. Look, over there is the portal; they must have already run through it." He dashed to where the portal swirled in between two large oak trees; it was stronger than most portals, more powerful.

Suddenly, Justahl grabbed the back of Seth's armor, which he wore at all times, "I hear something coming from inside. Quick, hide over there," he pointed towards the brush behind him. "We can surprise whoever it is, if we split up."

He began transforming into a tree- fairies can shift into anything they wish, as long as it is alive. His thoughts went to Peitar; this was the place he had died just three days before. A tear rolled down his cheek, cutting into his concentration. Gathering himself, he tried again, this time he succeeded, morphing into a tree in a matter of seconds.

Standing perfectly still, he prepared for battle. His bow and arrows hung high in his branches. They did not transform but, merely found other resting places other than his arms.

A tree was his favorite thing to become, it gave him extra senses. He couldn't see, taste, or smell but, he could feel and sense everything going on around him. With nothing left to do, he waited for the portal to release the intruders. This time they would all die.

Colors swirled around Gemedes as he was thrown through the portal. *I can't stand these things, someone needs to invent a teleportation device without the swirling colors*, he thought, *this makes me dizzy*.

Just then, without any warning, he was tossed out into the middle of a clearing. Trying to regain his balance, he smacked into a tree. At least he thought it was a tree. He fell to the ground and moaned, "Ughh….why is there a tree in the middle of this clearing? I could have sworn it wasn't in this spot before I left."

The tree shuttered and shifted back into a person. "That's because I'm a person."

Gemedes rose up from the ground and rubbed his head, "Justahl, is that you?" He asked.

"Of course it's me who else would it be you nitwit, Bigfoot?" Justahl glared at him.

Gemedes glared back, "Everyone knows Bigfoot doesn't exist." He stuck his tongue out like a five year old, "And next time, could you be a rubber tree." He touched his fingers to the spot which had whacked into the 'tree' and winced in pain, "I probably have a concussion from hitting you. What were you doing anyway? Is my head bleeding?" His thoughts jumbled his words, making him sound psychotic. Everything was swirling around him, he felt like he was on water.

Justahl ignored his second question, answering the first, "Seth and I have been out on patrol, watching for any suspicious behavior. Then, Seth noticed Harlem go through this portal so we came here. After arriving, we heard noises from inside the portal and prepared to fight whatever came through, which reminds me." He turned towards the brush, "Seth, you can come out now. It's just Jiminy."

"My name is Gemedes you big-"

Seth laughed, cutting off their bickering, "You two sound worse than an old married couple. What's going on? I thought you were with the brothers?"

Gemedes bowed to Seth, he was a Prince after all, "They were catching on to me. I had to leave or be killed."

Justahl giggled, "Well maybe you should have stayed."

"Stop it Justahl! Gemedes, come, you can tell me on the way to the castle. Aislinn is awaiting our return" Seth motioned to himself and Justahl, "But, I am sure she will be anxious to hear you have returned. It sounds bad, especially if they were already catching on to you." With that, he motioned for Justahl to go ahead.

After a few deep breaths to gather his thoughts, Gemedes began his tale with a warning, "Seth, you have no idea how bad things really are."

Aislinn sat on her white throne- which was located in the white throne room, given this name because the entire room was white and shone brighter than any other room in the castle- speechless and weary. She knew the moment she opened her mouth, the screams would betray her calm, collected appearance. On the inside she was already screeching in terror but, as the current ruler, she would not let anyone else know. Slowly she rose to her feet, peering down at Gemedes. He looked frightened, tired, and hungry. Had he eaten anything since he left? Knowing he couldn't refuse her hospitality, she came up with an idea that would buy her some more time with him.

"Your majesty," Gemedes interrupted her thoughts, "I know this is terrible news but, it's nothing more than the ugly truth. Please forgive me for having to relay this message to you." He bowed in defeat.

"Gemedes my friend, rise up. There is no need to feel like a bad messenger, you were brave enough to spy for our kingdom and we owe you our lives." Aislinn knew he would appreciate this remark and quit wallowing in self-pity, so before he could say anything else she added; "Now for your living arrangements, you will be staying in the castle until further notice. Inside these walls you will be protected, just in case your fears of being followed were a reality.

Nothing can harm you here. Since Thomas is no longer with us," she paused, sighing in frustration, "Justahl will have Chef Perdy add extra food for you at tonight's dinner. I am having the court members and their families over; I hope that will not disturb you?"

He shook his head, "Not at all, I love parties but, I am a little underdressed." Gemedes glanced down at his ragged clothes. When he had left on his journey, the clothes had been brand new-a gift from the king- but now they looked like a dishcloth that had been overused for centuries.

She giggled looking at the goblin, "I'm sure Thomas' room is full of clothes you can wear. Justahl could help-"

"No, I can dress myself thanks." Gemedes interrupted her before she could offer Justahl's help.

"Alright, well hurry off and get ready. Dinner will be served at eight and I expect you clean, dressed, and down in the dining hall by then. Is that clear?" Aislinn used a firm tone at the end to make sure he knew tardiness was not tolerated in this castle.

He nodded and hurried off through the golden double doors on the east side of the room. Aislinn couldn't be sure but, it seemed as though he wasn't telling her something. Before she could focus too much on this thought, Seth burst through the doors.

"Why are you still sitting in here? What do we do now?" He was frantically waving at her but stopped when he saw her face. "You look confused, what all did he tell you?"

"Enough. I had hoped my father would be back by now, because he could handle this situation better. I am a mess Seth, what do I tell people? An army of demons are coming with powers greater than any of us could imagine? It will crush all their hopes of survival." She couldn't help herself, tears escaped down her cheeks, which were hot with the anger boiling inside her.

Seth only nodded in agreement, "They must know all the risks; otherwise we are not preparing them for the worst, only covering it up. Harlem being on Cynric's right side may not be all bad." His eyes lit up with an idea.

Aislinn looked at him more confused, "What are you talking

about?" She raged with anger, her best friend was losing his mind. Harlem was evil and more powerful than any creature in existence, how could he being with the demon brothers not be a bad thing?

"Didn't your father use to tell you and Amara stories about Ananais, the last living half-warlock?" He looked at her and smiled.

"Yes but I hardly see how he can help us now. My father banished him from the kingdom over three hundred years ago. Even if he is still alive, which I'm not convinced he is because, no one has mentioned him since he left, what could he possibly do that would change the circumstances?" She was talking so fast, her head was spinning.

Seth laughed, "Just because no one talks about him doesn't mean he's dead. Aislinn, he may not be as powerful as Harlem but, he's our only chance at leveling the playing field at all. We have to ask around, see if anyone has seen him or heard anything that could point him out to us. We at least have to try." He lowered his head, waiting for her argument.

Sighing, Aislinn lifted his head. "Fine, but if we find out where he is, Justahl and Gemedes are coming along. There is no way I'm leaving them two alone in the castle. It wouldn't be here when we returned."

Seth jumped up and grabbed her into a bear hug, "Oh, this is going to be awesome. I just know he can help us, from all the stories your father told you, Ananais sounds like an amazing person."

With a roll of her eyes she exited the room, calling while she walked, "I just hope your right. For the sake of this kingdom, I hope he is alive and will help us." The doors closed as Aislinn hurried toward her room. She longed for her father's encouraging words. King Galiron always knew what to do in times of trouble but, it was her turn to make decisions. Even though she wondered why the king hadn't answered his device, she would make him proud to call her his daughter. Perhaps her luck was changing.

Chapter 5
In Dark Company

Galiron rounded the corner and stepped inside the meeting hall. The cavernous room had a blue cast from the fairy lamps, which were placed every few feet. There were several white columns reaching from the black onyx floor to the ceiling above; each carved with swirling marks and words of protection and honor. Queen Andorra sat on a large black throne on the far side of the room; she seemed calm enough considering the circumstances. Hundreds of smaller chairs filled the remainder of the room, several of which were holding a member of the court. This hall use to be the cathedral many years ago but, now it served a different purpose.

"Ah, welcome Galiron Celthric, King of the Mazikeen fairies." She announced him to everyone with a wave of her hand, and then motioned for him to sit beside her, "Please come in and sit down. I'm sure you must be tired." Her exotic, slanted eyes lingered on his, glowing a fierce golden white color.

Andorra's long black hair cascaded in ringlets down her back. Each strand was covered in small cherry blossoms, which seemed to sparkle with magic and explode with color. The smell of it made him long to be at home but, without the help of the Asparas fairies-

species of Japanese fairies- the war would be a disaster. Queen Andorra was his only option.

"Yes, it has been a long time." Galiron bent to kiss her delicate white hands, "I should visit more often. You grow lovelier each time I see you." He smiled at her and took his seat. Her blue kimono wrapped around her slender body, hugging each curve. The front of it was clasped together with a golden fish, covered with aquamarine crystals-a rare stone to find. A large black diamond, about the size of a half dollar, hung from the looping gold chain around her neck. Her crown was exquisite, with golden leaves and spirals, more black diamonds, and a great white diamond in the center.

The Queen's voice interrupted his thoughts, "Enough with the small talk, let's get down to the real reason you came here. What exactly do you need? I understand you told everyone on the island you were working out peace negotiations but, after the urgent message I received this morning, I'm assuming this is not true. So, let us know what we can do." She gestured for everyone in the room to take their seats so he could have the floor; all forty pairs of eyes were focused on him. The Japanese court was larger in number than his own, he liked things simpler.

Clearing his throat, Galiron stood and acknowledged each member before beginning, "I come to you, begging for your assistance my lady. Please realize you're my kingdom's best chance for survival. Without you, we will all die." He paused looking out over the crowd, "The Akassa brothers are housing an army of over seven thousand demons in Chicago and their numbers are increasing rapidly. They are being trained for one purpose, to destroy my people and myself." Their faces froze with fear but, he was not finished because he knew more, the ancients had told him many things. "Don't think they will stop there, they will come here next and destroy anyone who stands in their way. Cynric must be stopped."

The room fell silent, no one looked at him, and they all stared at their Queen. However, Andorra seemed calm, collected, and thoughtful. She wasn't shocked, or afraid, or anything, she showed no emotion. He couldn't put his finger on it but, there was a secret

60

there, one she didn't want anyone to know about. This entire situation was not quite right and he knew the moment he looked into her eyes, something was off.

Suddenly, she was on her feet and rushing out of the hall. She stopped before opening the double doors leading outside, "Everyone is to go home immediately, NO EXCEPTIONS! We will continue this discussion tomorrow at noon. Goodnight!" Without another word, the Queen vanished, leaving the entire court, including King Galiron, staring after her. Flowers floated to the ground in her absence, as if they were dancing to a sad song.

This is bad, he thought, *really bad.*

"What do you mean you can't breathe?" Arriann sat against the long brick wall, which surrounded the back of the alleyway. She brushed debris off her green dress in swift motions. The alley they had chosen was dark, dirty, and smelled horrendous; she longed to be in Chicago, at least the alleyways there had food; apparently Tokyo didn't have hobos.

Jamik coughed, making smoke roll off his tongue, the taste of bitter rage in his mouth, "I mean, you're sitting on top of me, now get off me humpty-dumpty." He jostled his partner with little success at freeing his trapped body. "Why are we here anyway? This alley looks more like a horror movie than a hideout." Glancing around, he noticed several barrels used by homeless citizens in the winter. He could also hear water dripping from some of the pipes snaking up the surrounding walls, and in the distance sirens wailed into the otherwise silent streets. To the left, was a large metal fence, blocking their only back-up escape if something went wrong. Arriann had told him not to worry but, he had his doubts. King Galiron was strong and he could easily take them both out if need be, they had to attack undetected.

"Ughhh…" She huffed, standing to release her friend. "We are here to capture the King you moron," she seized his throat and pinned him to the wall, "And if you EVER call me humpty-dumpty again, I will shatter you into a million pieces and set your entire body on fire. Do I make myself clear?" With those final words, she let him go.

"Crystal," Jamik slumped to the damp concrete below, pain shooting to his head as blood began circulating again, he hated being a human, it was so inconvenient. Humans were pathetic and extremely delicate; most of them could be killed in a matter of seconds. He would much rather be a demon any day, at least then he could protect himself against Arriann's strength. She was strong no matter what she shifted in to, his powers only worked when he was in full demon form.

Just then, two figures emerged from behind one of the barrels, covered in dirt, the smell of humanity rolling off them in waves of deliciousness. Jamik looked at Arriann, who was already sauntering to where the human children stood frozen with panic. He loved the taste of frightened blood and these little darlings would leave a perfect aftertaste. This would be pleasurable.

"Well, well, well," Arriann started, "It seems we have some eavesdroppers Jamik. What should we do about this?" By this time she had already reached the cowering children, closing them into a corner. Jamik was right behind her, savoring the smell.

Their hearts beat faster and faster, causing the delicious blood to course through their veins. He enjoyed seeing them shake, their eyes darting around for help; no one could hear them out here.

The scrawny one started to speak, almost whining, "We didn't hear anything w-w-we swear."

"Of course not," Jamik encouraged, "We are merely hungry and you two are just so, delectable." He scraped the scrawny one's arm with his nails, making blood bubble to the surface. It screamed in agony as the red liquid dripped from its fingertips. The other one was already pinned to the ground, Arriann on top of it, readying herself for a midnight snack.

She looked toward him, smiling with overwhelming delight, "Cynric will not be pleased with this, but I can't pass up this taste." She breathed in heavily, "You are going to be so good." With that, she leaned in closer, preparing to strike. The little girl squirmed underneath her, thrashing out with wild hands, smacking Arriann in the face repeatedly.

"That will only make things worse for you little girl," he stated, "She is a demon after all and we hate being slapped, especially by poor, helpless humans. It does nothing but pisses us off and make us torture you slowly, causing you as much pain as possible." He turned back to his prey. "Come child; lay down so I may feast on your flesh, blood, and bones. Don't be afraid it will only hurt a lot." He roared with laughter as his razor sharp teeth sank into the child's arm, making its shrieks fill the night air but, for once he didn't care. No one would be out at this hour and if they were it wasn't out of the norm to hear people screaming in terror. Cynric would be mad but, even he couldn't have passed this opportunity up. He began feeding more diligently, making sure to drain every drop before devouring the flesh and bones.

Arriann had the girl hanging limp in her arms, sucking the life out of her. The child's blood was getting thicker, she was dying slowly. Her cries for help were overrun by a rush of blood that trickled into Arriann's mouth, flooding her throat with strength. This was the best food in the whole world; a child's blood is untainted, pure, and complex. It holds many secrets and as a demon, each taste is more seductive than the last.

Too soon, there was nothing left but the rags the children had been wearing to cover their bodies. "Put their clothes in this barrel over here, it has gasoline in it. We should leave no evidence of our dining." Arriann dug in her purse for a match. "Step back," she yelled, throwing the lighted match into the barrel, it burst into flames and soon the entire alley was covered in a thick smoke. They turned to finish their task, just in time to see the King's white hair pass the opening.

The room was nice, too comfortable to be considered a cell but, a cell is exactly what it was meant to be. Cynric's two best demons had caught him and although it came as no surprise, their timing aggravated him tremendously. He had hoped they would at least wait until the Queen decided one way or another; his kingdom needed her assistance. Thinking back to the meeting, Galiron's mind flashed to her storming out of the hall without any answers at all. "We will continue discussing this tomorrow at noon," she had said but, her eyes already told the final answer, no.

He sat on the edge of the hotel bed; it had green sheets, a white comforter, and four fluffy pillows. *Demons usually didn't stay in five star resorts; this must have been Dimitri's idea instead of Cynric's.* Finally, he decided to look around, so he rose to his feet and walked slowly to the large bay window, which overlooked the main square of downtown. The city was absolutely breathtaking at sunrise, the sky was turning light pink along the skyline, business owners were beginning their daily routines, and cars began filling the streets below. It looked a lot like New York City only everything was in Japanese.

With a sigh he returned to his former resting place, he missed Roanke Island. The rolling hills, the green meadows, the dancing trees of Frost Forest, and as much as he hated to admit it, he even missed his young friend Gemedes. As the King it was considered weak to miss the hired help but, he thought of every creature as a friend, even the house goblins. He wondered how Aislinn was doing without him, would she miss him when he was gone. The answer was obvious, the entire kingdom would miss him but, he had to leave in order to protect his people. Cynric wouldn't stop until he was dead. Aislinn and Amara would both be fine, the ancients had told him this much, although his daughters' entire futures were unclear. *Seth will always be there*, he thought, *he will keep the girls safe and help Aislinn be a great Queen someday.*

Once, he had thought maybe Seth and Aislinn would get married and have children but, they seemed content on being just friends so he had dropped the suggestion. They were joined at the hip so to speak because, if she was in a room, Seth was not too far away. The King was grateful for the undying loyalty of the elves. He recalled the first time he met Ellyis.

Nearly four hundred years ago, when kings and queens still ruled most of the countries on earth; Galiron had settled down with his father and mother on what would someday become Roanke Island. His father had been searching for a secluded place to call home, somewhere humans wouldn't dare visit. So, when he found the small island off the coast of Northern Alaska, he started building homes, roads, and a large castle on the northern shore. This later became known as Mazikeen City but at the time, it was called Celthricton after his family name.

A couple of months passed and many fairies came to the island to live. Most found it simplistic, calm, and comforting but, he found it adventurous, wild, and undiscovered. As a teenager, he had made many friends; however, none of his friends could compare to his best friend Ellyis Arabiraheal.

Ellyis was the best fighter in all the land and also an elf prince. He even saved his life once on a rafting expedition with some fellow warriors. After this incident, the two had become best friends and hadn't been apart since.

The door flew open, snapping Galiron out of his reverie. Arriann entered carrying a large silver tray in her hands, "Your dinner." She thrust it towards him, then, turned on her heels and stomped out of the room.

This was weird, he never expected to get food; perhaps it was poisoned. Without another thought, he sat it down, it probably was poisoned.

The day was getting longer and longer, perhaps he could try and contact Gemedes again tonight, after everyone was out of the room of course. Honestly, how stupid can two demons be? They left him here for hours while they went sightseeing. Arriann would leave first, telling Jamik to remain next to his door until she returned but, as soon as she was gone, Jamik gathered his belongings and headed out. This left the room empty until around ten o'clock when he returned before Arriann could notice his absence. Their stupidity gave him free time to get the communication device he kept hidden under the bed and use it to contact the goblin. Each night, he waited until they left, grabbed the device, and gave instructions to Gemedes, so he could help Aislinn. He also asked for any and all updates concerning the army in Chicago. It surprised him, to find the young goblin back on the island. Galiron knew things were getting complicated back home and soon the war would begin. All he could do, is hope his people were prepared.

Eventually, nighttime had fallen over the city. The streets were still covered in cars and pedestrians but, everything seemed quieter than in the daylight hours. He loved looking out over the skyline as the sun descended; actually he loved looking out the window at all. Seeing the city lights, hearing the animals in nearby parks, and noticing the slight differences in the sky; it all made him feel less homesick. His stomach churned with the emptiness he felt in his heart. He stopped his thoughts, there was no time for this foolish nonsense, and he had a job to do.

After checking to make sure the witch twins-his nickname for his kidnappers- were out of the hotel room, he began rummaging under the bed for his device. Soon, his hands encountered a smooth, box-shaped object with tiny holes in it for the speakers and millions of tiny buttons all over the front. The device looked worn but, he knew it still worked like a charm.

Pressing the code for Gemedes' device into his own, he sent a message to his friend back home. 'Gemedes, are you there?' he typed, 'Please answer if you are.' Moments passed and nothing happened, perhaps he had done something wrong. He tried the message again, this time receiving an answer, although it was not the one he wanted.

My Dearest Galiron,

Did you think I wouldn't find out? How stupid do you think I am? The device you hold in your hand links you directly to me now. I figured you would know this but, I seem to be mistaken.

Even without hearing his voice, the King knew Cynric was the messenger; he could even hear him laughing at his lack of knowledge. Harlem had cast a spell on his device, making all his messages go straight to Cynric. He really hadn't seen this turn of events coming.

Please excuse the two idiots I left in charge of you for the time being, they are dreadfully unfortunate creatures. No one ever said demons were smart; skillful, evil and quick thinkers? Yes but, when it comes to brains, they lack even an ounce of common sense.

Enough with the chit chat. Understand your majesty, I will destroy your land, your people, and eventually I will even destroy you and there is nothing you can do about it. Don't worry though, my plan is working perfectly, I have ways of keeping your kind in the dark, even if they know about my army now. All in good time, you will realize I am the only ruler of this planet and nothing can stop me. So, farewell Galiron Celthric, I do hope you sleep well.

~Cynric
P.S. In the end, I WIN!

Rage rushed through him like an iron fist, smacking him down onto the floor. His hands flew out and caught the bed, flinging the entire mattress against the window in one swift movement. His mind raced ahead to the immense future but, all he could see was Cynric's face, mocking him while he died a slow and agonizing death. The image irritated him more, so he started flinging other pieces of furniture. Anything he could get his hands on quickly became a weapon to ransack the room. He couldn't breathe for the pain in his chest beating against his skin. Finally, he collapsed on the floor in defeat. There was nothing he could do now but, sit in this room and wait to die; karma had reared its ugly head and was headed straight for his heart.

"What the hell happened in here?" Arriann screeched, pushing Jamik out of the way to get a better look at the King's room. "Since when do tornadoes occur inside?" she yelled through the suite, "Have you seen this?"

He entered carrying a small bag of blood, slurping the contents out with a straw. He quickly glanced around the room; the only emotion on his face was complete shock at the damage in front of him. No words came out.

"Well?" Arriann knew he was lying now. He told her their prisoner hadn't made a noise all night, then, she came back to find a disastrous bedroom. The mattress leaned against the window, a chair lay broken on the floor, splinters of wood everywhere, all the lamps were overturned and smashed, and the King lay in a heaping pile in the far corner. More than likely he was unconscious. She turned back to her partner, "Are you going to explain to me how this," she gestured to the entire room, "happened, when you plainly told me he hadn't made a single noise all night? How did him smashing lamps and breaking chairs, not make a sound?"

Clearing his throat he began thinking. He knew he was dead, this much was fact but, he didn't need to tell her everything so he quickly came up with a suitable lie. "I heard a noise in the hallway around eight, so I walked out there to see what it came from. I saw a small creature run down the stairs, headed for the exit. Since it was more than likely a friend of his," he pointed toward Galiron, "I went after it. He must have done this while I was gone." The lie suited the situation perfectly or so he thought.

Arriann picked up one of the smashed lamps and knocked him in the arm, "Have you completely lost your mind? Cynric is going to flip if he finds out. How can you be so careless?" She hit him again only this time on the head. "Here's an idea, next time you see something or someone in the hallway, don't go after it unless it attacks you. Honestly what were you thinking?" Without another word, she stormed out of the room and slammed the door.

Jamik turned to follow her when a portal appeared in front of him. "ARRIANN!" He yelled for her to come into the room. She entered just as Harlem stepped out of the swirling vortex, setting his leather booted foot down on the soft, plush carpet.

Harlem stared at them, then, at the damaged room. "Hello, morons; I suspect you know why I am here?" He walked to the edge of the bed, taking off his signature leather gloves, and sat down. "Cynric is not pleased with you. First, you send spies, who died by the way, onto the island, which caused Iklin to show up for an unannounced visit. Then, you come here and leave the most powerful creature in the world, alone long enough for him to try and make contact with his house goblin. What does that tell you?"

Arriann started to say something but, thought better of it. Instead she replied, "This idiot left him alo-"

Harlem crossed the room in less than a second, seized her by the neck, and crushed her against the door, which opened into the large living room of the hotel suite. "Don't blame everything on him. You are just as responsible for this situation as he is. Luckily, Cynric requested I place a re-routing spell on his communication device. He thought you two would mess up."

He let go of her throat, forcing her lungs to start working again, "Look, we didn't know he would have a device. How mad is he?" She knew he was really upset. Cynric hated when people disappointed him.

"Trust me, you don't want to know. Let's just say if you two were back in Chicago, you wouldn't have your legs attached to your bodies." Harlem yawned with boredom, "I do hope he calms down before you return. He is beginning to get on my nerves."

Jamik looked at Arriann, "I think we should just remain in the room from now on."

She just shook her head and slapped him on the back, "You think."

Harlem waved another portal open, bid them goodbye, and vanished back to Chicago.

"I really don't like that guy." Jamik shivered with fear, "Couldn't Cynric find anyone else to relay that message?" He walked over to Arriann who just stared at him.

"Clean this up…NOW!" She barked, closing the door as she exited the prisoner's bedroom.

He picked up the mattress and threw it on the bed. The next few weeks were going to drag on forever, especially if she couldn't hunt. She tended to make his life miserable when she was hungry. Hopefully, they wouldn't have to be here much longer.

Chapter 6

Taste of Hope

He raced through the woods, screaming in pain. No one could help him, no one cared-he was alone and dying.

Sitting straight up in his bed, Justahl glanced around his bedroom. *When had he fallen asleep?*

His dreams were all quite strange lately. Every time he closed his eyes, he would find himself alone, in the deepest shadows of Frost Forest. The weirdest part was he couldn't seem to shake the feeling someone was after him-even in his dreams.

Quickly, he climbed out of bed, throwing the satin sheets onto the floor. After recent events, he was to remain in the castle until further notice. This wouldn't have been so bad if Gemedes wasn't staying two rooms down the hall.

Justhal couldn't stand the house goblin; he blamed him for Peitar's death. Gemedes was the one who sent a message to Peitar about the demon attack. Of all the knights on the island, he chose to send it to his brother. Anger coursed through him, making his entire body shiver with guilt and frustration.

"He wasn't the one who didn't help your brother," a strange voice echoed. *"You were annoyed with him and upset with the fact he was chosen for*

the knight competitions instead of you. So, you didn't care when he came and told you of the attack, did you?" The voice laughed at him.

He threw open the door to his room, checking the hallways for the creature who had spoken. The halls were empty-the only light coming from the golden fairy lamps, hanging every few feet on the otherwise dark, stone walls. Maybe this was a dream too?

"Nice try Justahl Lerin, but you will not find me in the castle, or even on the island for that matter. I speak to you from a different location, and this is most definitely not a dream, although I have been visiting you there as well." The voice seemed to shake the entire room when it laughed this time.

His head spinning, Justahl spoke to the strange voice, "Fine. If you will not show yourself, at least have the guts to tell me where you are." He sounded like an idiot, talking to empty space but, the voice sounded as if it were right next to him. Breathing down his neck.

"All in good time my young knight. You see how quickly I can manipulate you? Soon you will be unable to control your actions. I will drive you crazy with images of your dead relatives in every dark corner, hiding, waiting for you to join them in certain death. I will rule your entire body but, do you know why?" The voice paused for a moment before starting again, *"Because I am in your mind."*

The voice disappeared as quickly as it had appeared, only this time Justahl knew he wasn't dreaming.

Aislinn startled awake, not too surprised to hear a loud banging coming from inside the castle. The same noise had waked her to begin with.

Quickly, she grabbed her silk robe off the bedpost; where she had hung it last night, and threw open her bedroom door. Seth stood in the hall, armed and ready. His eyes were alert but the rest of his body screamed with the 'I just woke up so don't mess with me' look. She giggled to herself.

"Is something amusing you?" Seth's tone was bitter but, still held a bit of kindness towards her. "I'm sorry if my attire is not suitable for you but, it is two in the morning after all." He began walking down the hall, not waiting for her to join him.

Still giggling she answered, "It's just I didn't expect to see you this awake. It was odd that's all." They rounded the corner into the main lobby, which connected with the foyer on the other side. The room was dark, packed with unknown shadows, and cold. There were several paintings hanging on the stone walls, seating arranged in groupings to allow better communication when guests were over, and two large stone fireplaces sat on either side-neither burned even a single log tonight.

Seth looked at her, the apology hidden behind his crystal green eyes, "Forgive my rudeness, I'm not much of a morning person. Sorry I lost my temper."

She laughed in agreement, "I know and you don't have to apologize, I understand." The banging sounded through the room, filling the shadows with an unsettling echo. Noticing where the noise came from, her tone turned formal, "Who would be knocking on the door at this time of night?"

Grabbing her arm as she walked ahead of him to get the door, Seth argued, "No! I will answer, it is too dangerous." He pushed her so her entire body would be hidden by the door when it opened. *Just in case*, he thought. Then, without any hesitation, he opened the large wooden door and peered into the night.

A dark hooded figure stood outside the castle walls, drenched in rain. Seth forgot about the rain showers the island had been receiving on a daily basis. No wonder this creature was so persistent to get inside.

"May I come in?" The figure asked, his voice echoing through the castle with a hint of a foreign accent. "I am looking for Princess Aislinn. Is she here?"

Seth's entire body froze with fear. He raised his sword, raindrops glistening off of the silver edge like falling stars. "Who wishes to know?" His tone had turned deadly cold and calm, like his father's used to when something wasn't quite right. Lowering the sword to the figure's neck he added, "State your business with the Princess."

The creature stepped back, removing his hood in one swift movement and bowing in the next. "Forgive me. I didn't mean to alarm you my friend but, I need to talk to Aislinn. This is about her father."

Aislinn couldn't take it anymore. If this stranger knew something about her father, she needed to face him not Seth. Ignoring her best friend's motions to 'back off' she stepped into view. Without hesitation she spoke, her voice was still all business. "My father is in Japan. How could you know anything about him?" Her eyes met his then, immediately changing her tone. "Won't you come inside?" She gestured for him to enter before thinking, *why did I just do that?*

Seth gawked, his eyes nearly bulging out of his head before muttering in annoyance, "I don't see why I even bother trying to protect you. You always do what you want anyway…" He grumbled several profanities under his breath, while the fairy- the only explanation she could give a man with black wings and pale skin- walked into the foyer.

"Please excuse my friend," She elbowed him in the ribs, hoping it would leave a mark, "He hates surprises."

The fairy looked at her, honestly intrigued with her words, "Ah. But you like surprises?" His eyes were the color of blue crystals but, they sparkled like diamonds. He held his hand out to her in a gesture of friendly introductions, "How rude of me, my name is Dest Reimin. I am from the city of Tokyo, Japan, where I hold a seat on the council. Please know I am terribly sorry for the hour in which I made my visit but, I forgot about the time change."

Standing up, Seth mumbled something about "time change being a lousy excuse" and retreated into the other part of the castle. Yelling over his shoulder, "I guess I will go wake the others, since it seems we have a new friend."

Aislinn barely noticed the sarcasm his used to describe Dest, she was too busy trying to find her way out of his gaze.

Dest turned toward the lobby, "Shall we take a seat in there? I am so tired." He looped his arm with hers and together they waltzed into the other room, leaving complete silence behind them.

She noticed the heat that coursed through his arm to hers. It felt warm, alive, charged with nerves and something else she couldn't quite place. His wavy, golden brown hair swayed when he walked, making it seem as though each strand was dancing to hidden music she couldn't hear.

Finally, they made it in front of the left side fireplace. She nestled herself into one of the large chairs, trying to warm her cold body now that his heat was gone. "So, you are from Japan correct? And you have news about my father?" Aislinn shuddered at the thought of her father being in trouble. If he was in trouble, what did that say for the rest of them? She cast the thought out of her mind. They would survive. They had to.

Clearing his throat, Dest answered, "I'm afraid your father hasn't been seen or heard from for two days. Queen Andorra hoped he was back at home safe but, we all knew otherwise. No one disappears unless they have been captured or killed."

His words sent shivers down her spine. She was saved from speaking by the sudden crowd filling the room. Seth walked in followed by Gemedes, Justahl, Quid, and of course Amara. *The gang's all here*, she thought but, for once, she was glad.

Justahl was the first to speak, "You dragged us out of bed for this." He pointed towards Dest and shrugged, "So a new fairy shows up and captures the interest of your best friend. I fail to see how it matters to us?" He plopped into a nearby chair, "Please explain."

She looked at the ground, blushing since she'd been caught fawning over their guest. Was it that obvious?

Seth's face turned several shades of red before he spoke, "She isn't interested in him!" He raged with fury, "And DON'T speak to me in that tone ever again! I may not be a king yet but, I am still above you!"

Aislinn rose, taking a hold of Dest's chair. She didn't know why but, she suddenly had the need to be around him. Touching something he was touching or just touching him at all. "I think everyone needs to calm down. We are making a bad first impression on our visitor. Everyone this is Dest. He is from Japan." She turned toward Dest, whispering so only he could hear, "Don't mind them, they always fight at two in the morning. Please make yourself at home and we will continue our conversation at breakfast." Her soft

75

smile turned angry as she glared at Seth, "And since you woke up the entire castle, I guess you will be cooking breakfast. For EVERYONE! Oh and Justahl."

"Yes your majesty?"

"Make sure our guest finds a room suitable enough for his stay. One that isn't next to hostile neighbors." Without another word she left the room to get ready. She knew she looked awful and Dest looked magnificent in comparison but, nothing a hot shower and a quick change of clothes couldn't fix. Her mind raced through images of her father being kidnapped and thrown into a cell for safe keeping, or being tortured by two dark figures in swirling cloaks. She brushed the thoughts away. Perhaps what Dest would tell her wouldn't be so bad. Maybe her father was just sick or something. *Only one way to find out*, she thought and opened her bedroom door.

"So Dest, have you been in the council long?" Aislinn stared at the newcomer. He looked so put together, yet he didn't overdo it either. His clothes were neat and clean, and his armor was so shiny she could see her reflection in it.

Dest cleared his throat, probably nervous about having to speak in front of Seth, who stared him down intently. "No your majesty, I am fairly new to the whole council thing. My family is from a remote location. Not a lot of other fairies around to concern ourselves with councils and such. However, I have been with the Japanese council for about a year now so, I roughly know the majority about it. If you want, after breakfast you can accompany me on a walk down by the beach? I always go for a walk in the mornings; it gets me ready for the day. I could tell you more about the council."

Seth made a noise between a snort and a growl but, he quickly coughed to cover up his comment. "I love to go for walks too."

The entire room fell silent as everyone looked at him. Aislinn only laughed lightly, ignoring his attempts at protecting her, "I do believe he invited me. Plus, I need someone to run patrols until the new guards arrive. They should be arriving around ten, which will give you and Justahl plenty of time to scope out the shores for immediate danger." She turned toward Dest without waiting for the argument she knew would follow her last comment. "I'm sorry for his behavior and yes I would love to take a walk with you. Perhaps you could teach me some Japanese. I've always considered it to be quite a captivating language."

Dest smiled and took her hand. Kissing it softly he replied, "I would consider it a great honor."

Aislinn looked into his eyes again. Getting lost in their richness, swimming in their waves, and cascading down into his very soul. He was quite a gentleman; strong, faithful to his country and his people, and absolutely the most beautiful creature she had ever laid eyes on. It was at least ten minutes until she noticed all the eyes in the room were staring at her. She quickly coughed, using Seth's tactic to getting out of difficult situations, and ate a bite of apple off her plate.

Justahl saved her from speaking, "So, the princess tells us you have news of the king. Is he alright?"

"Oh, I completely forgot. Well, I guess I should start from the beginning. The king showed up about four days ago with news about the demon army invading you. He warned the queen, we would be next if we didn't help. Most of us just sat there in silence, waiting for the queen's answer. Would we go or would we stay? No one knew. But all she did was get up and tell everyone to go home. She said we would continue the conversation the next day. The king hasn't been heard from since."

She noticed his lack of enthusiasm at continuing on. He probably thought she was crazy, staring at him for as long as she had. She would make a note not to be so careless about her feelings from now on.

Seth spoke, "Maybe he got lost or he is sick. Have you checked all the hotels? All the roadways, restaurants, bars? He could have just left for a little while and hasn't returned yet. Or maybe he-"

"Enough Seth!" Aislinn was beginning to feel nauseous; her stomach did flips inside her body. It made her want to run away. Run away from everything, from the people in this room, the war, the island, the universe. Everything was poisonous. Nothing was normal or easy anymore. She needed a few moments to digest what Dest had told them. First, her father was missing and had been for days. Second, Japan wasn't going to help them at all except for sending this fairy over to tell them more bad news. And third, she was completely unable to lead an entire kingdom into a war she knew they couldn't win. She grabbed at the arms of her chair, the room swirling in all directions, and dashed out of the dining hall and into the foyer. Time was of an essence at the moment but, as a ruler she needed to always be calm. Right now she was seriously close to losing her cool. No one needed to see that.

Her gasps turned into long, deep breaths. Seconds ticked away on the large grandfather clock but, not even time was helping her now. What was going on? She never lost control like this. Ever.

Dest walked out, finding Aislinn slouched against the stone wall of the foyer. "You look awful."

"Gee, thanks. That is just what I need right now, more of the ugly truth." She paused looking up at him. "Oh, it's you. Please forgive my insolence. I am usually much nicer and less erratic."

"I don't mind. Actually, I'm quite use to it. My mother raised me and my siblings on her own most of the time since my father worked a lot; she had these days. Come on, I know what will cheer you up and relieve some of your stress. I can't imagine what you are going through. I mean your father left you in charge while a war is getting closer every day. Something like that has to be hard."

Aislinn looked at him, tears streaking her face, "You have no idea."

He helped lift her off the floor, gently taking her hand, "Do you need to tell them you're leaving for a bit?"

She shook her head, "Nah, they know what to do. Where are we going anyway?"

"Nope, it's a surprise. You like surprises remember?" His laugh echoed through the entire room, making her laugh as well.

He liked her laugh, it was subtle, sweet, and made her hair fall into her eyes. Without even thinking, he leaned over and brushed the lock of blonde hair away from her face. Her breath washed over him, flowing through his body like flames but, in a good way. It smelled like apples and maple syrup. Probably from the pancakes he had admired her eating earlier.

Stop! This is wrong, he scolded himself mentally, *and you aren't supposed to notice the small stuff. You're not supposed to notice her at all. Just a routine mission,* he reminded himself and quickly let go of her hand. Rushing out into the courtyard before he could get distracted again, he said, "Which way is the nearest beach?"

"Just through Frost Forest," She pointed to a winding trail, surrounded on either side by lush trees, shrubs, and flowers. It was the most magnificent place he had ever seen.

They set off in search of distractions.

Seth turned away from the door. Aislinn would come back any minute. She had to.

He should be out there with her, not Dest. If anyone knew what she was going through, he did. After his father passed away last year, she was there to help him through. So, why couldn't he make himself go to her?

It was like he was a puppet and someone else was pulling the strings. Stay or go he didn't have a choice. Something was wrong.

"Well done my young prince, you seem to have realized what's going on. Your friend didn't figure it out so quickly. He thinks he's going insane. Look at him."

A strange voice echoed in his ears but, when he looked around no one was speaking.

Justahl sat nervously ringing his hands over and over again but, nothing came from his mouth. Was he the one the voice talked about?

"Yes." The voice answered the question he hadn't spoken aloud.

He glanced around again, thinking he could catch the person playing tricks on him.

"You won't find me in that room Seth Arabiraheal, I am nowhere and everywhere. Trust me when I say, I will have my revenge and all of you will perish. Farewell and don't worry I will return."

With that the voice drifted away as suddenly as it had come. It was like the person could speak only for a short time. The worst part was Seth knew exactly who the voice belonged to but, he needed evidence before consulting Aislinn. He needed time alone to think and process the warning he was given.

"Justahl," He started, "I need you to take patrol by yourself this morning. It's important that I tend to a few things before going out again. I am sorry to leave you al-"

Gemedes' head shot up and he looked ecstatic, "No, no, he won't be alone. I can go with him. Please Seth. I promise not to be any trouble."

Justahl grumbled something like 'yeah right' under his breath but, didn't voice it aloud.

"Great. It's settled then, Justahl and Gemedes will go on patrol and you two," He pointed to Quid and Amara, "Will need to stay here until one of us return. Is that clear?"

Both Amara and Quid answered, "Yes sir."

"Alright now off with you all," He motioned for them to leave while he stayed behind to think. Nothing good could come of this situation and things were getting a lot worse since the new guy showed up. Maybe it was time to do a little background on Dest and find out everything he could. No one could be trusted, even if they did wear the face of a friend.

Leaving the dining hall, Seth set foot into the foyer. He hoped to find Aislinn still sitting there, waiting for him but, a quick look around proved his thoughts wrong.

The entire room was empty of life. No one had been here for at least twenty minutes. *So*, he thought, *she left without saying goodbye. Well, I sure hope this new guy isn't an axe murderer.*

Seth shook his head, then, headed off towards the library. Research always calmed his nerves, especially when it involved solving a mystery.

He had to figure out how Cynric was doing this and figure it out fast, before someone got hurt.

"How much farther?" Aislinn asked for the fifth time since leaving the castle.

"You're asking me?" Dest looked at her with a wild expression. "I've never set foot on this island, yet you ask me how much farther to the shore?" He shook his hair, laughing pitifully, "Come on, I think I hear the waves hitting the sand just up ahead."

He was right. Just after he finished his sentence, they stepped onto the first piece of sand.

"Wow," Dest gawked in amazement, "This place is stunning. No wonder all the fairies love it here." His eyes lingered on the sun-it was still early morning so it had not fully raised yet.

"I know it sure is something to look at. I can't believe you've never been here before. There were moments at breakfast I felt as though I have known you my entire life. Oh, well probably just the stress."

Dest laughed lightly, "Yes, stress. So, what do you want to know about me? I have heard so many stories about you, I too feel as though I know you. It has always been a dream of mine to spend a few hours with you, talking about life and stuff. Isn't it funny how some things just work out? I mean, this time last week I was just sitting in a room, taking up space. But now, I am out here with you in one of the most gorgeous places I have ever seen. How do you feel about this situation?"

"Ummm…" She paused. To be honest, she didn't know what to say. Her mind was screaming in protest for her to be more cautious but, her heart was screaming louder for her to tell him the truth. Plus, he talked a lot or maybe it was just nerves.

"I'm sorry. I didn't mean to make you uncomfortable. Please forget I even asked and feel free to ask anything you want. I swear I will answer truthfully." He looked at her; his blue eyes pierced her where she stood. His gaze held her in place.

"No, no. I'm fine it's just-" She paused again but, this time only for a second, "The truth is I feel like I can be myself around you. I feel safe, happy, and a little less stressed out. You have no idea how much pressure I am under. My father has ruled this island for hundreds of years and now he is missing. There is nothing I fear more than becoming the queen of this kingdom. I know the day is coming sooner or later but, really, I didn't expect it so soon. What if everyone hates me? Or what if I fail?" She dropped to the ground, placing her head between her knees-it always helped her to relax and breathe.

Dest sat beside her, only not quite hitting the ground as hard as she had. "Don't believe a word of it. They should recognize not every ruler will be like your father and you can't set yourself up to be just like him in every way. If you do, you will fail." He reached over, bringing her face up to meet his, "Look, I'm not saying you won't be a great queen because, I believe you will. I've only met you today and I believe that to be the honest truth."

"Then what are you saying?" His skin burned hers but in a pleasant way. It blazed through her and calmed her fears.

He laughed, "I was getting to that. All I'm saying is you will be a great queen in your own way but, no one is perfect all the time. Your father could even tell you that." His eyes flickered with a strange look before he gathered it back into his normal composure.

How odd, noticing his normalcies only hours after meeting him. She shook her head and sighed, "Thanks. I really needed to hear that, even if it was from a complete stranger."

"I would like it if perhaps we weren't strangers. Maybe we could have more talks like these."

"Where I completely lose control over myself and flee the room?" She giggled at the thought of Seth's face when he noticed her and Dest missing.

Dest laughed as well, his laughter carrying a melodic tune, "I didn't mean that." He nudged her arm with his, "I meant we should get to know more about each other while I'm staying here. My family would love to know more about the future queen of Roanke Island."

"I assume you have a large family?" She couldn't help herself from asking questions about him. He was new, exhilarating, and intriguing.

"Ah, the questions begin? Yes, you assume correctly. I have five brothers and two sisters, all of whom have either died in battle or moved to make their homes elsewhere." He must have noticed the sadness in her eyes, because he added, "Don't feel sorry for me, I like being alone."

"But, aren't your parents still around?"

"Yes and no. Yes, because they're still alive. No, because they still live in our old home and I don't see them much anymore. I used to visit all the time but, between the council and working, I hardly have the chance. However, I talk to them sometimes, on my communication device."

Aislinn was truly fascinated with this new creature; he seemed so content with his life. She wished for that luxury, "So, what do you do? I mean you said you work right, doing what?"

"I help around Andorra's castle. Paperwork, cleaning, delivering messages, and stuff. It doesn't pay much but, it gives me enough to eat and live."

"Hmm... Well, that sounds amazing. All you have to worry about is yourself; I have to worry about this entire kingdom." She motioned all around where they were seated. "I wish I could have a normal life."

"Being normal is quite boring. Look at your life. Excitement all the time, parties, battles, and now you get to spend time with me." Dest laughed heartily at his joke. "Tell me, what would you do if you weren't a princess?"

Aislinn was puzzled; she had never really given the idea much thought. No one had ever asked her that question before. "Well, for one I would get a job. Maybe working as a teacher, I do like children. Then, I would get married, have a family, and watch my own children grow into successful adults." She was satisfied with her answer; it painted an image of how things could be if she lived through this war.

"It sounds picture perfect. Would you choose a normal life?" His eyes pierced hers again.

Thinking about the question she chose the truth, again. What was with this guy? He could get her to tell the truth no matter what. "I think I would actually. Mainly because I wouldn't be leading my people to their death, into a war we can never win. Plus, no one knows when the war will start or how or even where, we just know it's coming soon. I can't face the entire kingdom and tell them to fight when I know they will all die either way. What am I supposed to do?" She felt herself slipping off the edge again, one question and she was freaking out.

Dest hugged her shoulders softly. Not long enough for her to feel the blazing heat but, long enough to get a whiff of his clothes. He smelled of metal and falling rain. It was wonderful.

He looked her straight in the eye and asked the one question she didn't want to answer, "Why is it hopeless? I don't mean to pry I'm just curious. If the war is against demons, we kill them all the time. No problem."

"Yes we do but, our entire island alone is no match for seven thousands of them plus Harlem."

She noticed his eyes darken at the mention of the warlock.

"Really, that many huh? Wow, I see your point. But isn't there anything you can do?" His voice faltered at the beginning, giving off the hint of something but, it was gone before she could catch it.

"Not unless Seth's plan works."

Aislinn thought about Seth and how he had been so keyed up with an idea to help them. She really didn't see Ananais helping them much, especially after the falling out with her father.

Dest looked interested, slightly too shocked to hear they had a plan. "What is Seth's plan?"

She couldn't decide whether to tell him or not. Yes, he was a fairy but, she didn't know that much about him. Could he be trusted?

"Come on I won't tell anyone I swear. Maybe I can help. That is if you want me to?"

"Well, Seth has this bright idea that Ananais is still alive. If we can find him, then, just maybe we can give those Akassa brothers a taste of their own medicine. However, there is a slight problem." She hesitated, "Ananais and my father had a huge fight, which led to him being banished from the kingdom. No one has heard from or about him since."

"I see. That is an interesting plan but, it seems as though you don't believe this Ananais is alive. Is that true?" He glanced out into the waves crashing to the shore.

"No and if he is, I don't think he will help us at all. He is quite angry with our entire family but, maybe with the right attitude and company," Now she nudged him in the arm, "He will."

Dest looked relieved and pleased with her answer, "I agree and I also thank you for inviting me. You don't have to be so kind."

He kissed her hand lightly, sending fire scorching through her veins and straight to her heart.

"I insist you join our adventure. It might help since Ananais is known for loving Japanese fairies." She laughed to herself.

"It would be an honor your majesty."

They continued talking for a while and before she knew it, he rose up from the sand, dusting off his gear, "I do think it's time to head back."

She looked at him, stunned. "Wait," She grabbed his arm, "Why must we head back so soon? We just got here."

He laughed, taking her hand and helping her to her feet. "Yeah, about two hours ago. Look at the sun; it must be nearly nine or ten." Pointing towards the sky he laughed again, "Don't worry I won't tell them anything you told me." He placed a finger to his mouth, signifying secrecy.

"Alright, if we must." She reluctantly took a step towards Frost Forest, only to be spun around into his arms.

"Thank you for this walk. It was nice and I find your life here fascinating." He hugged her for a while before letting go and taking her hand, "Is it okay for us to hold hands?"

"Of course, I'm a princess not a nun." She giggled as they walked onto the trail that would lead them back to the castle, the forest engulfing them in a giant green mass. It felt nice to finally feel normal for once, even if the creature next to you looked nothing less than perfect. Maybe with him here, she could find the courage to face the army of demons. It was a big maybe but, it was better than nothing at all.

Chapter 7

Search Party

Seth stomped ahead of them by several feet. He seemed to be taking Dest's arrival worse every day, and it didn't help any that she had invited him to join their search.

Since they left the castle, over twelve hours ago, he hadn't said anything to them except for once, when he was arguing with Justahl over which way to go.

"It's this way Seth. We'll encounter nothing but shoreline that way." Justahl explained.

"No! I think I know where we're supposed to go. I am the king." Seth pointed out sharply.

"Not yet you aren't and if you were, you would know this entire mission is pointless. No one can find Ananais; he hasn't been seen or heard from since the king banished him."

"I am well aware of how this search is going and I don't need help from you."

After the argument, Seth hadn't said another word.

Aislinn knew how Seth felt; it was all over his face. He was hurt because she was spending time with Dest instead of him. Of course, he wasn't in love with her, he just wanted to always know she was safe. He wanted to look after her, comfort her, and tell her it would be okay and now Dest did all those things. Seth was the big brother she had always wanted and never had; he was her best friend, and until Dest had shown up four days ago, he was her only friend.

Suddenly, Seth stopped. Every one of them froze, their bodies tensed for battle.

"What is it?" Justahl asked.

"Nothing, I just think we have gone all we can for the night," He glanced around, "It's getting dark and I don't feel safe traveling. We should set up camp here and continue at first light." Seth walked over to the nearest tree and sat down his bags. "I will be right back, I just need to scope out the perimeter."

Without another word, he darted in between two oak trees, disappearing into the woods.

"Is it just me or is he acting weird?" Gemedes spoke up.

Dest chuckled, "You mean he's usually not a raging jerk one second and completely ignoring you the next? Hmm…I thought that was just his normal behavior."

"No, actually he is quite cheerful when an entire army of demons are waging war on his homeland. I forgot most people are genuinely kind in those situations. My bad." Seth stepped into the light, which emanated from their fairy torches, an evil glare pointed directly at Dest

"Look I'm sor-" Dest started.

"Oh don't bother apologizing to him, he's being a baby." Aislinn interrupted him with a sharp voice, then, turned to Seth, "Start a fire and help Justahl and Gemedes pitch the tents. Dest and I are going to find food."

Grabbing Dest's arm, she dashed between the two oak trees, leaving a stunned and speechless Seth behind them.

It wasn't two seconds before the light from the fairy torches disappeared, replaced by the light of the moon. Dest opened his mouth to speak. "I have to say I'm beginning to think you're more ready for this war than you let on. What you just did was amazing. Seth's face was priceless!" He nudged her in the shoulder, placing his hand in hers.

The gesture heated her entire body like a pleasant fire, making her glad she had let him in the castle last week. "Well, I suppose I'll have to apologize later. It's not very queen-like to be yelling at another king, even if he is being a jerk. Thanks though, for the compliment about the war. I just hope you're right."

"Aislinn, you are one in a million. You are beautiful, talented, smart, and kind-hearted. No one will ever be as great as you are. You're going to make an amazing queen and don't worry about the war, I have a plan that just might work." He smiled a brilliant smile, his teeth glistening like diamonds in the moonlight. "Do you think we can find this…Ananais or whoever?"

"If we don't I'm afraid we will all die." She sighed, "Alright, enough talk about war and death. I get too much of it at home, it's all the council discusses anymore. Come on, let's go find some food before we give Seth another reason to hate you."

"He hates me?" Dest looked sarcastically shocked, "I thought he absolutely adored me. Why else would he look at me with those glaring eyes of love and kindness?"

They both burst into laughter as they edged into another clearing.

Glancing around, Aislinn noticed several small bushes blossoming with tiny teal berries. She paused, trying to remember the name for those plants. Nothing came to mind.

Dest ran forward, dropping her hand and picked a berry off the nearest bush, "This is amazing, dream berries!"

"What did you call them?" She looked at him shocked. All her life she had been walking through these woods. Her and Seth played hide and seek here when they were younger. However, in all those years, she had never seen this berry. It was like they were placed here by magic.

"These are dream berries." Dest ran back to her side and opened up his palm to reveal the tiny fruits. "They are known for their rarity, only blooming once every two hundred years. My father use to send me and my siblings out all the time, to search for these things. Some say they're magical and whoever eats the first one, will receive the wish their heart desires most." He held up his hand, balancing a single berry in his palm, "Here, take it. Perhaps you will get your wish."

She looked at the round fruit, taking it out of his hand and placing it into hers. After examining it, she raised her hand and plopped it into her mouth. The taste was sensational. It made her feel like she was floating on air, sucking in sunshine, and savoring every last drop of sweet dreams in one bite. The taste flowed down her throat and made her feel happy, strong, and perfect. It was the most outstanding fruit she had ever consumed and unlike anything she had ever ate.

"Well, did you make a wish?" Dest looked at her curiously.

Aislinn thought about everything her heart desired but, every wish involved him. His eyes cast a deep shadow down his face, the moonlight sparkled in his ice blue eyes, and he looked like an angel. She had everything her heart desired and more, when he was around. The only thing that was missing was his lips on hers. Then, she wished.

"I made my wish." She stared into his eyes, getting lost again, but noticed something off about them. He seemed unhappy about something. "I'm sorry, if you wanted the berry, you could have eaten it."

"Oh, no, I'm sorry. I shouldn't be alone with you; we need to get back to the others."

Without another word, he turned and fluttered away. So much for the magical powers, she thought as she flew after him, catching a few fish, from a nearby stream, on the way.

"Well it's about time you came back," Seth scolded. "I was beginning to think you were lost. Did you at least get some food?"

Aislinn stepped into the campsite, two paces behind Dest. He didn't look at her. "Oh, keep your pants on, we weren't gone that long." She held up her hands and tossed him the fish, trying to hit his face but, sadly she missed. "Here, I caught those on the way back. Hope everyone likes trout."

Gemedes' head shot up in response, "Trout! I love trout!" He glanced around at the others, "I mean…Yeah. Trout is cool."

Justahl and Dest laughed heartily before taking a fish and skewering it with a sharpened stake from their travel bags. Dest still didn't make eye contact with her or anyone else for that matter. Something was wrong.

She turned toward Seth, "I'm sorry for snapping at you earlier. Forgive me for losing my temper."

Seth looked at her, a smile lighting his face, "There is nothing to forgive. I am the one who needs to apologize. It seems our guest will be staying longer than I expected, therefore, I should treat him with more respect." He glanced over at Dest, "I'm sorry and I hope you can look past my unorthodox behavior and just call it truce. I will try not to be such a jerk from now on."

"Umm. Okay...sure. Truce." Dest nodded, shaking Seth's outstretched hand.

Aislinn smiled to herself. Seth was truly an amazing liar, even to complete strangers. She would have to thank him later for at least trying to end the madness.

A noise broke through their chatter, making all of them on edge.

Justahl was the first to break the silence, "What was that?" He peered around into the woods, which encompassed them on all sides.

The noise sounded again, only this time it was closer. Something or someone was screaming in agonizing pain but, not one of them could see anything.

Seth shot up from his seat on the ground, grabbing his sword and bow in the blink of an eye. "I don't know but, it's getting closer. Quick Aislinn, take Gemedes and get inside the tent. Don't come out no matter what and be armed for anything. You two," He pointed at Dest and Justahl, "Come with me."

In an instant the three of them were dashing through the tree tops, running parallel to each other. Aislinn grabbed a frozen Gemedes, and shoved him into the tent, then, she began chanting a protection spell in order to block intruders and make the entire campsite seem empty. Neither of them made a sound and she could no longer hear the others or the screams.

"Got you," Seth yelled to the hiding creature. "I have him; you all can come out now."

Justahl and Dest fell out of two nearby trees, landing on the balls of their feet.

"Well done Seth. I was beginning to think it had gotten away." Justahl stepped forward, slapping him on the back.

The cloaked figure squirmed in his grasp, "Let me go!"

"QUID! Is that you?" He dropped the creature, letting it smack to the ground with a thud.

Quid lowered his hood, "Hey guys, what's up?" His tone was casual as if they had found him in the castle playing video games.

"WHAT'S UP?! You're joking right? We followed your screams and now you're having a casual conversation with us. Were you not just screaming a few moments ago?" Seth felt the heated blood rush to his cheeks, rage coursed through his veins. "By the way what in the hell are you doing out here anyway? Didn't I tell you to stay home? Is anyone else with you?"

"Calm down. No, I came alone and yes, you told me to stay home but, I hate staying home, I miss all the fun." Quid looked down, kicking a pebble with the toe of his boot. His head snapped up, responding to another question, "Wait, what do you mean you followed my screams? What screams? I wasn't screaming."

Seth looked at the others and shrugged, "I guess we better get back to Aislinn." He shook his shaggy, blonde hair, "Come on Quid, it seems you will be joining our search after all. But don't think you're off the hook, a week of extra chores will do you some good." Without another word, he took off into the tree tops again, heading back for the campsite.

Justahl looked at Quid, "Are you coming or what? I doubt whatever was screaming will leave you alone. You might be safer with us for the time being." He patted Quid's arm laughing to himself before following after Seth.

"Shouldn't we go check on them," Gemedes questioned. "They have been gone for quite a while." He glanced around quickly, listening for the screams or footsteps, whichever came first. Only silence was heard.

"Calm down Gemedes. Nothing is wrong and no, we can't leave the tent remember." Aislinn shook her head, a laugh hanging in her throat. Gemedes was always worried about something or someone but, usually his worries didn't involve Justahl. Perhaps they had come to like each other.

After a few moments of huffing and sighing, Gemedes gave up and went to sleep. Aislinn found the silence captivating and well needed. After all, she had been through a lot lately. First, she finds out an army of demons is being created to destroy her land and her people. Then, Dest shows up and tells her, her father has been kidnapped, and to top it all off, her best friend is acting really weird, or weirder than usual.

Ever since Dest had shown up last week, Seth had been complaining about nightmares which involved voices in his head and ultimately ended with his lifeless body on the ground. When she asked him what happened, he would just shrug and say it was no big deal but, she had her doubts.

Then, there was Dest. He is absolutely the most amazing creature she had ever met and to top it all off, he was gorgeous. Every time she was with him, it was like her heart beat faster, her palms got all sweaty- which may have been because of his natural body temperature-, and her mind raced, making the words in her head not match the ones she ended up saying aloud. Finally, there was that kiss, or rather the almost kiss.

She wanted to know the feeling of his lips moving with hers, making ripples of rhythm as they kissed for hours and hours. Nothing would satisfy her more but, he disappeared. One perfect moment, turned into her looking pathetic and stupid. She felt completely absurd for ever having made that wish.

Footsteps were heard, followed by voices, which made her come back from her memories of earlier tonight. Gathering her thoughts, Aislinn lifted the spell and climbed out of the tent.

"Aislinn," Quid cried.

Quid. She looked at him, momentarily confused. What was he doing here? Did Seth know?

"Yeah, Seth knows I'm here."

He answered her unspoken question, which was odd. She glanced around, trying to figure out where Seth was, to no avail.

"He should be here in just three...two...one."

Quid turned toward the two oak trees, just as Seth, Justahl, and Dest leaped to the ground.

"Hey, I see you have found our uninvited guest," Seth made a low growl in his throat. "We didn't find anything unusual in the woods, just him." He pointed toward his brother before taking a seat against a nearby tree trunk.

"Ah. Well, welcome to the team Quid," She paused looking at Seth, "Where is Amara? Did she come too?"

Quid giggled, "Nah, she stayed at the castle. She said she didn't want to witness Seth ripping my head off when he found out I followed you guys." He sat next to Dest, who automatically scooted over in response.

Aislinn frowned, "I see. Seth," She stared at her friend relaxing against the tree, "Can I speak with you for a moment? Alone."

Seth scrambled to his feet, the hint of a smile crossing his lips as he looked at Dest- rubbing it in. "Sure."

They disappeared into the darkness of Frost Forest.

Aislinn paced in front of him, "We must figure out more about Dest. Find out about his family, friends, distant relatives, anything that may link us to who he truly is." She rang her hands on her dress nervously.

"What, don't you trust him?" Seth mused, "I thought you two were in looove." He burst into laughter.

"Oh shut up!" She punched him in the side, probably harder than necessary. "I just want to know more about the fairy who has taken up residence in my home that's all. Don't you find it odd he showed up right after we found out about the army? It is like he timed it perfectly."

Seth huffed, "I have only been trying to tell you this since he got here but, you have been too busy getting all googly-eyed when he's around. I see the way you look at him and quite frankly I find it disgusting." He sighed, "However, since I am always the brains in this friendship, I did some research."

Aislinn threatened to punch him again but, she refrained, smiling generously for him to continue. She was smart too, just not around Dest, which was weird.

"Nothing. I found absolutely nothing about him anywhere and I even had a friend of mine check the Japanese councils' records." He shook his head, "It's like he doesn't exist."

"Really? That's all you found? Nothing?" Aislinn looked at him, worry creasing her forehead. "I don't understand."

"I wasn't finished." Seth laughed, "Yesterday, I received a message from my friend in Japan, telling me all about our new guest."

"Great, what did he say?" She looked at him curiously.

"Everything and nothing at all. He told me exactly what Dest told us when he showed up, even the part about being on the council. It was strange."

Stunned, Aislinn smiled, "What do you mean strange? Your friend told you the truth and so did Dest. What's the problem?

"The problem is it's too perfect. It's almost like it was planned. You don't think it's odd that last week my friend couldn't find anything on this guy, then, all of a sudden, poof, a perfect record of his life. Do you not find that strange?" Seth looked at her kindly.

"No! I think your friend made a mistake and Dest has done nothing to you. Plus, I thought you were going to try to get along with him? What happened to that?" She was furious. Her best friend was accusing Dest of being too perfect. It was absurd. Of course her mood swings were absurd as well.

Just five minutes ago, she doubted Dest. Now she was protecting him at the expense of calling her best and only friend, a liar. *What is going on*, she thought.

Seth sighed, "I told him I would try to behave less like a jerk, I never promised I would trust him."

Without another word, he turned and walked back toward the light of the campfire.

Aislinn was alone. Again.

Fighting back tears, she ran a shaking hand through her rough, tangled hair. She was a mess, had been for over two weeks now. The war raged not only on the outside but, on the inside as well. Her emotions were up, down, and everywhere in between. But, the weirdest part was Dest.

Before he showed up on the castle steps, she was perfectly content with being alone all the time. The only person she could truly count on was Seth and even he left her alone most of the time.

"You are a loner, sweetie," Her mother had said once. "No one can control you and you should never let them try."

Her mother always knew what to say, always had. She was perfect. Beautiful, self-less, and completely in love with her father but, now she was gone forever.

Aislinn dropped to the cold ground, the tears she had been holding back released in long streams down her burning cheeks. "Get a hold of yourself Aislinn," She scolded rather loudly into the night air, "A queen never loses control."

A twig snapped behind her, making her jump up in surprise. An unfamiliar velvet soft voice, sounded in her head or beside her, she couldn't be sure. "You seem upset Princess. What could ever be wrong? The war? Your father?" The voice disappeared in a tiny laughter, then, it sounded again from farther away. "I feel like we got off on the wrong foot, where are my manners. It's me, Cynric. I seem to have stumbled across someone very important to you."

"What are you talking about?" The words escaped from her mouth before she had the time to realize what she was doing.

Cynric laughed, appearing beside her, staring at her with piercing gray and black eyes, "Don't worry your heiress, your sister will be just fine, as long as you do everything I say."

"I will NEVER do what you ask and leave my sister alone, she has nothing to do with this!" She screamed into his calm face.

He smiled, shaking his head, "Pity. I had so hoped for us to be best friends forever," He smiled lightly, "But it seems we must settle this the hard way." With that, he disappeared.

"WHERE IS MY SISTER?" Aislinn wailed, "Please don't hurt

her!"

Just a single phrase slithered through the air but, it ripped her to pieces, "She is with me."

"Wake-up! Come on Justahl. Gemedes. Wake-up!" Seth whispered frantically before kicking them both in the side.

Justahl shot up, his hand automatically going toward his sword in response. "Huh. What is it?"

"I need you two to run patrol. Check out the perimeter and see if it is safe to travel yet. Think you can manage that simple request?" Seth turned and sauntered out of the tent, leaving them in silence.

Moments later, Justahl emerged, followed by a still sleepy Gemedes.

Rubbing his eyes, Gemedes looked around, "Why are we the only ones awake? Why not send the new guy? Desk or whatever."

Both Seth and Justahl burst into laughter at his mispronunciation but, Seth laughed the loudest. "Because, he's not here."

Justahl immediately quit laughing, concern filling his eyes, "What do you mean he's not here? He was here when we fell asleep."

"I mean what I said. When I went to wake him," He shrugged, "His tent was completely empty. Nothing left except his neatly folded blankets. He took his belongings at least. Maybe he won't return."

"I wouldn't count on that, he likes you too much." Justahl mock-punched him in the arm, then, burst into laughter again as he walked over to gather his other weapons.

Seth shook his head, "Gemedes?"

"Yes sir." Gemedes looked up at him.

"Do you have weapons?"

"I know how to use a sw-"

"OH NO!" Justahl yelped, "I agreed to do a patrol with him but, he can carry this," He thrust a fairy torch in Gemedes' open hand, "I don't trust him. The kingdom might need another new knight when we return."

"Suit yourself." He shrugged slightly, "Get going before Quid hears your two bickering, and wants to go too. Go!" He pointed toward the trail, which lead to the road they would travel again today.

Justahl looked at Gemedes, "Come on. Let's just get this over with but, stay at least three feet away from me, understand?"

Gemedes smiled and nodded; grasping his torch with both hands he followed his new partner into the woods.

Seth sighed, they are pathetic, he thought, before returning to his post. He watched and waited for them to return.

Gemedes looked around. *The woods seem fairly quite this morning,* he thought. He paced himself three feet behind Justahl, who hadn't stopped walking for over twenty minutes. However, he didn't mind at all. Justahl's lack of attention, gave him time to think about the council. *How wonderful would it be for them to give the goblins a seat, he thought, and not just any goblin? Me.*

He was pondering the thought when suddenly he heard screaming. *Where is that coming from?* He wondered. Quickly, he looked around, noticing for the first time where his torch was pointed.

Justahl ran around in circles in front of him, frantically patting his left wing. Trying to put out the raging flames that burned him.

Finally, the fire ceased and left behind a charcoaled skeleton of Justhal's former wing. Gemedes looked down at his torch, which was pointed directly in front of him instead of toward the sky. He had set Justahl's wing on fire. *Oh no,* he thought.

Justahl turned on him, fury in his eyes. He growled, "WHAT THE-" He stomped over to Gemedes, "Give me that!"

In an instant, the torch was out of his hands and lying on the ground in a crumpled mess.

"I'm so-," Gemedes started but, Justahl held up a hand in protest.

"If you value my sanity at all, you will refrain from apologizing for what just happened. Actually I would prefer you never mention it again." Justahl slammed him into a nearby tree, "Understand?"

Gemedes gulped, sweat rolling down his forehead, "Understood."

Justahl let him go and turned back toward the campsite, "I think we have done enough patrolling for one day. Seth can go with you from now on, I'm out."

Neither of them said another word the entire way back. Even

when Justahl's blackened wing flailed in the wind.

Chapter 8

Ananais

Seth listened, waiting for Justahl and Gemedes to return. He knew it was silly, being on edge all the time about things but, he also knew what Cynric was capable of. Cynric would destroy all of them, including his brother and as much as Quid got on his nerves, he loved him and would rather be tortured than see him killed.

The voice, His voice, sounded through his ears. "Ah. Alone again I see. What no protection spells or voodoo rituals to keep me away?" Cynric laughed.

"What do you want from me?" Seth shouted, fury coursing through his veins, lighting his entire body with a raging fire of hatred. "Leave me alone."

"Hmm, nope! I'm having way too much fun. Aren't you?"

"I would be if I could sleep but, someone keeps me up all night with dreams about my death. I wonder who would do such a thing." He mused.

Seth knew better than to piss off Cynric, he had been there the last time, when Modric attacked the island. Cynric would stop at nothing to avenge his father's death and he was the only one who could stop him.

Suddenly, he was flying across the clearing, headed straight for the tent where his brother slept. Slashing open the door with a dagger, he stepped inside. Something was wrong. He would never go into his brother's tent while he was sleeping, especially with a dagger pointed at his heart. Seth stopped and spun, looking for a reason he would have done this but, all that remained in the clearing were the fairy torches, which were going out due to the sunlight peeping through the trees.

"Don't fight this. He will never know what happened. Consider it a favor for your sake. I would kill him but, thanks to my new powers, you get to kill him instead-NOW MOVE!"

Seth dropped to his knees, the dagger still in his hand. He let out a low growl before plunging the tip of the blade into his brother's body, piercing his heart.

"Seth. Seth." Someone shouted his name, "Hey Seth, wake up. What are you doing?"

Someone shook him violently awake. He shot up like a bullet, gasping for relief from his latest nightmare. This time, he didn't know if he was dreaming it had seemed so real. Grabbing his sword, Seth ran into Quid's tent, nearly tearing it down in the process.

Justahl cautiously walked to stand behind him, placing a hand on his shoulder, "Seth is everything alright? Why are you waking Quid up so early? Seth?"

He sighed, noticing Quid's tiny body wrapped in his blankets, still sleeping in all the commotion. *Lucky*, he thought before returning to his post at the base of the tree. Slumping to the ground, he realized it had all been a dream. "It was a dream." He spoke aloud on accident, making everyone else look at him like he had lost his mind.

"What are you talking about? What was a dream? You running around the campsite like a mad man, tearing tents open, and babbling like a fool?" Justahl paused, laughing out loud, "Nope that was all real."

For the first time, Seth noticed Justahl's wing, which hung limply at his side, completely charred. "I could be asking you a million questions too but, let's start with the most curious one, what happened to your wing?" He smiled up at his injured friend.

"Why don't you ask him?" Justahl pointed at a stunned and silent Gemedes.

Nodding and laughing again, Seth added, "Well I sure hope you do better in the battle, otherwise a damaged wing will be the least of your worries." He burst into a roaring laughter, successfully waking up everyone else. "Seriously, who knew the most arrogant fairy on Roanke Island, not to mention the head knight of the council, could get beat up by a house goblin. I find it rather-"

Justhal leaped at him, both of them tumbling in a mock fist fight. Aislinn stepped out of her tent, momentarily ending their argument. "What is going on out here?"

Seth helped Justahl to his feet, looking at the princess, "We were just having a bit of fun. Sorry we woke you." He bowed in apology.

"No need to be sorry, I needed to be awake anyway. Where is Dest? I desperately need to talk to him about something." Aislinn glanced around.

He shrugged, "I don't know. When I went to wake him this morning, he was go-"

"It seems I arrived just in time. Glad to see your admiration for me hasn't changed Seth." Dest walked into the clearing, carrying three large fish. He stood beside Aislinn in a matter of moments, placing the fish on the ground next to her feet. "Good morning. I trust everyone slept well." He looked directly at Seth, his eyes relaying an unspoken message.

"We all slept fine. Thank you for breakfast." Aislinn turned back towards her tent, then, she glanced back, seeming to have forgotten an important message, "Oh yes. Justahl?"

Justahl's head shot up in response, "Yes your majesty?"

"I do hope Gemedes didn't hurt you too bad, we don't have time to find a replacement for you as well." Her eyes focused on the goblin, who was sitting beside the fire, warming his hands, "I trust you will be more careful from now on." With that she walked into her tent and zipped it shut.

Dest looked at all of them and was about to ask the obvious

question when Justahl answered, "Just drop it! I DON'T want to talk about it." He disappeared into the woods, leaving Seth laughing, Gemedes in silence, and Dest stunned.

"I wonder what that was about?" Quid asked. He stepped from his tent, rubbing the sleep from his eyes.

Seth stared at him in amusement, laughing again, "Sometimes it's better not to know. Trust me."

Aislinn knew she would eventually have to face Dest again but, how could she after their previous conversation? He obviously didn't like her, his sudden shut-down made this fact perfectly clear. Yet, there was the way he looked at her.

There was a noise just outside her tent, followed by the zipper being zipped down to allow entry. She couldn't deal with this right now, Seth surely knew better than to intrude on her dressing.

"Excuse me Princess, are you dressed?" A familiar voice echoed through her large tent. "I really must speak with you about something."

She stepped into the larger part of the tent, gesturing down her dress, "Of course I'm dressed, otherwise I would have screamed when you opened the door." Aislinn noticed the visitor as Dest, "Oh. Hello."

"Hey." Dest replied shortly. He held a strange emotion behind his calm eyes. She guessed he was waiting for her to break the awkward silence.

"Er. You wanted to talk to me. About what?"

"Yes. I feel as though we got off on the wrong foot last night and I was hoping for another chance to get to know you." His smile glittered in the morning light, shining down through the roof of the tent.

The tent she slept in was quite large, with three rooms. A large room, a smaller dressing room, and of course the room in which she slept. She had wanted a much smaller tent, a normal sized one but, her father insisted on only the best for his daughters.

"I-I guess so, if you really want to." Aislinn paused, thinking about her sister. Could she tell this stranger what had happened in the woods after he left? She decided not to for the time being. Some things are better left untold in situations such as these. Plus, she wasn't sure but, something was telling her it was better to keep it a secret until she found out for sure. Maybe it was all a dream.

"Princess?" Dest stared at her curiously. "Are you alright? You look pale." He placed his hand on her shoulder, sending thousands of electric currents, pulsing through her body.

"Um. Yes. I'm fine." She looked away, pulling her shoulder away from his touch as well. "I'm just worried about my sister. She's alone in the castle."

"Ah. I see. Well, perhaps you could use my communication device and contact her. See if she's okay." He smiled at her again. It lit up the entire room.

She had to tell him, "I would but, I think something's happened to her. Something bad." Her heart seemed to race out of her chest when she said it, her mind miles away, back at the castle. She knew better than to leave her sister alone, now she was paying for her mistake. First, her father disappeared and now this. Nothing would ever be the same if she lost her entire family. *The war can come,* she thought, *and I don't care.* For a moment, she let herself sink into the blackness that had been haunting her for weeks. It ran through her veins, causing her to shiver from the coldness it left in her frail bones.

A hand came down, pulling her out of the swirling darkness. She gasped for breath. "It's going to be alright. Your sister is fine. Don't worry." His voice calmed her, soothing her nerves. He sounded so sure of himself. "Don't cry, Aislinn." She hadn't realized she was crying but, his lips moving to say her name was the most beautiful thing she had ever seen. He leaned closer, placing her in the fold of his arms, closing the small gap between them in the blink of an eye. Her body immediately warmed, causing her to relax automatically.

"Thank you Dest. I'm sorry for losing my self around you. I don't understand why this always happens. Usually I'm much better at hiding my true emotions." She wiped her eyes with the sleeve of her emerald green dress. It hugged her curves perfectly, with her curly blonde hair cascading down the back of it in ringlets. It had belonged to her mother and now it was hers.

He pulled away. The sudden rush of the cool morning air was like drowning in ice water after stepping out of a burning fire. She longed to be back in the comfort of his arms but, she knew a true ruler would never admit to needing someone so badly.

"Is something wrong?" Dest asked.

"No. No. Everything is fine. Thanks for always being here for me when I lose it." She smiled at him, trying to portray happiness even though she felt empty inside.

"Come here," He said, smiling to himself. Her heart started beating faster and faster, making her wings respond to the movement as well. She knew that look, reading novels as she had throughout the years let her know the look he wore very well. He was going to kiss her. Finally, her wish would come true. Granted it was a day late but, she didn't care. She stepped closer. His hand cupped the side of her face, his fingers sliding down her jawbone, making an invisible line down to her throat. It felt amazing. He interrupted the silence, "I feel like I know you better than I know myself sometimes." Then, without another word, he pressed his lips against hers.

He kissed her softly at first, his lips moving lightly with hers, letting her feel every nerve in her body ignite with passion. She wanted more of him so, she pressed closer; molding herself against his body. Her arms wrapped around his neck.

He froze, pushed her away, and walked out the door without a backward glance.

That was weird, she thought before the blackness overtook her again and tears rolled down her cheeks in hot streams. She was alone, completely and utterly alone. Dest had kissed her, she knew that much but, why had he pulled away so fast? Was he afraid of getting too close to her? She was a teenager after all, only seventeen and he was at least twenty-one but, did that make a difference? Nothing about him made sense-

A loud crash made her jump, she ran from the tent to see Quid lying on the ground laughing. "What is going on out here?" She

106

screamed.

Seth looked at her from across the clearing, "We were just trying to clean up. Are you ready for us to pack your things?"

"Yes, I am definitely ready to get out of here. All this closeness is making me claustrophobic." She knew it was a lie but, she couldn't dare tell them the truth because, she was suddenly very aware that Dest was nowhere to be found. "Where is Dest?"

"Er. I'm not sure." Seth answered, glancing around in confusion. "He was just here a few moments ago." He shrugged, looking rather bored with the subject, "Oh well, who needs him anyway? You got us."

"I was just curious that's all. I would rather not have to explain his disappearance to Queen Andorra if he were to get killed." Aislinn smiled to herself, thinking about him dying. He deserved it after treating her like he had. She was a future queen and he had treated her like a prostitute.

"Well, if he decides to grace us with his presence, you'll be the first to know." Seth added before walking over to finish cleaning up.

It is going to be a very long day, she thought.

Justahl returned about an hour later, laughing at some joke no one else had heard. Dest followed two steps behind him.

"Where have you two been all morning?" Seth questioned. "We have been waiting for over an hour."

Justahl quieted his laughter and looked around, "I see you still remember how to clean up Seth, I'm impressed."

Seth rose from his resting place under a tree in the clearing; his face filled turning blood red in anger. "I ought to char your other wing you ungrateful little-"

"ENOUGH! From both of you!" Aislinn walked to where the two stood arguing. "I am quite ready to leave if you don't mind. We still haven't found anything even remotely close to Ananais's house and I'm sure we haven't much more free time to look."

Justahl spoke up, "Actually your worries are unnecessary. We," He pointed to Dest and himself, "Think we may have found Ananais's house about a mile up the road. It shouldn't take too long to get there."

"Ah. Well in that case, lead the way but, I still don't want to hear another word out of either of you. Understand?"

"Yes your majesty." Seth and Justahl answered in harmony before grabbing their belongings and heading toward the road.

Aislinn was about to leave when she remembered something she had been meaning to talk to Dest about. She walked to where he stood gathering his things. "Dest. May I speak with you for a moment?" Her voice sounded so childish. Like it had when she was eight and had broken her father's favorite vase.

He turned and faced her, staring with those blue eyes. "Of course. What seems to be bothering you Princess?"

So formal, she thought, *why did he speak to her like they hadn't shared more than just stories?* It was as if he didn't want to remember the kiss at all. "Well, to be quite honest, you are bothering me. One minute you are all over me and the next you're disappearing without so much as a single word to tell me what I did wrong. What is that about? Oh, and dare I mention anything about this morning in the tent. I mean do you just feel sorry for me? Am I some pity case so you can return home and brag about how you fooled the Princess? Because I'm not just some-"

His lips pressed down on hers with passionate force, momentarily cutting into her concentration. She couldn't think when he was so close. Staring with eyes like ice, freezing her to one spot. It was too much for anyone to handle. Did this mean he liked her or was this just another pity kiss? For the moment it didn't matter.

All that mattered in that moment were his lips on hers, moving in synchronizing patterns. It was the kind of kiss that made you blush and sent your heart into frenzy at the same time. The only bad part about the moment was time. There was never enough time to fully be satisfied kissing him. To be honest, she knew that if given the rest of eternity to kiss him, she would still long for more and more.

He pulled away and looked at her. "Aw Aislinn. You are too good for me and you don't even know it. I'm tired of pretending to not care about you because, I do care. I care too much sometimes." He sighed, taking her into the fold of his arms.

Confused, she asked, "What do you mean you care too much sometimes? That doesn't make any sense." His arms were so warm and strong, they made her feel safe.

"I mean, you're are a Princess and I am nothing. You rule kingdoms; I sit and do what I'm told. You live here," Dest gestured openly around them, "I live in Japan. Do you get the picture?"

"So, you're saying all this time you've been running away from me because of who I am and where I live? That's absurd. You could live in the castle with my family; my father will absolutely adore you. And don't worry about the lineage thing because, none of that matters to me. You are just Dest to me and I am just Aislinn. But, I'm tired of you treating me one way and then, two seconds later treating me as if nothing happened."

He pressed her closer to him. "I'm sorry. Please understand this is all new to me. I've never cared about another person outside of my family and it's difficult for me to be myself around you. You're always so open with me and I love that about you but, I just need a little more time to adjust before I spill my guts out so to speak."

"So you're saying I just need to let you storm off without any explanation, even when I feel like it's my fault and that you may never come back?"

"I will never leave you unless it is absolutely necessary; no matter what anyone else says about it." He answered.

She could sense a hidden meaning to his words but, when she was about to ask about it, he kissed her again. This time she knew it was real.

"The house is just around this curve. It won't be long now." Justahl explained.

"Well it's about time. My feet are killing me and my stomach is growling like a vicious mountain lion." Seth replied to no one in particular. He was still a little aggravated because of what had happened at the campsite before they'd left. After waiting for a good twenty minutes or so, he had gone back to the clearing to find out what had been taking Aislinn and Dest so long. Nothing he could have imagined prepared him for what he saw.

The two of them were kissing passionately and hadn't even noticed his arrival. He stepped around a tree, clearing his throat, "If you two are done, the rest of us would like to start today's journey. That is if you don't mind?" He spoke harshly, perhaps more harshly than necessary but, he couldn't help feeling a little jealous. She was acting childish and Dest was just getting on his last nerve.

Finally, they broke apart, embarrassment written plainly across their faces. Dest was the first to speak, "We were just-um-" He looked at Aislinn for help explaining their current situation but, found no help. She just nodded, letting him know it was okay to continue with the truth. "Well Seth, we were kissing. I really like Aislinn and I think she likes me too. Of course one never can be one hundred percent sure in these cases but, she did kiss me back, so there's hope. Anyways, we are happy to follow you now, so please lead the way." He gestured toward the road.

Seth huffed and mumbled something under his breath before walking away. Dest and Aislinn followed hand in hand the whole way.

Snapping out of his memories, Seth realized everyone else had stopped about thirty feet back. He cursed and swung around to face them, "What in the blazes are you doing? Why did you all stop?"

The entire group laughed and Justahl answered, "Were you planning on stopping at Ananais's house or did you just want to know where it was?"

"I didn't realize we were there yet." Seth headed back toward the others.

Aislinn looked at Justahl, "Do you think he will recognize me?"

"Of course, after all you are the Princess and he is a warlock." Justahl replied.

Dest spoke up then, "I thought he was only half warlock?"

"Yes my dear boy but we magic folk don't like to rely on labels." A small voice sounded through the woods all around them.

All of them glanced around, looking for the source of the strange new voice. Seth and Justahl's hands twitched toward their weapons in response.

"Those are not necessary unless you plan on losing your arms. Please come inside. I understand we have much to talk about." The voice disappeared, leaving the six of them in complete silence.

Suddenly a low grinding noise was heard from under their feet. They all jumped back. Gemedes' legs twined with Justahl's, knocking them both flat on the ground.

"Get off of me you stupid little gnome." Justahl roared with anger.

Gemedes shot up, dusting himself off. "I'm sorry; did I mess up your dress sweetie? And I am a goblin not a gnome you idiot."

Seth looked at both of them, "Will you two please stop bickering. You're on the same side so just stop!" He was really getting annoyed with them but, in reality he was venting his anger on them instead of Aislinn and Dest. Noticing the hole that had formed in the exact place they had been standing a few moments earlier he added, "Look. I think he wants us to come inside."

"Are you nuts?" Justahl screamed. "It could be a trap. If he wants us to come in, he can just come out here and-"

Aislinn glared at him. "I didn't come all this way to ignore an invitation. You can stay out here if you like but, the rest of us are going inside. Does anyone else object?" She glanced around. "I didn't think so."

They all headed into the opening in the ground. Justahl and Gemedes brought up the rear, just making it inside before the hole closed tightly above them. They were cast into complete darkness.

"I was hoping you would get the hint." The voice came back. "Welcome to my home."

The entire cavern lit up, tiny fairy torches lined the entire room. They stood in what seemed like an entryway. A large chandelier hung from the ceiling, casting fairy light all around them. It was the most extravagant place Seth had ever seen, even if it was underground.

"Come in my travelers. I sense you are weak and in need of some refreshments." The voice was followed by a tiny figure stepping out of the shadows to their right. In full light, the figure transformed into a tall bearded man who wore a long black cloak. The hood fell back revealing his strong features and golden eyes. He was beautiful for sure but, he also carried a sparkle of magic with him and when he moved, it shimmered around him like fire blazing in an open hearth. It was magnificent.

Aislinn looked at him and asked, "Are you Ananais?"

The man laughed heartily, making the lights in the room shake with laughter also. "I am just he and I know what you have come for. Please let us retire into the dining hall so that we may discuss this subject more." He didn't wait for a reply, he simply turned and walked down a long corridor, lights flickered on as he passed.

After a few brief questioning glances, they all followed the warlock into his home.

Chapter 9

In Truth, Find Lies

"I want to thank you again for inviting us into your home." Aislinn started, "It is quite lovely down here."

"Yes. I assumed it was only a matter of time before you all found me. Of course, I was expecting your father's apology before now but, that's another conversation entirely. I don't wish to portray your father for his true nature."

Seth eyed Ananais, "And what may I ask is his true nature?"

"I'm not getting into that today Mr. Arabiraheal and I suggest you don't either." Ananais's voice rang out harsh into the dining hall. The room was rather cavernous with tall walls, covered from floor to ceiling with burgundy draperies. In the middle of the room sat a large dining table, with carvings of stars, moons, and all sorts of magical symbols representing the warlock history.

Aislinn wanted to know more about her father, she barely saw the man anymore. He was always away on business or in a council meeting. It would be nice to see what others thought of him. With her mind made up, she asked Ananais to explain more.

"Oh alright but don't blame me if you don't like what you hear. Your father and I have been friends for nearly three thousand years.

During those early years we spent most of our time tracking and killing demons and unruly creatures of evil. He was always friendly to me and very courageous but, everything changed about a thousand years ago, when Modric started to rule the demons.

I told him not to go after Modric that night, it would only get him killed and the entire world would be doomed for all eternity but, your father was just as stubborn as he was kind. He went to Modric's castle in Moliston and killed nearly all the guards the demon king could conjure up. That was until Modric summoned the most powerful demon known to mankind, Geroeth. See during that time, Geroeth was the most feared and hated monster in the universe. The beast could kill a man in the blink of an eye and never missed. Your father was one of the unlucky few to make it out alive."

"What do you mean unlucky? And how did he survive if this demon is so evil?" Aislinn was truly intrigued now.

"Let's just say the man which emerged from those walls was no longer Galiron."

"What do you mean?"

"Think about it. Do you honestly think a fairy, no matter how strong, could defeat Geroeth? The thing possessed Galiron's body that night. I assume that is how the legend was started, although they were off about it being a curse."

"A curse?" Aislinn couldn't make the words fit together. Her father, the man she admired and looked to for advice, was a really a demon just using his body? If this was true, where did that leave her and her sister? She didn't dare ask, at least not with the threat of war breathing down her neck. There were already too many problems to deal with, no sense and adding another one now.

"According to my research, which I've done a lot of in the past one thousand years, the being that slays Geroeth will be cursed for an eternity. He or she will be forced to kill the ones they care for most."

"But I thought you said he was possessed?"

"I said there was a legend about a curse, not that the legend was true. Although the demon possession could make it seem like the person is cursed, it's really just Geroeth acting through him or her;

using their life so to speak to gain something of importance to him. Your father has killed many creatures in the last ten centuries, or rather the demon inside him has."

"Alright, so basically what you're saying is my father isn't King Galiron?" She asked lightly, the initial shock wearing off some as she spoke.

"Not exactly. I have a theory that my old friend is still in there somewhere, which would explain his acts of kindness and selflessness. But most of the time no, the man you encounter on a daily basis is not the real King Galiron, even though Geroeth is known for playing the role of his victims quite well. It took me nearly four hundred years to notice any drastic changes in his personality. Before then, he seemed normal." Ananais ate a few bites of his lamb stew, savoring the aroma and trying not to think about his lost friend.

"So is that why Modric was left alive that night?" Seth asked the question before she had the chance to.

"Yes. Geroeth formed a plan which involved Modric. I can't tell you everything, because I don't even know the entire plan. What I can tell you is this; he promised to give Modric enough time to find and train a suitable heir to the demon throne. A son so to speak. Then, when the time came, Modric would put together an army and invade the island. However, right before he died, he was to complete one last task, which was to make his heir promise to get revenge at all costs. Modric already had two demons under his control, Cynric and Dimitri."

Seth spoke up, "That doesn't sound so bad. I mean King Galiron couldn't just leave the demons without a ruler, perhaps he thought the son would be less evil. Why should we believe this nonsense? Why would Geroeth need to operate through Galiron when he is powerful enough to accomplish it on his own?"

"I said no 'man' could stand against him but what if the entire supernatural realm teamed up? Could you imagine anything surviving that?" The warlock waited for an argument. "I thought not. If he doesn't handle the situation carefully, meaning killing everyone who knows anything at all, the creatures would destroy him. They won't attack someone who wears the face of a friend, especially when he's their king, no matter who he kills in the process."

Seth's head shot up, "What do you mean? Who all has he killed?"

"Geroeth is very cunning, like all demons are, and like most demons he has an act for killing things that get in his way. Take your father for example-"

"You mean he killed my father?" He looked like he was about to throw up. "I don't understand. He told me my father was killed in battle. I saw the demon marks on his chest, where it ripped out his heart." He shuddered at the memory.

Ananais sighed, "I told you the legend held some truth behind it. Geroeth never expected anyone to find out about his plan. So, when Ellyis started getting too close to the truth, he had to be dealt with. He made Modric do it for him, that way no one else would get suspicious. In the end though, it was his decision to end your father's life, not Modric's. I'm sorry I couldn't tell you the truth sooner but I needed to know for sure first. It has been rough enough knowing the truth; I couldn't bear to let anyone else suffer as well. For years I've torn libraries apart, searching for a reverse spell or anything that could possibly save my friend's life, but unfortunately I've had no such luck. The only way to get the demon out of him is to kill him, and even then Geroeth will just possess someone else. He won't stop until his ultimate goal is complete."

Aislinn found her voice in time to ask the obvious. "What do you mean his ultimate goal?"

"After this new battle, during which this entire island and the Akassa brothers will be wiped out, the final step in his plan will begin. Harlem will be spared long enough to create a new supernatural world and crown Geroeth king, then, he will be used for magic purposes only. More than likely caged underground somewhere until he's needed but never mind that. This new kingdom will contain all the creatures it does now but, they will all be under Geroeth's command."

"So what you're saying is, my father schemed up this entire battle just to destroy us all? That makes no sense."

"That's not what I'm saying, the demon wants you dead and the only reason you're not is because of Galiron. He has a plan of his own, and he and Geroeth have come up with a little agreement. This agreement was made so you could win both battles. The demon would have killed you long ago but your father is fighting like hell to buy you some time, hence the reason for the battle with Cynric's army. It just may be harder than he expected. I don't think Galiron intends on surviving the attack, which may be one of the reasons he was captured in Japan. If he times it just right, he can sacrifice himself in order to spare you and your sister. It's a constant fight, trying to keep the demon down long enough to do all this, but I know he believes it will work."

His words sunk in, making her feel lousy and scared. What if she failed and her father risked all this for nothing? How could she bare to let him die for her sake? This was getting more and more complicated. *What's next*, she thought, *flying monkeys who shoot lasers from their eyes?*

"Try to realize what's at stake here princess. The real Galiron would want you to carry on, even if it meant you had to do it without him. Losing one life compared to thousands is no contest, especially when it must be done. I will help you all I can but I need to know you can handle this. Can I count on your word?" Ananais stared at her, his eyes holding a million untold stories of her real father, someone she barely knew.

"Yes, you have my word." She turned to face the rest of the table. "We will continue with my father's plan. I expect each of you to act like nothing has changed and what we heard today wasn't true. There will be a battle and we will be ready for it. Seth, you and Justahl will begin overseeing the weapon productions. We'll need a lot of them if we are to win. Ananais I need healing potions, protection spells conjured, and enchanted weapons for the soldiers. That leaves you two," She pointed at Gemedes and Quid. "I realize neither of you are properly trained for combat so I am designating you official messengers until further notice. Are there any questions?"

The room fell silent, every pair of eyes trained on her, as she spoke. Then, without a word, everyone bowed in agreement.

As soon as everyone stopped bowing, Ananais grabbed Seth's arm and lead him into another part of the house. Justahl and Quid began talking about some sports match they had attended last week, and Gemedes started roaming around the room in search of something interesting to mess with. This left her, sinking into a bottomless pit with no way out. She had made it seem like she wasn't afraid anymore, that her father being possessed by something so evil was no big deal, but in inside she was terrified. Her heart rammed in her chest at a million miles an hour with no sign of slowing down. Unexpectedly, a hand came down on her shoulder and a sense of utter calm rushed through her veins. She didn't need to open her eyes to know who it was.

"I think you forgot about me Princess." Dest spoke. "I do hope I can help too."

She couldn't believe it, she had forgotten about Dest. The one she had just kissed moments earlier. He stood there in the same room as her, a mere ten feet away and she had forgotten all about him. She twined her hand with his and pulled him into a long corridor. This time the lights didn't come on as they made their way into the living quarters of the house. She glanced around, unsure where to sit but Dest maneuvered them onto a nearby couch, letting her fall into his lap.

"I'm so sorry Dest. Please don't think bad of me for forgetting you it's just too-"

He cut her off with a kiss. It warmed her body and made her heart slow to a steady beat. She was once again thankful for his strange way of always knowing when she needed him most. "There is nothing to forgive. You've been through a worse hell today than any demon has in a lifetime. Don't fret the small stuff, I am here whether you remember me or not." He chuckled lightly, sending ripples of happiness through her skin. It was almost as if they were one in the same. If he was happy, she was happy too.

"You always know exactly what I need at every moment yet, I can't even remember you're in the same room. How awful is that?"

Without warning, tears started streaming down her face and onto his chest.

His hand rubbed her back in small circles, "Shhh. Don't cry Aislinn. Everything will work out for the best, I promise. You have nothing to fear."

"How can you say that?" She sobbed, "You heard Ananais, my father is a demon. He killed Seth's father and countless other creatures and I never knew it. I've been living a lie my entire life and the man I looked up to for the last eighteen years isn't who I thought he was. What am I supposed to do now? Kill him? I can't do that Dest, no matter what he is or what he's doing, I can't kill him." Her tears flowed heavier now, making a large wet spot on his shirt. She wiped at her eyes, "How silly of me, I shouldn't ruin your shirt just because I can't keep it together."

He tightened his grip on her and placed her in the fold of his arms. "Don't ever think for one second you are expected to kill your father. No one will ask that of you and if they do, I'll handle it. Cynric will take care of that creature, all you need to do is let the plan unfold and I swear he will be destroyed; even if I have to kill him myself."

Aislinn knew she should be angry with him for confessing to kill her father but, she wasn't. Actually she was relieved because, even if she failed, that thing would never win. It was rather comforting. She raised her head and kissed Dest lightly on the cheek, "Thank you."

"For what?" He asked.

"For just being you. And I promise to try to remember you from now on." She started to pull away, to go back to the others but, he wouldn't let go. "What?"

He laughed, and then kissed her. As always, his kiss sent sparks through her, making her forget where she was and what she was about to do before he kissed her. All she knew was how his lips fell on hers, making her feel whole and happy. She remembered the way the dream berries tasted, how they made her feel alive and light as a feather, but the feeling she got when he kissed her was even better than that. The kiss was soft at first but then became more urgent. She wrapped her arms around his neck and pulled him on top of her as they fell onto the couch. This was the kiss she had been waiting for. His hands slid up her neck and traced the line of her face, then, swept down her arms and grabbed her legs. Her legs responded by wrapping around his, forcing him to get closer still. Their breath came out quick and rapid, the closer they got the better she felt.

This new found obsession with him was growing on her. She didn't know what it was that kept her wanting more and more but it overpowered her. His constant closeness and unexpected surprises sent her into frenzy, but it was worth it. Everything she did now was either about him or for him, even going along with the whole save the universe thing. She knew deep down if it hadn't been for him, she would have ran away, probably screaming. He made her strong but he also caused her mind to go hazy, although wrapped up with him like this made it harder to see that truth. Her decisions were centered on this creature in her arms and the strangest part was she didn't care. What was happening to her? Was she mad or was it something else entirely? Whatever it was, at that very moment, she didn't want to know the answer.

They could hear footsteps coming down the corridor, quickly ending their little make-out session. She shot up, throwing him to the floor with a thump. He rose up and stifled a laugh as Seth opened the door.

Looking at the two of them, his smile faded into a frown, "Ananais requests your company in the dining hall. It seems he has an interesting theory about Gemedes. But I fail to see how it could be more interesting than this." He glared at them both, before stalking out of the room and back down the corridor.

Now she was trying not to laugh. "I guess we should go see what's going on."

His hard expression returned, which annoyed her to no end. "Yes. I suppose we should." He didn't even take her hand as they followed the path back to the others.

It was weird how one minute their relationship was intense, passionate, and out of control, and the next moment he acted civilized and structured. Almost as if he was embarrassed to be seen in such situations. Perhaps his father had had a strict no public display of affection policy. Either way, it wasn't normal and definitely needed to be addressed at some point. This fairy was beginning to get more and more confusing.

The lights dimmed as the finally joined the others, casting an eerie shadow on their previous encounter.

Gemedes stood in the middle of the room while Ananais read in one of his volumes of books. Everyone in the room looked between him and the warlock, waiting for the verdict no doubt.

To be honest, he had never thought about being special enough for one of the most powerful warlocks to be interested in. This would definitely make his list of bragging moments. Of course he was also very aware that the warlock could find something horribly wrong with him, and then what would he do? Justahl would get a kick out of throwing it in his face again and again, plus, maybe he didn't want to know if he was special or not. It didn't matter one way or another, to most people he would always be just a house goblin.

Quid stepped over and placed a hand on his shoulder, leaning in he whispered, "I don't think of you as a house goblin. You have risked your life so we could be prepared in the upcoming battle. And don't worry about Justahl; he's just jealous because the king chose you instead of him for an undercover mission. He's wanted one since he was born, probably even before then." He laughed and stepped away.

Gemedes thought about Quid and how he had been able to know exactly what he was thinking without him speaking a word. Actually, now that he thought about it, Quid had done that a few other times in the past couple of days as well. Perhaps he wasn't the only one who was special. Could it be true that an elf could read minds? If so, what did this mean? He wasn't sure but, he was going to find out soon enough.

Ananais closed his large, leather bound book and crossed the room to where he stood-motionless considering he was in the presence of a warlock, even if this one didn't use his control. The warlock glanced about the room and when he had everyone's attention, including Justahl's he spoke loud and clear, "I believe we may have a protector in our midst. This young creature is special, very special indeed. I call him a protector because of what he can do."

He began pacing the room, "You see many years ago, before all the goblins were sentenced to eternal service and nearly all the warlocks were wiped out, there was a small tribe just north of here who called themselves protectors. This tribe was made up of a family of goblins and three warlocks, Mavelin, Venice, and Nester. All three of those warlocks began conducting spells on the goblins, forcing them to drink potions, possess demons, and all sorts of other dreadful things. Then, one night Venice mixed up a rare potion that had only been brewed one other time in history but, no one has a name for it. Either way, he made it and gave it to the last living goblin among them; I think his name was Dresver. After he drank the potion, he passed out and they couldn't get him awake. So, they decided to burn him like they had the others; however, when Mavelin started to light Desver's body on fire, nothing happened and eventually the flame went out altogether. Scared that they had upset the forces of power among the spirits, they quickly cleansed themselves of all magic and left for another location.

Years later, Venice was out taking a walk when he caught a glimpse of Dresver. He thought he was crazy so, he brushed it off and went back to his walk. Then, a few days after that, a letter came to his door addressed from Dresver. In the note, he described everything that had happened from that night he drank the potion until the time he had sat down to write the letter in perfect detail, including how Dresver had stopped the fire. Venice knew he had successfully created a protector and as for Dresver, well many say he still protects the royalty in Europe but, I believe his spirit resides with those who need him most."

Ananais walked back to where Gemedes stood, still frozen with the knowledge that he was a protector, "As for you my friend, I believe that you are a direct descendent from Dresver and have therefore received the power to protect those around you."

Justahl rose from his seat on one of the many faded couches in the room, "Well I don't care what any of you say, that thing there," He pointed at Gemedes, "Is no more a protector than I am the Queen of Egypt. Who says you're not just making all this up to get our guard down?"

Aislinn spoke up then, "JUSTAHL! That is quite enough out of you! Ananais has been gracious enough to help us in the upcoming battle and I will not let you disgrace him in his own home. If you can't control yourself I will have to take more drastic measures, do I make myself clear?"

He bowed, whether in shame or in defeat Gemedes couldn't be sure but he didn't say another word.

Ananais looked at Justahl, "Come here boy." He gestured for him to stand next to them. Justahl followed his command and in seconds stood where the warlock had motioned. "Now, Dest."

Dest looked up, "Yes?"

"I want you to try and attack Justahl with that sword." Ananais smiled as Dest made his way across the room to where they all stood in a line. He raised his sword and nothing happened. Justahl opened his eyes and looked at Dest then, at Ananais. Ananais clapped his hands together, "Magnificent. Did you feel anything Justahl?"

Justahl shook his head, still in shock.

"How about you Gemedes?"

Gemedes looked up at the warlock, "Nothing."

Finally, Ananais turned to Dest, "And you? Anything?"

Dest nodded, "Yeah, I felt a jolt go through my sword like I had struck an iron shield or something. It was weird. Did he do that?" He pointed at Gemedes.

Ananais beamed, "He sure did. I told you he was a protector. This creature can block anything or anyone from harming the people who are closest to him. Of course, we will have to practice with him to get it perfect and to see how many people he can protect and how close they have to be but, altogether truly extraordinary." He clapped his hands together again in triumph.

Aislinn, positive that the warlock was done with his demonstrations, rose from her seat and spoke, "It seems we are more blessed than I thought. Perhaps we can win this war after all." Glancing around the room she added, "Are we all ready to return home? I'm sure the council will want to hear all the good news and I desperately need to check on my sister."

Everyone agreed that it was past time to be going back and started gathering their things. Ananais prepared a portal for them so they could return to the castle faster and safer. Gemedes was about to step through when he noticed that Ananais wasn't packed to come with them.

"Aren't you coming?" He asked, "I thought you were going to stay at the castle until the battle. You know, to help me prepare?"

Ananais shook his head, "I will accompany you at the castle tomorrow but there are a few housekeeping things I need to attend to. Don't worry my young friend I will make sure you're ready for battle when the time comes. Now hurry before the portal closes." He motioned for him to step on through, sending him into a vortex of swirling colors and voices, one of which he had never heard before. It was a girl's voice and it was speaking to Ananais but, Gemedes knew it was just the portal playing tricks with his mind. No one else had been at the warlock's house except them and he was the last one to go through. *Yes,* he thought, *it was just my imagination.*

Chapter 10

Evangeles

"Father?" Evangeles called to him from her room, which had been blocked from his previous company.

Evangeles was Ananais's daughter and she was also full witch. Her mother gave birth to her just days before being destroyed in the cleansing. The cleansing was a nice description for the decision made in 1809 by the supernatural realm, that all magical beings, old or young, should be destroyed for fear that they were part demon in nature and hated humankind. Ananais's young bride, Cynthia, hid him and their new baby girl deep underground and forced him to place a blocking spell around them so they couldn't be found. She was killed; however, during that night he realized his daughter was extremely powerful. The block that went around them was more powerful than his usual spells and since they were the only two in the hole, he knew it was her helping, even in infancy. Now, since they were the only magical beings left in existence, except Harlem, he kept her hidden from all eyes except his own for fear that someone or something might find her out and destroy her. Through the years he had made himself known, since no one believes warlocks are evil anymore, but even King Galiron didn't know of Evangeles existence.

Today's visitors were no exception of that rule.

Placing a hand in the air beside him, he released the block and soon heard his daughter's footsteps on the floor. She sounded upset.

"I don't understand why you have to keep me hidden. You always go on and on about how no one believes in destroying us anymore, so why hide me? I want to go out and see the world." She plopped down on the couch, making dust fly off in clouds, and crossed her arms in anger.

He sat beside her and wrapped an arm around her, "My sweetheart, you must understand nothing is as it seems and that goes for the people in the world. They accept me but, that could be because I am friends with the King and I am only half warlock. You are full witch. Your mother was a very powerful witch and it got her killed. I couldn't bear to lose you too."

She pushed him away, "I don't want to hear that. It's been over two hundred years since mom died and I know you are in love with Queen Andorra. You fawn over her every time she comes to visit, which, I might add, is a lot more than she visits anywhere else."

Ananais looked at his daughter, "How do you know all this? Have you been using those window spells to see out of your room again? I told you not to-"

"Oh, chill out. I only use the one-ways and they're completely harmless. Nothing can get me if no one can see me so relax. Besides," She shrugged, "I only use them when I get really bored, which is more often these days. That reminds me; I overheard your conversation with the Princess and her friends. When is this battle occurring and can I help?"

His body froze at the thought of her out there on the front lines, in plain view of all the demons, including Harlem and Cynric. Not to mention the fact that it would be hard to block her and distract Harlem at the same time. He turned on her, his voice louder than it should have been, "Most definitely not. I will not risk you even being on this island during the battle let along helping. It is completely out of the question. Why on earth would you think I would let you help? I don't even let you go into town or leave the house for that matter."

Evangeles raised her voice in response, "I am two hundred and two years old, and I don't have to answer to you anymore. This isn't about just you anymore father. The entire kingdom is in danger and if you all fail, the world and all of humanity is in danger. What do expect me to do, just sit around and do nothing? Mother would have wanted-"

"You have no idea what your mother would have wanted. She risked her life to save us both and now you just want to go out there and risk your life for what? Humanity? That is the most absurd thing I have ever heard. You never even knew your mother so you have no idea what she would have wanted." He regretted the words as soon as he had said them but it was too late to take them back now.

She shoved off the couch and towered over him in an instant, "I may not know who she was but, I do know this much, she risked her life so someone else could live and now all I'm asking is for the same chance. You don't know how good I'm getting. I've been practicing day and night to get better, ever since I overheard you talking about the impending war in your study three months ago. I'm ready for this father and I know with my help they can't lose. All I'm asking for is your blessing and a chance to prove myself."

Ananais rose and stared her down, "NO! It is absolutely not going to happen. If I have to chain you down and force you to leave I will. I don't want it to come to that but, I will protect you no matter how much you hate it. Now go pack your bag, this discussion is over." He began to leave the room when he was stopped by her growl.

His head spun around just in time to see her lift her arms above her head. She whispered a chant under her breath and in an instant they were standing in a field of green clover. In the distance he could see and hear a waterfall falling into an unseen river below. Birds flew in the sky above, singing their harmonious melody, and tiny animals played in the woods surrounding them. He glanced at his daughter who had changed entirely. She stared at him with a smile on her face, one that screamed 'I told you so.'

Evangeles opened her mouth and began speaking before he could even think of the words to say. "I told you I was getting good. You never taught me a transfer spell and yet I can do it. I read about it in one of those books in your study, although I don't recall which one exactly. Anyway," She shrugged, "What do you think?"

Ananais gaped at his daughter for a few more minutes before finally finding the strength to question her. "What is this place? Did you create it?"

She giggled, "Yes I created it, so don't worry it's safe to be here. No one can see us here but, do you know why?" Her eyes lit up with excitement.

He shook his head. Turning to take in the entire scene around them. It was like a dream only more realistic. Here he could smell, hear, see, and feel everything around him. He could probably even taste it if he wanted to.

"This is my special place. I come here when I need to think and get away from everything and everyone. It's the one place I can come and truly be alone. But the reason no one can find us or see us here is because it is in my head. This is all from my own creation. Every tree, bird, stream, and blade of grass I made with magic." She walked over to him and took his hands, "Please father, give me just one chance to truly shine. I need this. Please!"

Ananais knew he should let her help in the battle but, he just couldn't. If Cynric and Harlem knew of her existence, they would neither one rest until she was destroyed. Sending her to Japan was the only way to keep her safe.

He tilted her head to meet his eyes and spoke in a sincere voice, "Please, don't make this difficult Evangeles. I need you to do this for me and keep yourself safe. It isn't going to end badly but, it would if you helped. I can't explain it to you because it is too complicated but, please trust me and do what I tell you. I promise you will get to help one day but just don't make it this time. Please!"

"Alright, what do you need me to do?" She answered and in a flash they were back in their home underground, the beautiful dreamland a distant memory.

"You will leave out tonight through a special portal. Queen Andorra will be waiting for you on the other side to seal up the portal and give you further instructions. Please, follow everything she says without argument. She is kind but not open to negotiation. I will send for you when the war is over and then, I promise to teach you everything you need to know to be a great witch." He answered calmly, wrapping her in his arms for a hug.

She held him tightly for a few moments before retreating into her room to pack. It would be the hardest goodbye he would ever say, counting the time he had said farewell to her mother. Evangeles was like her in so many ways. Strong, willing to sacrifice herself for everyone else, and just as stubborn too. However, unlike her mother, she had just begun to discover her powers. He had seen a prophecy that revealed her at her most powerful state. It was scary and breathtaking at the same time but, that was a different situation altogether. For now, he had to prepare the portal to send his daughter away, knowing it could be the last time he saw her. The war was coming and they all had to be ready to die, even him. One way or another, this battle would change everything. Whether it would be good or bad, he couldn't tell.

Chapter 11

The Night of a Thousand Screams

"Try harder Gemedes," Ananais shouted over and over. Every time he failed to block Justahl, he would yell at him. "Alright, enough for today. We will start again at dawn." His hand came down on Gemedes' shoulder, "I know this is hard but, it will be worth it if you can block Aislinn and Seth. Especially if they're miles apart. You are doing well but we need great."

Justahl rolled his eyes and pushed past them grunting, "Yeah, great. Give me a break." He turned to them with hate filled eyes, "We've been doing this for over a week now. Ever since you," He shot a finger at Ananais, "Came around, I haven't got any sleep. Between training for the battle with the other fairies, helping him train with his protective abilities, and I'm not even going to start on his," He glared at Gemedes, "Sleeping habits. Let's just say last night I nearly burned to death in my own bed." With that, he stalked off toward the castle, his almost healed wing fluttering in the wind.

Ananais cast him a sideways glance, "Do I dare ask what he is referring to?"

Gemedes threw his hands in the air in exasperation. "It was an honest mistake. Really. I was in my room as usual but, I heard strange noises coming from Justahl's room, which is right next to mine by the way. I ran in there thinking something might be wrong but, nothing."

"Nothing?" Ananais questioned. "You mean nothing was in there? Where was the noise coming from?"

"I don't know for sure. I think it may have been somewhere else and after I got up it stopped." He shrugged.

Ananais shook his head, "I fail to see how this relates to him burning to death."

"Well, I was getting there." Gemedes huffed but quickly changed his tone when he saw the warlock's face. "Okay. Okay. I'm sorry. Well, after I went into his room, I looked around for the noise and found nothing at all. Then, I noticed his bedside torch was still lit so-"

"No. You didn't touch it did you?" Ananais gasped, "Really Gemedes, I thought we had already discussed this, gracefulness is not one of your more redeeming qualities. What happened?"

"I didn't fall over anything thank you very much. However, when I stepped over his bow and arrow, it shot out and launched right into his mattress. This caused feathers to fly everywhere and also caused him to wake up. I had just reached for the torch when he shot up and scared me, I screamed and the next thing I know I'm running around the room looking for anything that could put out a fire. Needless to say, he has a new room now." Gemedes laughed dryly. "He didn't like that room anyhow, so technically I did him a favor."

"Yes, of course because everyone dreams of being burned to death while a goblin, who is clumsy I might add, looks for a pail of water. I don't see the problem at all." Ananais laughed sarcastically and slapped him on the back. "Well, we better get back in the castle by night fall," He looked around cautiously, "I don't trust these woods. Come on and try not to set anything on fire tonight. I think it will be your responsibility to look after Justahl since Aislinn and Dest are going out tonight."

The two walked for a while before Gemedes realized Ananais

hadn't mentioned Seth all day. He looked at his friend, "Where's Seth if Aislinn and Dest are going out?" Normally he didn't worry about the soon to be elf king but, for some reason he felt like there was something wrong. He didn't know what but something was up.

Ananais smiled, "I believe he is helping train Quid. I offered my skills but, I think Seth needed to talk to him so, I stayed out of it. Why do you ask my young friend?"

"I just have a strange feeling. It's something I've never felt before." He saw Ananais's concern and added, "It's probably nothing. Don't worry."

They began walking again and didn't speak another word the entire way back to the castle. The feeling never faded.

Aislinn hurried about the castle, trying to secure everything before she and Dest left for the evening. "Every candle has been hidden, all the torches are blocked so no one can touch them, and you put all the weapons in the safe room right?" She looked directly at Dest.

He cleared his throat and answered, "Yes, but do you mind telling me why we needed to child proof the entire castle? It's not like you're leaving it in the hands of two toddlers. Justahl is a hundred years older than you and Gemedes is what, pushing four hundred now? They're quite capable of surviving for one night."

She shook her head, clearly amused by his comparison. "I don't think you realize how dangerous it is to leave those two alone in an unsupervised environment. Sometimes it's worse than leaving toddlers behind. Besides, you should see them at the annual Christmas ball we hold every year." Her head snapped up as if she remembered something important, "That reminds me, will you be staying long enough for Christmas? You really must see the island during the holidays, it is quite magical."

"More magical than usual?" He began laughing heartily. "Of course, I wouldn't miss it for the world. When is it?"

Dest looked up when she didn't answer immediately, surprised to find the hallway completely empty. That's odd, he thought. He wondered where she could have gone so fast and why she had just disappeared so suddenly. Without thinking, he headed off to try and find either Aislinn or the others but, something was wrong. The halls appeared to be melting right down to the floor boards and the air smelled of burning sewage. His heartbeat picked up as he raced further down the hall, almost at a dead sprint. He had completely forgotten about his wings and when he finally remembered them, it was too late; he was standing in a graveyard. Alone.

Spinning, he noticed this wasn't just any graveyard; it was where his parents were buried. What he didn't understand was why he had shown up here? Finally, he found the familiar tree, under which were his parents' tombstones. He knelt and placed his hand on the cold granite.

It seemed like such a short time ago that they had died, although it had been years. He wiped a tear from his cheek, it burned like fire. There would never be anyway to escape this pain, it had him by the neck, choking him, making him beg for some kind of mercy. It was the worst pain he had ever felt. His life was filled with hurt and death, it was part of the job but his parents had been such loving creatures, especially his mother. He closed his eyes and could almost hear her talking to him but, of course that was impossible.

The memory hit him like a hammer to the head, forcing him to look, feel, smell, and taste it entirely. His mother sat by their old fireplace, rocking back and forth with something cradled in her arms. He saw his former self, around ten years old, walk into the room and up to his mother, a tiny hand reaching for the new baby.

"Can I hold her?" He heard himself say. "I will be very gentle."

His mother looked at him and smiled, rising from the chair so he could sit down. After he did so, she placed the swaddle in his arms. Now he rocked back and forth, cooing to the baby and making kissing faces.

Dest stepped back, making the memory drift away until he was back in the graveyard. It was hard enough to think about his parents without having to think about his little sister too. She had been so innocent, so fragile, and so-tiny. That was the day he had lost hope in the world and now since he had an ounce of happiness back, he was forced to linger on the ghosts of his past. It wasn't happening. He closed his eyes and thought about Roanke Island, the trees, the waves on the shore, and finally he thought of Aislinn. Her face so warm, beautiful, and perfect in every way.

Then, he was back in the castle, in the same hallway he had been before his journey. However, Aislinn was still missing. His mind thought of every horrible thing that may have happened to her but it was unnecessary because before he could take a step, she appeared behind him, a hand placed on his shoulder.

"Are you coming or are you rethinking tonight's plans? I completely understand if you-"

She looked so lovely in the dim light, he couldn't resist cutting off her words with a kiss. "I wouldn't dream of it. Come on, let's get out of here."

Without another word, he grabbed her hand and pulled her into the night, dropping light kisses on her all the way to the beach. Tonight was about forgetting. Forgetting that there was a war coming, forgetting about their pasts, and most of all forgetting that they shouldn't be together. If this was the last night they had together, he couldn't think of a better way to spend it than holding her in his arms until dawn. Nothing would come between them, at least not at this moment.

Gemedes laughed, "I told you not to open that drawer. Why does no one listen to me?"

"Perhaps it's because you're always knocking stuff over and running into things all the time." Justahl laughed bitterly, "I'm just saying it could be a possibility. That's why I don't listen to you anyway." He threw his arms up and kicked the dresser.

"It's also why you can't find your sword." He pushed past the fairy. "Move, I have a knack for finding weapons." A few seconds passed and before Justahl could speak another word, he tossed a shining sword in his direction. "There. I told you I could find it."

Justahl just huffed, "Thanks."

"Wow. That must have been hard for you." Gemedes poked.

"You have no idea. So, what are we-"

A scream sounded through the castle, cutting off their

conversation.

"What was that?" He asked.

"I don't know. Come on." Justahl motioned for him to follow as he headed off toward the scream, his sword ready to slash whatever caused it.

The two ran through the castle, cautiously looking for anything that may have made a scream. They were about to round the corner into the foyer when Justahl grabbed his arm, forcing them both against the stone wall.

"Shh…" Justahl put a hand around his mouth to silence him, "There are demons in the castle. We have to be quiet; there may be a chance they don't know we're here."

Gemedes pried his hand away with a nod, before take a quick look around the corner into the room. "How did you know there were demons in there?"

He just looked at him like he was an idiot, "The odor. It smells horrible in there. My guess is it's a group of around ten or twenty lynx demons. Nasty creatures but, not very smart. If we're careful we can sneak up and attack them." He paused as if waiting for Gemedes to protest. "Keep moving, don't turn your back on them, and don't forget to shield yourself from their tails."

"Why?" Gemedes asked, truly curious. He had witnessed thousands of different demons during his stay with Cynric but, he couldn't remember hearing anything about lynx demons.

Justahl huffed, "Because, their tales are lined with poisonous thorns that can kill you if one gets in your skin. It's just best to kill them all without letting them fight back." He looked at him and smiled, "Are you ready?"

He nodded, "Let's kick some demon butt."

All at once, they were in the heat of what seemed like a giant battle, even though there were only a few demons present. The foyer suddenly seemed very small in comparison as he and Justahl bounded through the herd, slashing at the demons, and sending them back to where they came from. Gemedes remembered his talk with Iklin, the demon of death. He had told him he was always present when a demon died, in order to take them back. He wondered where Iklin was now. Was he here in this room? Would he notice him?

Just as he was about to turn his attention back to the battle, he heard a weird gurgling sound coming from behind him. He had forgotten one of Justahl's rules and had turned his back on the demon. When he spun around he saw Justahl curled up on the floor writhing in obvious pain, tiny thorns eating away at his flesh. His stomach turned, causing him to lurch over like he was about to be sick but, nothing happened. He quickly swung his sword and slashed the demon in two, right across the middle. It disappeared a moment later, leaving the room silent and completely trashed. They had defeated them all, but his pride was short lived because he remembered the fairy lying at his feet.

Reaching into his pocket, Gemedes retrieved the tweezers he had gotten while in Chicago. One by one he plucked the thorns out of Justahl's deteriorating skin, poison oozed out of the wounds and his body lashed on the floor with every pluck.

"Hold still," Gemedes yelled, "I'm almost done. Just a few more."

Justahl moaned in response. "I told you to watch your back you ignorant," He screamed as the last one came out, cutting off his banter.

"I know. Please don't yell it will only make it worse. I'm going to go call Ananais on the device in the king's study. Don't move." Gemedes rose to retrieve the device.

"Like I have much of a choice." Justahl coughed and vomited a fountain of blood on the marble floor.

Gemedes knew he didn't have much time, he just hoped Ananais knew what to do. For the first time in his existence, he was putting his faith in a warlock. Hopefully this one wouldn't disappoint him. He dashed from the foyer, leaving Justahl in a pool of blood.

"Alright Quid, now do exactly like we practiced only this time try it upside down." Seth nodded as his brother climbed up in the rafters of the training house. Since it was cold outside, they had to train inside, which made it harder to train him properly.

Quid looked down at his brother, "I don't see why I have to do this upside down. Since when have we battled while hanging from rafters?"

"Well, we may not battle from rafters but, we are put in dangerous situations which require us to be flexible on all accounts. Hanging upside down and blocking is one way to increase your versatility and help you remain balanced. Now block my arrows. Ready?" Seth loaded his bow and began firing arrows one after another. He was surprised to see Quid successfully blocking them all without as much as a flinch. Maybe his brother had what it took to be a knight after all.

Once the arrows were gone and Quid was safely on the ground, Seth decided it was time for a break. So, they went outside to get some fresh air.

"How am I doing?" Quid asked. "Do you think I'm doing alright?"

His brother was so innocent, so carefree; it reminded him of how he used to be before his father died last year. He looked at his brother, "You've done well but, we are far from done. I suspect we will have to do this for at least three more weeks and then we will start on your mental training." His hand came down on Quid's back. "I feel like I owe you an apology. I never wanted this life for you because I never wanted this life for myself. If I could take you away from all this, trust me I would but, I realize now that although we can't forget this life of hate, dying, and destruction, we will always have each other. You're my brother first Quid and I owe it to you to teach you what father taught me. I really think you will be a great knight one day and when something happens to me, you will make a great king."

Quid smiled, "Thanks Seth. I think you will make a great king too and if you ever need me, I'll be right here by your side."

Seth wrapped his brother in a hug and ruffled his hair before looking back out at Frost Forest. He noticed a dark figure moving in the shadows, which made him jump up in response. "Get out your sword Quid. It's time to put those skills you just learned to good use. Come on."

Without another word, he dashed after the figure, Quid dead on his heels.

"Alright, that should stop the poison from entering your bloodstream." Ananais stood and started wiping his hands on an old cloth. "How did those demons get onto the island, or better yet, how did they get into the castle? I thought there were enchantments, spells around the perimeter to keep out such things?"

Justahl started to speak, "I don't know and yeah, there are blocking spells placed throughout the island and one surrounds the entire castle. The only way they can be broken is by a-" His expression turned thoughtful as he remembered what his trainer had taught him about spells.

"Any warlock or witch can break a spell as long as another warlock or witch hasn't cast it. If a magical being performs the spell, it can't be broken by anyone except the witch or warlock who cast it." His trainer had explained.

Gemedes looked at him, clearly confused considering his jaw hung limply to his neckline. Ananais looked relieved.

"Well, in that case, it seems I have some spells to cast." Ananais began pacing, "Hmmm, I also need to brew a few healing potions. One for Justahl and several to keep on hand, at least until I can get the blocks back up." He turned to Justahl, who was still leaning against a chair in the foyer. "It appears that our friend Harlem took it upon himself to break the blocking spells. I do hope they haven't been down for long or we will have a bloody mess on our hands. Where is that communication device? I think we need to check on the others." He began pacing and talking to himself again, "First things first, get the block around the castle, then, we can worry about the other blocks throughout the island." As quickly as he had come, he left the room. His only words were, "Hurry." As he sauntered off down the hall towards his room.

"Seth behind you." Quid screeched as his sword sliced through another demon. "Where are all these coming from?"

His brother looked at him while beheading another creature with one swipe across the neck. "I don't know, there shouldn't be any demons on the island. They must have broken the blocks that are around the island. We need to get back to the castle." Another swipe at two progressing demons, they disappeared in a puff of dust.

Quid was trying to kill as many as he could but, every time he killed one, two more would take its place. "There's too many of them Seth." He was losing stamina fast, he was also injured. His left leg had been sliced open by a gorge demon when he was fighting off a horx. Blood flowed willingly from the open wound, soaking into the grass below.

"Just stay with me Quid. I will try to build a portal. Here," He tossed him his bow and arrows, "These will give your sword a rest while I open the portal.

He grabbed the bow in time to shoot an arrow between the eyes of another horx demon. "I can't do this any-"

A second horx demon had appeared behind Quid, piercing his stomach and cutting off his words. He fell to the ground in a thud but not before sending an arrow into the creatures head.

"QUID!" Seth screamed. He rushed to his brother's side, momentarily forgetting their escape plan. Hundreds of demons swarmed around them, hissing, growling, and flinging poisonous thorns at them. But none of that mattered to Seth anymore. All that mattered was the end of the horx tail sticking out of his brother's chest. "Try to breathe slowly Quid. It won't hurt as bad."

Quid looked at him and tears filled his eyes. "Did I do good Seth?" He coughed and blood splattered his lips.

Seth wiped the hair back out of his brother's face and smiled. Of course he would be thinking about how well he did at a time like this. "Yeah. There are no more left."

The demons in the woods around them snarled in protest to his words but, for once Seth didn't care. Quid needed medical attention, fast. He gently laid his brother's head back down on the ground, trying not to jar him too much, as he opened the portal that would transfer them back to the castle. The demons would have to wait.

As his foot stepped over the threshold of the portal door, he leaned down to place a kiss on his brother's forehead. He couldn't die. Not like this. He had to survive. He just had to. The swirls swallowed them up and the demons disappeared behind them.

Chapter 12

Punch In the Heart

Ananais leaned over Quid's body, healing him. He seemed to be handling things well, so Seth stepped out into the hall. Waiting for his brother to die was hard enough; he didn't need to add to the pain by watching as well.

"If it hadn't been for you, your brother wouldn't be lying there almost dead." Cynric's voice echoed in his head. It reminded him of being in someone else's thoughts, something he didn't do very often because it hurt. His head throbbed in response of the crowdedness in his mind. As he slumped to the ground in defeat, the voice chuckled, "You seem to be taking this well enough young prince. What, no 'hello, how are you doing?' I am hurt Seth." His head rocked with laughter.

"I am not a puppet on a string," Seth started, "You can't keep pulling my strings at will. What do you want from me?"

The voice was silent for a moment then, answered, "I want you dead but, that won't come until later. First, I want you to suffer like I suffered the night my father died. He was everything I knew and he died so I could carry on for him. I have to do this, can't you see that? I have to kill you and every being on that island. It's what my father wanted and it's what he will get."

All at once, the voice shifted out of his mind, into a form in front of him. He slunk back until his back was nearly pressed into the wall. How can he be here? Seth wondered.

"Understand this," The figure grabbed him by the neck and thrust him up, "I will come in the night, silent and deadly. No one can stand against me and no one will survive. Head this warning, Seth, if you want to live, join me. Together we can make over the world and rule for all eternity. No more death, no more pain, and I will even spare your brother's life."

Seth looked at him in response, "You would let him live?"

The figure, which he had identified as Cynric, smiled. "Of course. He is of no importance to me but, if you join me, I won't kill him. What will it be elf?"

There was only one way to save his brother and he couldn't think of anything he wanted more. So, without hesitation, he answered, "I will join-"

The door behind him swung open and the warlock stormed out into the hall, his hands raised in response to the visitor. "You are not welcome here demon. As for you," He pointed his finger at Seth, "I am disappointed that you have no confidence in me. This creature cannot be trusted, no matter how good his words sound. He is a liar and never helps anyone unless it helps him in some way. Goodbye Cynric. See you in battle."

Cynric swirled in on himself and disappeared in an instant. Seth slammed against the cold, stone floor below, his heart racing and his eyes filling with tears. "I wasn't going to…"

Ananais glared at him, "Yes, you were and for good reason. Your brother is the only thing you have but, to trade your soul to the devil himself won't help you. I can promise you that."

Seth stared out into the hall; it smelled like the chef was preparing dinner. *Roast and potatoes*, he thought. Before he could think about it more, he remembered his brother, still lying on the bed in the room behind him. "How is he?"

"He's doing alright. His body is weak, so traveling through the portal must have knocked him out cold." The warlock wiped a hand across his forehead before continuing. "I have done everything I can; now we must wait and see if it works." He turned to walk down the hall, his body looking ragged and tired from exerting so much magic. But, before he completely disappeared he turned and spoke a few final words to Seth, "Just know that horx poison is tricky and I can't guarantee any results. Are you prepared to let him go?"

Seth nodded.

"Well in that case, now I have done everything I can. Goodnight young prince. You may have my room tonight; it is right next to his. Sleep well and I will send Gemedes to protect you, just in case our previous visitor decides to return." Without another word, Ananais disappeared down the next corridor, leaving Seth alone with his thoughts.

He walked slowly into his brother's room, taking the seat next to his bed. Quid looked peaceful as he slept, it didn't even seem like he had been hurt at all. Seth took his hand in his, wrapping it in a warm embrace. "Don't die Quid. You're all I have little brother. Please, please, please don't die." It wasn't proper for him to cry but, he let a few tears stream down his face, betraying his prideful spirit and shattering his already broken heart. He fell asleep with Quid's hand in his.

"I hope Gemedes and Justahl didn't cause too much damage to the castle. I can't leave to get more furniture." Aislinn pushed the heavy wooden door of the castle open, flooding the foyer with moonlight. She glanced around, surprised to see no lights on. Everything seemed to be cast in shadows, daring her to come inside and join them. They mocked her and made her uneasy.

Quickly, she returned the light to the fairy lamps, which ran on fairy energy. The room glowed, revealing the damage from the night's battle. Now she wanted the shadows back.

Aislinn's jaw hit the floor, as she gawked at the ruins of what use to be a beautiful entryway. Her hand came down, to steady herself, on what appeared to be the remains of a chair, of course she couldn't be sure.

Dest walked in behind her and froze. "What happened in here?"

"I don't know but, I plan to find out." She cupped her hands around her mouth and shouted, "Gemedes. Justahl. Seth. You all better get down here and explain yourselves." She waited for a response but, no one came or answered back. "Seth? Justahl? Gemedes? You guys here?"

She looked behind her at Dest, who just shrugged in response. However, before she could shout again, an exhausted looking Ananais stepped into view. His tired eyes scanning the room. "Welcome home princess." He slumped into the only chair standing, his eyes immediately closing. "I assume you wish to know why your friends are not answering, and why the castle looks so, well, ruined."

Aislinn stated, "Yes, I want to know. Just tell me what's going on. Where is everyone?"

Ananais spoke, his eyes still closed, "Well for starters, the blocks are broken throughout the island but, don't worry I will have them back up as soon as I heal."

"What do you mean heal? What's wrong? Are you hurt?" She rushed to the warlock's side, kneeling beside him to examine him closer. "You appear fine; tired perhaps but, it is four in the morning."

He smiled, "Yes, it is and you two have been out all night." He must have noticed her expression because he stopped his thoughts. "Alright, alright, I guess I should start with the beginning."

As soon as Ananais had completed his story of the night's events, Aislinn rushed off to find Seth. She found him, lying next to Quid, his hands wrapped around his brothers'. "Seth?" She nudged him lightly, hoping not to startle him too badly. He had been through enough.

His eyes fluttered open as he slowly turned to look at her. "Oh, hey; when did you get in?'"

"Just now. You look terrible Seth, maybe you should go lie down in Ananais' room, its right next door. I could keep an eye on him and if anything happens, I'll let you know." She placed a hand down on his shoulder.

He turned, throwing her hand off his shoulder, and glared at her.

"You have no right to tell me what to do and thanks for telling me I look terrible. Need I remind you, you would look worse than me if it was Amara lying here nearly dead, instead of my brother? And where were you while Quid and I were attacked? What about Justahl and Gemedes? Were you here when the demons attacked them?" His face turned red as fire and his hands were shaking as he spoke. "NO! While we were all fighting for our lives, you and Dest were out canoodling. So, no I shouldn't go rest in Ananais' room while you watch over Quid because, you should have been watching out for all of us. That's what a real queen does. Now, if you would be so kind as to leave, I need to make a bed in the floor, unless there's anything else you think I should do?"

Aislinn was dumbfounded, her jaw hanging limply at her feet. She had never had anyone, especially Seth, her best friend, speak to her like he just had. His words tore at her chest, making her sick. She wanted to leave, run and hide somewhere. Somewhere no one could find her but, her legs wouldn't move. Her eyes started burning as she let tears stream down her cheeks. Hatred, pure hatred was all she felt. She wished it had been Seth who was hurt instead of Quid; she wished it more than anything else.

As she finally turned to walk away, she found the courage to say what she wanted to say. "Seth Arabiraheal, I wish it was you in that bed." She had almost made it out into the hall when he replied.

"Yeah, me too." The door slammed behind her, closing her off from the only person she could ever really trust. She needed to escape.

A knock sounded on the door.

Who can it be now? Seth thought as he climbed out of his pallet on the floor. Creeping slowly across the wooden panels, he made his way to the other side of the room. In one swift motion, he swung the door open, stepped out into the hall, and closed the door softly behind him.

He quickly glanced around; looking for any sign of a visitor but, all he found was an empty hallway. Just as he was about to go back inside, a hand came down on his arm.

"Wait," A familiar voice echoed off the stone walls, "I came to talk to you."

Fed up with secrets, Seth screamed, "THEN SHOW YOURSELF COWARD!"

Out of the shadows, stepped the one fairy he didn't want to talk to, Dest. He looked too perfect, too calm, and just plain weird. Not a single strand of hair was out of place, his wings looked magnificent as the light from the fairy lamps seemed to dance off of them, and his eyes stared through Seth's very soul. It was a little creepy, to be honest.

"To what do I owe this spectacular visit?" Seth spoke sarcastically. His words almost made him laugh but, Dest seemed not to notice his joking tone at all.

"You need to watch yourself elf. Prince or no prince, you don't need to treat people like dirt. Especially when that person happens to be your best friend." His voice boomed through the hall but, his facial expression remained calm the entire time.

Seth stared in horror, "You mean to tell me you came all the way down here to tell me to be nice to Aislinn? What is it any of your business? You're a visitor here and I think I know her better than you. Besides, no one asked your opinion our friendship. So, BACK OFF!"

Dest didn't flinch, not even when Seth got right up in his face. Instead, he smiled. "I don't think you know her as well as you let on. She is an extraordinary creature and I am honored to even spend a moment with her. Do you have any idea what this war is doing to her? No, you don't because you're too busy worrying about whether she likes me or not. Well here's a news flash buddy, I love her and if I'm lucky enough she may feel the same. So, why don't you," He poked him in the chest, "Back off before you get hurt. Understand that?"

Anger coursed through his body. This fairy was getting on his last nerve. Showing up without any warning and keeping his best friend away from him for days. Now, he was threatening him? "It's coming through loud and clear. Now, why don't you turn around and go back where you came from before you get hurt."

In a flash, Dest had him pinned to the wall, his face inches from Seth's. He slammed a fist into the side of his face, causing his entire body to shake. Then, Dest turned and stormed off down the hall, leaving Seth's body in a pile on the floor; blood trickling down his swollen face.

After washing the blood off his face and hands, he returned to Quid's room. He had just closed the door when he heard a small voice, "Seth? Is that you?"

Momentarily forgetting his smashed up face, he dashed to Quid's side. "I'm here brother. How are you feeling?"

Quid looked up at him, meeting his eyes for the first time since the attack. "A little sore but," He coughed, "I'll be alright. Where are we? Did we kill all the demons? Is the war starting? How am I alive?"

Seth sat down beside Quid, his eyes filling with tears. "Calm down. Relax. Everything is fine. We are in the castle and Ananais healed you. There were too many of them Quid. I couldn't battle them alone so, I brought us back through a portal but I'm sure they're all either dead or gone. Don't worry about that now, all that matters is that you're alive and healing. Rest now, everything is alright. The war is not beginning anytime soon, so rest."

He placed a hand over Quid's heart, near where the horx tail had pierced him, and let out a sigh of relief. His brother was fine. As Quid closed his eyes, Seth found himself regretting his words to Aislinn. Perhaps he could find her and apologize. *Later*, he thought, *but for now I will stay with my brother.* He closed his eyes too, finally at peace.

Dest ran a hand across her back, comforting her while she lost it completely. How could Seth have talked to her like that? She wasn't going to get over this. He was her best friend and now he hated her. The worst part was she had no idea why.

"It's alright Aislinn," He whispered in her ear. Trying to calm her and get her to stop crying. "You have done nothing wrong and he is not worth those tears. Trust me. I have spent many nights crying over things I cannot hope to change, it only makes me weak." He took her face in his hands, turning her to face him in the dim room. "You are definitely not weak and nothing he says will ever change that. Come on, don't cry anymore. Please."

She cast a weary glance in his direction before turning away again. "I have never felt so alone and I can't expect you to understand how this feels. Seth is everything to me. He is my best friend and for some reason, us being together is killing him." Without hesitation, she rose from the bed, which they had been sharing for the last few nights, and walked to the door. Opening it she stated, "As much as this hurts, I have to let you go. I can't lose him over someone I barely know. You are more special than I can even imagine and no one will ever take your place in my heart but, this is what's best for now. Seth is in pain and I need to be with him now."

Dest winced at her words, his mouth hanging open in surprise. "Are you seriously breaking up with me? Now? Like this?"

"I'm so sorry but yes I am." The tears she thought were long gone returned, streaking her face in hot streams. The creature in front of her was magnificent in ways she could never describe. He was breathtaking, perfect, and she loved him but, she had to let him go, for everyone's sake. She threw the door open, the light from the hall flooding the doorway. "Please just leave now so I can't hurt you anymore. Goodbye Dest. I will never forget you."

As he walked out the door, he turned and laid a final kiss on her cheek. It still burned even after he was long out of sight.

Her hand shook as she closed the door and before she could even make it to the bed, she fell into the shadows that had haunted her for weeks, only this time Dest couldn't come pull her back to reality. They engulfed her completely and she never came back.

"Where's Aislinn?" Seth asked Ananais. The warlock had been silent since Dest left a few nights earlier. It was unusual.

He looked pointedly at him, rage flaming up behind is otherwise calm expression. "I don't know. Probably still in her room. She hasn't eaten or moved for three days. Ever since-" His words stopped, "You know what, why don't you just leave it alone? I don't see why you care anyway? There was no reason for what you said to her the other night but, that's beside the point. You got what you wanted, no matter who else it hurt in the process. She is miserable but don't worry she will survive. My only question for you Seth Arabiraheal is will you?" Without another word, Ananais got up and evaporated, probably returning to his room.

A few moments later, Quid walked into the dining hall. His wounds had completely healed and he seemed to be in a pretty good mood. That was until he looked at his brother. "What the hell happened to you? You look terrible."

He sat beside his brother in one of the twelve oak dining chairs, his hands reaching for a muffin in the same second.

"Thanks. I feel like I've been stabbed in the back with a stake but, that could be because everyone hates me." Seth snapped, "I'm just saying."

Quid giggled, "Everyone doesn't hate you. In fact, I can think of three people who don't hate you who are in this very castle. Justahl doesn't hate you."

"That's only one Quid." Seth frowned. He loved his brother dearly but, sometimes he could be so dense.

"I wasn't finished yet so, no I'm not dense thank you very much. Now, I don't hate you, that's two people." He held up two fingers, "And Gemedes is too busy hating Justahl that he doesn't have enough time to hate you too."

At that, they both started laughing.

"Yeah. I guess that is three but, Aislinn hates me and I don't think Ananais has ever liked me much, even before the other night." Seth sighed.

Quid looked at him, a weird expression coming over his face, "What do you mean Aislinn hates you? I do believe she made Dest leave because his being here was hurting you. In my opinion, that is the opposite of hate. She told him to leave and it killed her but, she did it for you. Now, what are you going to do about it?"

His brother was actually smarter than he gave him credit for and he was right. Aislinn didn't hate him, yet but, if he didn't get Dest back she would. Forgetting his brother's presence, he summoned a portal that would show him where Dest was. After a few moments, he saw him walking along a path in Frost Forest. Time was of the essence so, without thinking about it, he ran to into the foyer and grabbed his cloak. Heading out into the morning sun, he knew what he had to do and he had to do it fast. Luckily Frost Forest wasn't more than a few feet beyond the castle gates.

Chapter 13

Falling

"Dest, if you would only come back, I swear you won't hear another complaint out of me. Aislinn is lost without you." Seth begged him over and over again but, nothing seemed to shake him. He stood, leaning against a large tree, his black wings fluttering slightly.

"I fail to see how any of this should matter to me anymore. She told me to leave so, I left. Case closed. End of story. Whatever you want to call it, it's over between her and I so, please just leave me alone. The last thing I need is some elf telling me what I should or shouldn't do," Dest shoved a finger into Seth's chest, "Especially you!" He started to walk away but, Seth refused to move out of the way.

"Just come back until after the Christmas Ball, then, if you still want to leave you can. She cares for you Dest, I don't know why but she does. I never thought it would hurt her to let you go but I was wrong. Way wrong." Seth looked at him, trying to read his emotions but he couldn't pick up on anything at all.

Dest just glared at him, "What do you expect me to do? Go and beg her to take me back? I can't and won't do that. Now if you could be so kind as to get the hell out of my way, I need to be leaving. Unless there's anything else I can do for you?" He paused, "I thought not.

In a flash, his wings burst into full shape, shading an arc of about five feet around him. With no sign of stopping, he flew off into the treetops.

Seth knew he had to do something so, he grabbed the biggest rock he could find, loaded his bow, and shot it. In a matter of seconds, the fairy lay flat on the ground, the rock at his side.

"What on earth are you doing? You could have killed me." Dest roared.

Laughing, Seth walked over and picked up his weapon. "I'm sorry, next time I will use a flaming arrow instead of this deadly rock." His entire body shook as he leaned against the tree for support; his laugh could have been heard for miles.

"Ah. Well either way, I don't appreciate your behavior. One minute your all 'Get away from me. I'm in pain. Blah, Blah, Blah. Now all of a sudden you're begging me to come back. Could you explain your true feelings for me because, quite frankly I'm confused."

They both sat on the ground in silence for a moment. Seth was contemplating what to say. Dest contemplating his next exit strategy since flying away wasn't an option.

Seth let out a huge gust of air and turned toward him, "I-"

A screech broke out through the woods, followed by the sound of someone or something running towards them. The two rose to their feet.

"What is that?" Seth asked.

Dest shook his head, "I don't know but whatever it is, it's coming this way. We need to take to the tree tops, if it's a demon, we can surprise it by dropping in on it from above. You take that tree," He pointed to the oak tree behind him, "I will take this one. Don't make any movements until you see me signal. Understand?"

Seth looked at him and nodded, "Except what if it isn't a demon, then what?"

"We will cross that bridge when we come to it, for now we're betting on the demon. Alright, up you go." He motioned for Seth to take his station in the tree.

"Wait. What's the signal?"

"Er." Dest thought for a second, "When you see me jump down, just guard my back."

This time, Seth leaped into his tree. Dest followed his motion and flew into the tree directly across from him. Now, they waited.

Moments passed and nothing happened. Birds flew by, animals scurried around like normal, and there was no sign of danger in any form. Dest was beginning to think the forest was playing tricks on them. Suddenly, a gust of wind howled through the trees, leaving a black form behind as it dispersed.

The creature looked sickly, bones protruding from its black skin, which looked burnt and rotting. Its eyes were sunken in and cast a vicious glare as it stared around. Oily black nails curled out of its long, bony fingers and there were sores all over its body that seeped with an oozing puss. The worst part was smell of rotten sewage that rolled off of it and its teeth, which snarled back in response to its surroundings, were jagged and resembled broken glass.

Dest crouched down to peer at the creature closer, his legs arching just slightly so he could get a better view. He knew this particular demon quite well; his family had dealt with them for centuries. Back home they were known as Ravarks, which was translated into 'Hell's Angel.'

Trying to be subtle, he retracted his wings, letting them fall silently behind him. He started to descend from his hideout, going down the back way. Out of sight. Once he made it to the ground though, he took off like lighting, his sword drawn high above his head as he charged the beast in front of him.

As his blade pierced into the monster's flesh, another screech went up into the woods. Dest dropped the sword and shielded his ears, knowing the sound would make him pass out if he listened for too long. However, he had forgotten to mention this point to Seth, who fell out of his tree, his head smacking the ground with a thud.

The beast stopped screeching and turned to see the fallen elf. As he neared Seth's body, all Dest could think about was having to take his dead body back to Aislinn. She would think it was his fault, even after he explained the entire story. Plus, he didn't know why but, there was just something about Seth that he found intriguing.

Quickly and quietly, he dashed up into what use to be Seth's hiding spot. He knew that if he could get high enough, he could stab the demon in the back and he would disappear. His father had taught him how to send demons back to hell, something he would never forget.

As soon as he reached the top, he leaped from the highest branch, plummeting towards the demon below. Finally, the blade of his sword plunged into the Ravark. It didn't even make a sound before it disappeared.

Since the demon was gone, it was safe to check on Seth. His body still lay crumbled on the forest floor, his eyes wild with horror. He wasn't dead, yet, but he would be if they didn't get help.

Sheathing his sword, he lifted Seth's limp body into his arms and formed a portal at the same time. Momentarily forgetting his fight with Aislinn, he stepped into the vortex. After regaining his thoughts, he made a mental note to drop Seth off and leave as soon as they were back. No need to linger where you're not welcome.

"Hold on." Gemedes called as he raced across the foyer to the large wooden doors. The foyer was returned to its former glory shortly after the demons' attack. It looked exactly the same except for the antique clock King Galiron had sitting in the far left corner, it was past repairing so, they sent it off to be recycled. As he reached the door, he paused, thinking of who it might be so late in the afternoon. It was too early for guests to be arriving for dinner but, too late for council members to be dropping by unannounced. However, after a moment of hesitation, he thought it might be urgent and opened the door.

Dest stormed in before he even had time to release the door handle. Seth lay limply in his arms. As soon as they were both in safely, Gemedes shut the door and ran to Dest's side.

"What's going on?" He asked. "What's wrong with him?"

"I need you to get Ananais quickly. Seth and I were attacked in the woods and he is in desperate need of medical attention. Hurry!" Dest shouted.

Gemedes started to run off but turned instead to ask another question, "Should I retrieve Aislinn as well? She will want to be here you know." He knew better than to ask him this after what had happened but, he didn't want to hear it from her later. She would find out one way or another, she always did so, he didn't want to get in any more trouble. Dest would be gone soon anyway but Aislinn was soon to be his queen.

Dest frowned, "Yes. You might as well get her down here too. I will just leave as soon as you return. Now please hurry, time is running out."

With that, Gemedes raced out of the foyer towards Ananais' room. He really hoped he was available.

In a matter of minutes, the foyer was overflowing with people. Ananais had come in first, carrying his bag of goodies in one hand and a glass of something black in the other. It appeared to be some sort of electric potion, since it was shooting out purple sparks every few seconds, but Dest couldn't be sure.

Soon after his arrival, Aislinn and a very distressed Quid entered the room. Each looked devastated and absolutely crazy with guilt. Dest longed to have his arm around Aislinn's shoulders, comforting her during this tragic time but, he knew it would only bring her more pain. She had made her feelings quite clear earlier so, there was no need to relive the misery he had already felt. Once was bad enough.

Eventually, the room was filled with six other creatures besides himself and Seth. Gemedes couldn't keep anything quiet. He had even told Justahl and Amara, who just stood back and watched as Ananais cast spells and gathered things from his medical bag.

He decided now was as good a time as any to slip out so, he bowed to Gemedes, thanking him for his help, and retreated out the door. The air was growing cooler as he exited and quietly shut the door behind him.

Before the latch caught though, a figure appeared in the doorway. Aislinn stood with her bright purple eyes pointed right at him. His heart skipped a beat because of the pain he found there. He felt it too.

She didn't say a word as she ran into his arms, tears falling in streams down her cheeks. Dest knew he should push her away, tell her how unsafe she was, that he was dangerous and not worthy of her at all but, instead he wrapped his arms around her and pulled her to him as close as he could. Immediately, he forgot everything that had happened that day. She was here, in his arms, and that was all that mattered to him. It was weird how one action could change the course of his entire future. He no longer regretted the day before it began, he welcomed it with open arms and a smile, and it was all because of the fairy he held in his arms. She was the one creature who had melted his hard exterior and touched his heart. He had been lost for so long and thought his life was hopeless. Doomed to spend the rest of his days in misery because of someone else's mistakes. Now all he wanted was to spend the rest of his existence right where he was, with Aislinn and no one would take that from him. Not even Cynric.

After too short a time, she pulled out of his embrace, her eyes still glistening with tears. "I'm sorry Dest. I never should have said all those things to you. Perhaps then Seth wouldn't have felt obligated to go after you and he wouldn't be injured." Aislinn leaned against him for support.

As he rubbed her back he replied, "Don't think for one second this is your fault. None of this is your fault. If anything it is mine. I shouldn't have been all over you all the time. Things did get a little carried away."

Aislinn smiled and looked up at him, "Yeah. Well I allowed them to happen and started a few myself. Either way, we need to be more careful and respectful of everyone in the castle, not just Seth. He can be a little overprotective at times but, it's only because he considers me his sister. We've practically been together our entire lives so, I owe him to at least stop being all over you all the time."

"Agreed. From now on, I will try to control myself and only kiss you on the cheek when we are in the room with others." Dest nodded in agreement to her request. It was going to be hard considering he was used to having what he wanted, when he wanted it but, it was a small price to pay to stay with her.

She laughed and once again, he found himself lost in her laughter. It was mesmerizing and truly unique. He felt alive when she was happy. Something he hadn't felt for a long time. At last, he was home.

Seth had made a full recovery by the next day and was back to himself, or rather the guy he was before all the war stuff happened. Aislinn noticed his attitude toward Dest and her relationship had changed. Actually, he seemed to be taking it quite well. His moods had changed too, he had been grumpy for so long that it was shocking to see him smiling and laughing when she had entered the dining hall Saturday morning.

"You are up awfully early," She exclaimed. "I didn't expect to see you around much today. Are you feeling alright?"

Seth smiled and nodded before turning back to Justahl and Dest. The three of them were discussing what to do about Gemedes this evening.

"I wanted to take Aislinn to see a waterfall I found yesterday but, if we need to stay here, we can." Dest explained. "We don't mind do we?"

Aislinn shook her head, "Not at all." She was still shocked to find them all getting along so well.

Seth looked at the two of them and smiled, which surprised her even more. "I really need to help Quid train. He's improving but, he still needs a lot of work before the war. Justahl would you be willing to keep an eye on him for a couple hours? Quid and I won't leave until around two and we usually return by eight. Plus, we will just be at the training grounds and I will take a communication device just in case something goes wrong this time."

Before Justahl could answer, Dest added, "Yeah and I don't want to get to the waterfall at least until six or seven so, we will be here until then. You will only be alone with him for two hours tops."

Justahl nodded in agreement, "Yeah, why not. It's not like I have any plans this evening." He sighed, "I need a girlfriend."

The three started laughing again before changing the subject back to battle strategies. Aislinn made a quick exit in order to find Ananais; she needed to see how Gemedes was doing with protecting.

Once she was in the hall, it was just a few steps to the foyer and a few more out to where Gemedes was training. Ananais looked aggravated and Gemedes just looked tired.

"Hey you two," She called, "How are things going?"

Ananais looked at her and laughed, "About as well as they were last week. He has all the skills but I think he lacks motivation. Do you think you could help?"

Confused, she walked closer to the pair. "What did you have in mind?" She asked.

"Well, I know your father asked him to protect you at all costs so, I believe if I threaten you, he will be forced to protect you from me. Are you ready?" Ananais explained calmly.

"Do I just stand here?"

"Yes. I will only attack your mind for now. Then, if he can master that, we will move on to physical attacks. Ready Gemedes?" He called to the goblin.

"Yeah." Gemedes answered slowly.

"Alright now just relax Aislinn. I will try to make this as painless as possible. One…two…three." Ananais shouted.

All at once, the image around her changed, shifting into an entirely different setting. She was still in the entryway but, it was all wrong. The ground beneath her feet was cracked every few feet and hot steam rose from the cracks, making it hard to breath.

The trees in Frost Forest were still there but, they appeared as though flames were licking the bark right off of them. It was strange but, only because she had no idea what was going on. Everything seemed so real and she could feel the steam, smell the burning trees, and taste the saltiness of the breeze coming off the nearby ocean. She was at home but, it was definitely not real. Closing her eyes, she waited for Gemedes to block Ananais and keep this particular image at bay.

Just like it had started, it stopped. Instantly. One minute she was trying to stay away from the fire which was growing to where she stood and in the next, she was back in front of Ananais; no flames in sight.

Ananais clapped his hands together in satisfaction, "Excellent. That was amazing Gemedes. You blocked me in less than five minutes. This is definitely the route to take when training you. Good thing you're protecting her and Seth, otherwise you couldn't stay focused. Extraordinary!" He shouted over and over again.

Aislinn was also happy for Gemedes but, mainly she was glad to be rid of that nightmarish image. She hated thinking about death, it made her feel weak. Something a true ruler would never show to anyone.

After deciding to skip the physical attacks for the day, the three returned to their normal schedules. Aislinn had the weekly council meeting to attend to in just one hour, Gemedes had taken on Thomas's responsibilities until they could find a replacement, and Ananais was heading into town for a bit. They all played their part and forgot about the impending war for a little while. It was nice to just relax sometimes and not worry about the future.

Dest guided her though the woods, gently leading her to their destination. Aislinn knew the waterfall well but, there were still butterflies in her stomach as the neared the familiar clearing. Of course, she always got butterflies when she was around him. Tonight was no exception to that fact.

They finally reached the clearing and stepped out onto the riverbank. The water rushed over the cliffs in front of them, it was truly amazing. She could remember the first time she had seen the waterfall but, this time it seemed more beautiful and spectacular than it ever had. It made her heart stop to see the crystal blue water flowing down into the river below; the moon hit the water causing a rainbow of colors to be reflected into the night air.

Everything seemed tinged with life, silent but out of control at the same time. Fireflies danced all around them, the flowers seemed to be exploding with vibrant hues of blue, teal, pink, and orange, and thousands of fish swam around in the pool below. She longed to just dive in and become one with nature, the way she had countless other times but something held her back, rather someone. Dest. He stood staring up at the endlessness of the night sky, his arms wrapped around her, holding her in place, refusing to let her go.

"What are you thinking?" She asked as she turned and began tracing lines on his chest. It was warm and buzzed with life as well.

Instantly, he stared at her, forgetting the stars. "I'm mustering up the courage to sing you the song I wrote." His face fell and for once he looked sad.

Lifting his face to stare into his eyes, she replied, "I was wondering why you brought a guitar. I didn't even know you played. Can I hear the song? Please."

He laughed, "I knew you would ask eventually but, I must warn you it's not finished yet and I'm a little rusty. It's been years since I played."

Aislinn only nodded for him to continue. Without another word, he sat her down on a stump and retrieved his guitar, which was leaning against a nearby tree. He began strumming and in a matter of seconds, he was playing the most beautiful song she had ever heard. It made her want to cry but, only because she knew the message. The notes told the story of two creatures who were destined to be apart but, couldn't stay away from each other. They traveled for years in the dark and when they finally met, it was like the world was all colors.

As he neared the chorus, the atmosphere around them changed, matching each note exactly. The wind softened and blew with the harmony. All of the flowers swayed along with the melody and the fireflies danced along with the beat. It became almost impossible for her not to start dancing too; like magic.

Eventually the song was over and his guitar lay on the ground but, the sounds of his strumming still lingered in the air. Aislinn looked at him smiling, "I can't believe you think it's not finished. What's wrong with it?"

Dest wrapped her in his arms again and planted a small kiss on her lips. "Nothing. It's absolutely perfect. All it needed was you."

"That is truly the most wonderful thing anyone has ever done for me. Thank you." She pulled him down and kissed him again, only this time she didn't stop. It wasn't until Dest pulled away that she even noticed what was happening at all.

"Not tonight. I want everything to be perfect when we finally do that." He touched his lips to hers once again before leading her back to the riverbank. "You want to go for a swim?"

Aislinn only grinned in response and leaped off the cliff into the water below. Dest followed a moment later, his shirt lying with his guitar. Both of them forgot the hour and just focused on each other. It was like a long lost dream come true.

Chapter 14

Hunger

"Ananais is working Gemedes, so get lost." Justahl demanded. "I'm not going to be responsible for letting you interrupt him. What do you need anyway?"

Gemedes smiled slightly. "I was just wondering when he was going into town. Aislinn needs him to pick up a few extra things for the ball tonight. I'm completely here on business."

"Right. Business. I'll believe that never. Just tell me what she wants him to get and I'll make sure he receives the message." He added.

"No. Aislinn told me to talk to him personally, if she wanted you to do it, she would've asked you, not me." Gemedes shoved at him, trying to get him to move. "Could you please get out of--"

The door to Ananais's room flew open, causing Justahl to fall back across the threshold. "What are you two bickering about? Is it too much to ask to get a little work done around here, without having to worry about finding earplugs to block out your constant yelling?" He looked straight at Gemedes, then, added, "Ah. My young friend, how is the protecting working out for you?"

"Good as far as I know. Aislinn says her dreams have been rather pleasant considering the train wreck they were before. I was just coming to give you a message from her when he," Gemedes pointed to Justahl, "Stopped me."

Ananais turned on him, "Why didn't you let him in?"

Justahl was at a loss for words so he just shrugged.

"Well, please come in Gemedes. I need you to give something to Aislinn too." The warlock added peacefully before returning back into his room. Gemedes stuck his tongue out at Justahl, then, followed obediently.

Once they were all inside with the door closed, Ananais began scurrying about the room, gathering things here and there as he went. Justahl lounged against the far wall nearest the door, trying to remain unresponsive.

"It will take a moment for this potion to be ready so, why don't you tell me what Aislinn wanted while we wait." Ananais implied.

Gemedes nearly dropped the bottle he was looking at but, caught it before it could crash to the floor. "She wanted to know if, when you go into to town, you could gather a few supplies for her. I'm guessing they're for the ball tonight but, she wouldn't tell me for sure."

"Of course. Let me just grab a piece of paper and a pen." He answered while glancing around. Once he had his pen ready with ink, he asked Gemedes to continue.

"Um. She needs turmeric, quail eggs, frog eyes, and a vile of dragon blood." Gemedes stood there for a minute then, nodded as if that was all.

Ananais smiled as if the list pleased him, although Justahl had no idea why. To him, the list seemed odd and surely Gemedes knew those supplies weren't for the party tonight. In fact, they sounded like ingredients for a potion of sorts but, before he could ask Ananais to explain, the warlock was already exiting the room.

"I won't be gone long." He exclaimed as he handed Gemedes a tiny bottle, filled with a swirling orange liquid inside. "Guard this with your life and make sure it gets to Aislinn personally. You must not give it to anyone else. Understand?"

166

Gemedes only nodded in agreement and placed the potion in his pocket for safe keeping. In a flash, Ananais had on a long, hooded cloak, which concealed his entire body, a pair of boots, and was heading out the front door of the castle.

"So, let's get that bottle to Aislinn." Justahl announced, clapping his hands together.

"Er. I can't yet." Gemedes explained. "I think I forgot something in Ananais's room. Be right back." He yelped behind him as he ran off down the hall.

"But...I thought...Where are you going?" He yelled after him. It was no use, the goblin was already halfway there, all Justahl could do now was follow.

The smell of fresh blood encased him, filling him with the hunger he desperately tried to force down. He knew he shouldn't hunt here, it was wrong and he would get caught but his need overpowered everything else. It intoxicated him, driving him closer and closer to the final choice. He would choose one or the other. Either let them live, or end their life to satisfy the monster inside him. If he was back at home, the choice would be unanimous but out here, his motives changed. Right now he was spying, learning all he could about them without being recognized. Killing one of them in broad daylight would get him noticed for sure and now wasn't the time to alert anyone of his whereabouts. But, the blood smelled so good.

"Ughh." Cynric shouted in frustration before grabbing his mouth. He quickly looked around to make sure no one heard him but, his fears were short lived. The town square was bustling with fairies, elves, and the occasional goblin or two. It seemed as though they all had somewhere to be, something more important to tend to; more important than his momentary lapse of control.

In a flash, he was in an abandoned alley, peering out into the busy cobblestone streets in front of him. The sun beat down on them, making them all the more tempting and seductive. Their sweet blood beckoned him forward, begging him to lose control again and just feed but, he knew what his task was and eating was not a priority right now. He would just grab something once he was safely back in

Chicago.

To be honest, he hated the city life. The constant noises, from the sirens to the gunshots, it drove him crazy. And he wasn't even going to think about how furious the incessant music from the ice cream truck made him. It had to be the most dreadful noise in existence and Chicago was overrun with them. Late at night, while he studied over last minute details, he swore he could hear the song blasting through the streets below. He was glad this battle would be over soon, he greatly missed his home in Moliston.

Thinking about Moliston brought up another priority, Harlem. The warlock was supposed to meet him over an hour ago. Wondering where he was, Cynric stepped towards the mouth of the alley, just far enough to see down all the streets that lead away from the square. Nothing. Either Harlem forgot or something was wrong.

Just as he was about to pull out his communication device to summon him, a portal appeared deep within the darkest part of the alley. It wasn't smart showing up through a portal in the daytime but, Cynric assumed the creatures of Roanke Island were used to Harlem's uncustomary ways by now. He had lived here for over fifty years.

"Cynric," Harlem began, "I see you have made it safely. Are you enjoying yourself?"

Cynric looked at him in complete awe, "Are you serious? This place is horrid and I fail to see how anything, let along you, survives here. Is it always this crowded?"

Harlem laughed heartily before answering with a flat out, "Yes. It's always crowded in Mazikeen City. However, it is particularly crowded today because of the ceremonies later this evening. The castle will be hosting its annual Christmas Ball tonight and of course, yours truly," He made a wide gesture to his entire ensemble, "Has made the guest list. Care to join me? The invitation stated I could bring a friend and since we both know I have no use for those, I guess you will do."

"As flattering as that sounds, I decline. You can go if you wish but, no part of me wants to be anywhere near that castle until I'm destroying it next week." He answered sarcastically.

"Suit yourself. Perhaps I will ask Amara, she seems innocent enough." Harlem replied casually, then, his tone changed drastically. "Look, over there." He pointed to a figure in the distance, "Is that? No it can't be him."

Cynric was confused. He stared intently at the hooded creature on the opposite side of the large fountain that sat in the middle of the square but, no one he knew came to mind. "What are you talking about? Who is it?"

In the time it took him to turn around for an answer, the warlock was already halfway across the square. He was headed straight for the figure in black. All Cynric could do was follow. Luckily he had splurged for the twelve hour transformation potion instead of the four hour one he and Harlem had agreed on at first.

Harlem was just touching the creature's shoulder when he arrived to stand beside him. His face was full of questions he knew couldn't be answered right now.

The figure turned and nearly backed into a rolling cart of apples. Quickly, he tried to turn and leave but, Harlem was faster. Grabbing him by the arm, he turned the poor thing around and got right up in his face.

"What are you doing Ananais? I thought they killed you centuries ago." Harlem roared.

Ananais turned his gaze to them both, his eyes sizing them up. Possibly debating on whether he could take them both on. Cynric assumed he decided against it, for now anyway. In a quiet but harsh tone, he spoke to Harlem for the first time. "Well, well, well, if it isn't my old friend Harlem. Let me guess, you're coming to buy an outfit for this evening?" Harlem just glared. "No, well in that case you must be here to scope out the area for next weeks' battle, right?" Ananais laughed heartily at what appeared to be an inside joke.

Harlem wasn't amused but, Cynric was the first to speak. "How do you know when the battle will be? Are you psychic?"

This Ananais fellow looked harmless but, something about the way Harlem glared back at him made it seem otherwise.

"You must be Cynric. I'm sorry we haven't officially met. I've been meaning to contact you for months but, time flies when you're training a goblin to protect against mind control. Which reminds me, I fail to see how either of you came up with such a brilliant plan. It was hard for Seth and Aislinn, for a few weeks, but I would gather you already knew they weren't affected anymore. Hence the reason for your visit to the island." Ananais smiled viciously. "As for you Harlem, I suggest you find yourself another date for this evening because, I can personally guarantee he," he pointed in Cynric's direction, "won't be on the guest list." With that, the man turned on his heels and started to walk away but, at the last minute he shot a mischievous smile straight at Harlem. "Play nice Harlem, I'm not dead and I'll be watching your every move." Then, he vanished, leaving them both stunned.

"What the hell was that about?" Cynric turned on Harlem for answers but he quickly regretted it. The warlock was having some kind of episode and appeared to be hyperventilating. They needed to get off these crowded streets and find somewhere to regroup.

Just then, Cynric spotted a young female fairy. Her hair hung down past her waist in rings of golden brown and her eyes were a fierce teal color when the sun hit them just right. He knew it was risky but, Harlem was going to freak out if they didn't find somewhere quieter to be. Turning towards the girl, he all but shouted out, "Where is the nearest hotel? My friend is in desperate need of a place to lie down. He has panic attacks."

In a matter of seconds, the girl was leading them down the streets and away from the square. The farther they got, the more relaxed Harlem became. By the time they had reached the hotel, he had calmed down completely and looked more furious than crazy.

Cynric bowed to the young fairy, whose cheeks flooded with blood, and literally ran through the doors of the hotel. He had to get away from her scent, it was driving him bonkers and the blushing didn't help at all. His hunger had returned and although he didn't attack the girl, he couldn't say the same for the room service guy. The monster had come unleashed. Now the only evidence of the fairy's existence was his ragged, bloody clothes which lay strung around the room. He was a demon again.

The room seemed out of place when Ananais wasn't present. Almost eerie but, Gemedes knew what he came back for. He raced across the stone floor, nearly slipping on the Oriental rug in the middle of the room. Glancing around, he noted several potions sitting on countless shelves, thousands of books in numerous languages he couldn't speak, at least a dozen ingredients in jars he had no name for but disgusting, and finally the largest book in the room jumped into focus. A warlock's spell book is just too tempting, he thought, then, he snatched it up in his hands and placed it on a nearby table.

Skimming through the pages, he began noticing how complicated some spells really were. After a few moments, he found one that looked simple enough to conjure, so, he read off the supplies he needed to complete it.

A Simple Transformation
Ingredients:
Someone or something to transform
Fairy Dust

Only two ingredients, he thought, that should be easy. He looked around for the dust and an empty container he could change. When he found that, he went back to the spell and read the directions. Following them exactly, he placed the container on the floor behind him, grabbed a handful of dust, and had just released the dust over his shoulder when he heard it.

Justahl ran into the room and began shouting, "What are you-"

Gemedes turned when the light flashed behind him, his palm pressed over his eyes. Opening his fingers slightly, he peered out, fearing the wrath he knew was coming for him in a matter of seconds. To his surprise, all that stood behind him was a goat. A goat. He raced to its side and picked up the container he'd meant to transform.

"If the container is still intact," He wondered out loud, then, it sunk in and he didn't dare finish that sentence.

Even as a goat, Justahl was scary. He cried out, his hoofs reaching up to knock at Gemedes's face.

Gemedes backed into a corner, holding up his arms in defense. "I'm sorry man. Really. Please just calm down and I will find a counter spell to change you back." He begged again and again.

Ananais stormed through the door, "What is going on in here and why is there a goat in my room?" The warlock screamed.

"I can explain." Gemedes started but, decided it was better to just leave the accusations up to him.

"Also, why is my spell book out? Gemedes, have you been doing magic?" He asked calmly while placing the book back on the shelf.

"Um. Yes." He answered quietly.

Ananais was still calm as he politely told him to get out before he caused more damage. "I'll get Justahl back to normal. Just please do what I asked. Alright. Nothing else."

Gemedes just bowed and left the room quickly. He was still apologizing when the door shut behind him.

Harlem hurried about the hotel room, wiping here and there, searching for any evidence Cynric might have left behind. He knew it was pointless to be so obsessive but, a bloody hotel room could cause real problems in the city. Problems they couldn't afford now that Ananais was aiding the princess.

"Tell me again how you know Ananais and how he being in the square was a bad thing? You seemed surprised to see him alive. Why?" Cynric was still asking questions he couldn't answer just yet. He still needed time to process everything.

Ananais was helping the fairies, that much was obvious but, to what extent? Was he just around to scare them off or was he actually planning on fighting in the battle? All these questions and more flooded Harlem's mind, making it impossible to concentrate on Cynric's constant interrogation. He needed a moment so, he fled from the room to collect his thoughts. No one, not even the demon king, was ready to see him lose his mind.

Cynric didn't follow, which was best. After making sure he had secured the room, he retreated back out into the streets of Mazikeen City. He still hadn't found an outfit for tonight's celebration and the hours were ticking by faster than he wanted. So, with his demon comrade in for the night, he decided to go shopping. He would need a grand ensemble and luckily he knew exactly where to go to get one.

Seth was filling hundreds of bowls with green and red glistening balls while Dest helped Justahl hang the lights and garland throughout the castle. Tonight's ball had to go off without a hitch, otherwise Aislinn would have them all hung up in the dungeon for sure.

She and Amara were off getting ready somewhere, leaving Seth in charge for a while, which infuriated him even more tonight than usual. He was about to just throw the lot of decorations out the nearest and highest window he could find.

Celebrating, he thought, with a deadly battle getting closer every day. It was sheer madness but Aislinn assured him cancelling it was out of the question.

"If I cancelled the party Seth, it would only make things worse. I'm trying to lend comfort to the families in the kingdom right now and not celebrating Christmas would just make them crazy with fear." Aislinn had practically shouted at him just for mentioning such a thing. After that he had dropped it completely and decided it best to just go along with whatever she wanted. At the time, he hadn't realized he would be the head of the decorating committee.

He threw his hands up in the air, nearly knocking over three bowls in the process. "I've had it. This is worse than our senior prom last year. Aislinn dragged me into decorating for that as well and I hated it. I'm not about to get manipulated into another job like that again. She gets me to help and then, when it's time to decorate, she disappears, leaving me to do everything. Well, not this time. I'm done with this."

Justahl just burst into loud guffaws of laughter while Dest just stared in confusion. "I didn't know you all had a prom. I thought that was a human tradition?"

173

Seth knew he shouldn't laugh, it broke into his manly outburst but he couldn't help it. "People always give credit to humans, when in fact, the idea to hold a dance to symbolize one's ascend out of one stage of life into the next, is an ancient Gaelic tradition. We only call it a prom to mock the humans of earth. It's quite silly, parading around in extravagant ball gowns, pretending to be happy about becoming an adult. Actually, it's just the opposite feeling for most of us because, we know we can no longer hide behind our innocence. We must grow up fast, become warriors for the cause. Does that sound merry to you? No, it doesn't. The humans on the other hand don't have to worry about being in constant deadly wars, they can choose their own destiny and joining their army is optional. Here, on Roanke Island, it's mandatory and punishable by death if you refuse." He paused for nothing more than a dramatic effect, then, answered sharply. "But, all that aside, yes, we have a prom. Anything else you want to know?"

"Nope," Dest shook his head, his mouth still gaping in shock. "I think I better go find Aislinn, since her head of decorations has gone mental." He disappears out of the foyer in an instant.

Justahl comes over and slaps him on the back, "You really know how to put on a show." Then, he looked down at his hands, "Can you at least help me finish hanging these lights? I can get Gemedes to finish the bowls and stuff."

"Exactly how are you going to get him to agree to help you? I thought you shunned him after he turned you into a goat earlier today?" He asked, trying not to start laughing hysterically.

"I'm still not entirely over that one but, I'll manage if it means you don't lose control over your emotions. We all know how that works out." Justahl replied with humor.

Seth nudged him in the arm, "Oh shut-up and hand me those lights." He began climbing a ladder to reach the ceiling. "I'm sorry about going completely insane since Dest arrived. It's going to take some getting used to. Plus, with Quid's training and the coronation ceremony only a month away, my emotions are through the roof. Is it wrong for wanting my brother to still need me to protect him? I feel helpless now, unwanted. He seems so in control of everything, I sometimes wonder if he should be king instead of me."

"Don't say that. Your father was a great king and you will be to, you just have to allow people to help you. No one can carry the weight of the world on their shoulders no matter who they are. Not even King Galiron can do everything by himself. Why else would he have asked your father to rule over the elves? Sometimes it's okay to show weakness because, it makes you human. Lose your humanity and you're no better than the demons we fight to destroy every day."

Seth allowed Justahl's words to sink in, causing him to remember King Galiron and his father's last moment together. Yeah, some friend he turned out to be, he thought but all he said was, "To be quite honest, I just wish I could take Quid's place forever. He's all I have left and I can't bear the thought of losing him. You must know how I feel?" He put down the lights he was holding and turned his body so he could look down at his friend.

"Better than anyone." Justahl smiled. "If I could have split myself apart and took Peitar's place, I would have but, he knew what he wanted. Just like Quid knows what he wants. It's our job to support their decisions and be there to back them up." His head bowed slightly just as a tear ran down his cheek. "I only wish I could have come to this revelation before he was killed but, I don't want you making the same mistake Seth. Your brother is stubborn but he knows what he wants just like your father. It's hard to accept but, that's the way things are. I guess what I'm saying is, just be there for him and always back him up no matter what. You never know what could happen to him. One day he will take over for you and you're the only one who can prepare him for that."

They both stood quietly for a few moments before Seth spoke up. "Thanks Justahl but, I don't know that I'm ready to be king yet, let along set an example for him to be.

"Yeah. Sometimes I feel the same way about being a knight. I constantly ask myself whether I'm good enough, especially after Peitar's death but, then I remember what my father told me once. 'Being a good fighter doesn't make you a good person, it just makes you faster than the rest. A good person is someone who can love with all their heart, believe in the impossible, and follow what they know is right.' In my opinion, if you can say you do all those things, then, you're ready to be king. You won't always know the answers to everything but, if you believe in yourself and trust your heart, it will never let you down. I'm not worried about you Seth; you're a good person, well when you're not armed or aggravated. I truly think you'll be an amazing ruler, just like your father."

"That means a lot to hear you say that Justahl. Really. I think Peitar would have liked this side of you, you know. He was always telling you to let your emotions show and tell people how you really feel. This Justahl would make him proud to call you his brother and it makes me honored to call you friend." Seth replied softly before stepping down off the ladder he had been using to reach the ceiling of the foyer. He walked back to the far side of the room and gazed out at their work. "It's fantastic. Aislinn will love it."

"What am I going to love?" A voice sounded behind him, nearly making him jump out of his skin.

Turning, he noticed her face was only half made up, which made him giggle in response. Other than that, she looked absolutely radiant. Her dress was made of a deep red silk, covered by a layer of tiny green stones. The bodice matched the green jewels and wrapped around to lace up the back. The arms were long, green, and nearly touched the floor. It was the most amazing dress he had ever seen her wear and the shoes on her feet matched perfectly, glistening green with red rubies all over them.

Dest's arms wrapped around her. "Doesn't she look ravishing? I mean, really Aislinn, where did you find this dress?" His hands skimmed down her bodice.

She blushed, eyeing him shyly. "I had it custom made for this occasion nearly five months ago, although at the time I wasn't sure if we would be having a ball or not."

"Well, it's a good thing you are. No one will be able to keep their eyes off you. I'm afraid I won't get a chance to dance with you." He laughed lightly.

"Don't worry; I'm saving a special dance for you. Now, if you three are good on decorating, I will finish getting ready." She eyed each of them before lightly kissing Dest on the lips and disappearing back down the corridor to her dressing room.

"You two seem happy." Seth noted.

"Yeah. I really like her. Actually I think I've fallen in love with her. She's so perfect and I can't imagine my life without her. That's why I'm going to ask Queen Andorra if I can move here permanently but, don't tell Aislinn. I want it to be a surprise alright?" Dest whispered.

Justahl only nodded in approval before leaving to retrieve Gemedes to help finish.

Seth just stood there, shocked, horrified. Not only was this creature stealing his best friend for a few months, now he had to make it all official and stay forever. It was cruel and nothing good would come of it for him. Aislinn already spent every waking moment, and well sleeping moment, with him. How would it be if he lived here in the city or worse in the castle? After the battle was over, he and the other elves would return to Elventrale where he would be crowned king after the New Year. Where would their friendship be by then? Nonexistent? She would never admit it but, it was true. They had finally grown apart. All these years of growing up together, spying on the council meetings, building clubhouses in Frost Forest, and skipping rocks on the river. Everything they'd been through would be nothing but a distant and hazy memory. Dest living here pretty much put the icing on an already cooled cake.

He realized a moment too late that he had been staring Dest down like a lion on the hunt because, Dest was already shaking him out of his silent thoughts. *Good going Seth*, he thought, *now he really thinks you're a mental case*. So, before he could embarrass himself more, he left the fairy standing alone in the foyer. He didn't know where he was going to go but, anywhere was better than there.

Chapter 15

Silent Promises

The guests were making small circles on the dance floor. Round and round they spun as the orchestra played. Everyone seemed happy and the room was filled with laughter and smiling faces.

Harlem leaned against one of the marble columns of the council room. He used to love the Christmas Ball. In fact, before meeting Cynric, this event was the highlight of his whole year. Since he was always the best dancer and always the best dressed, he knew how to make an entrance. This year, everything about this celebration made him sick. If Cynric's plan went off without interruption, every creature in this room would be dead; with the exception of one.

Well, he thought, *there's no reason why I can't have a little fun tonight.* Perhaps he could call in a few dragons or start a fire in the kitchen. *Anything to liven these creatures up a bit.* Then, he remembered the one person in the room who would stop him no matter what he tried. So, whatever his plan was, it had to be subtle and he had to keep Ananais in the dark.

"Who are you trying to keep in the dark?"

His voice was in Harlem's head before he appeared. Ananais stood beside him, a too friendly smile sweeping from ear to ear across his face. "I see you still know how to appear out of nowhere."

The warlock, who he still couldn't believe was alive, clucked his tongue in disappointment. "Still not convinced that I know every move you'll make before you decide it yourself?" He shrugged, "I guess time will tell. Anyways, I just came over to make sure our guest of honor was enjoying himself this evening?"

"Hm." Harlem replied. "I think the party is lacking in excitement. Don't you? The food is-"

Ananais cut off his words, "Speaking of the food, doesn't that pig look," His eyes cut over to him, "Succulent?" Bursting into hysterics, he disappeared.

It took all of Harlem's already shaky control, to keep from going after him. But, this act would only jeopardize his chances of speaking with Amara later tonight. His old nemesis would get what was coming to him but, not here, not now. However, the images of his childhood couldn't be controlled like his anger. Reigning in those memories would be impossible.

It was years ago, when Ananais and he were the best of friends. Actually, they hadn't become enemies until Ananais married and moved to Roanke Island instead of remaining in Russia, where they were born. Harlem could never shake the feeling of abandonment, it pierced into his soul, turning it black and unforgiving. He hadn't forgotten it but, was forced to relive it every night when he went to sleep. Everything from their warlock training at school, to the afternoons they spent dueling in one of their backyards. There was one memory he wanted to forget, the afternoon when Ananais turned him into a pig. They were both eleven and had just got home from learning transformation spells at school that day, when it happened.

"This won't hurt a bit Harlem. I promise." Eleven year old Ananais called, as he gathered fairy dust in his hands and began reciting the spell. Then, a flash of smoke went up and Harlem's body was replaced by the body of a fat, pink pig.

"Ah. Fun times. Fun times." Ananais's hand came down on his back, snapping him out of his reverie.

He turned around, glaring into his eyes. "I would appreciate it if you would be so kind as to leave me alone! What are you playing at?"

"Me? Playing? I would never."

In the same second it took Harlem to wrap his hands around Ananais's throat, he was back across the room, twirling a fairy around on the dance floor. Sighing, he mumbled under his breath, "I won't stoop to your level. I've grown up since then."

"So have I." Ananais spoke inside his head, while his body spun to the music.

As Harlem ascended the stairs, he had one last thought. *This battle should be interesting.*

"Or not." Ananais appeared, then, disappeared again.

He was about to leave, but her glittering golden wings stopped his retreat. Now was the time to speak with her. So, after taking a deep breath to calm his nerves, he stepped into her path.

"Oh. Hello Harlem. I didn't expect to see you here tonight. What no menacing demons to keep you company?" Amara laughed bitterly, stepping around him in the next second.

"I just need a moment of your time." Harlem pleaded, his hand coming down on her shoulder.

She giggled, "I'm sure I don't want to hear what you have to say. You must want to talk to my sister, since she's the leader of this army. I am but a mere weapon in her eyes; something to use in order to destroy Cynric's plans. Now, if you would excuse me, I see one of my school friends." Her wings fluttered as she tried to pull away from his grasp.

He looked down at her outfit for the occasion. It was magnificent. Deep green with a golden, swirling design which could only be pure gold and that was just the skirt. The top was a corset, revealing just the very top of her breasts; it was pure gold as well, with long, velvet green sleeves that cascaded down to her waist. Then, there were the accessories, which included; a golden crown encrusted with emeralds and jewelry to match. No wonder her wings were gold tonight, instead of the usual teal hue.

"This is about your sister." Harlem whispered, then, he started walking out the doors to another part of the castle. Privacy was the number one priority.

After allowing her to catch up, he found a deserted sitting room in the west wing. He had to hand it to Galiron, he sure knew how to decorate. The room was mixed with shades of red, gold, and orange. It was warm and inviting, which would work to his advantage since he was about to discuss Amara becoming a traitor. "Sit down." He spoke with just a hint of hostility, making sure she knew he meant business.

"Just who do you think you are, ordering me around in my own house?" Amara scowled, her eyes trying not to look directly at him. She failed miserably and as soon as he caught her eye, she fell onto the couch behind her.

Harlem was glad he had mind control on his side. "I've called you in here to discuss something with you. First, I want you to tell me the truth, how do you view your sister?"

She shrugged, "I don't know. She's trying her best to prepare everyone for this war but, I fear she can't do it alone and she refuses any help I offer." Amara paused for a moment, then, continued. "My sister still sees me as a child, too young to be involved."

"Trust me, Aislinn won't hesitate to involve you in the battle." Harlem pushed. "What if I told you she's just denying you opportunities to show you're better than her? I see it in your eyes; you're in desperate need of adventure. You long to be free from her constant authority. Right?"

"No. I love Aislinn, she's my sister and only wants to protect me. Although, she could loosen up a little now and then, but I don't mind too much. She's trying to ensure my safety." Amara rebuked.

"Yes, because your safety is the only thing that matters." He argued sarcastically. "Don't you see? She's not worried about you anymore, or at least not the way you think. Aislinn is a leader now and just what do you think would happen if your father wasn't around anymore? Well, I can tell you. She will take over as queen and you will have no choice but to bow to her. Nothing you say will matter because she'll be constantly in council meetings or traveling around the island. You will be nothing to her. I wouldn't be surprised if she didn't force you into the human world and make you go to college. Think about it. Do you really want to sit here and let her take over?"

Amara just sat, staring at him in silence as the words sunk in. Then, she spoke with hesitation, "What are you getting at exactly? How can you offer me anything more?"

Harlem smiled. This was the response he was wanting, and he didn't even have to push her into it. "I can offer you a life without want. After Damien and I infiltrate this island next week, nothing will be spared unless one of us says so. Therefore, if you agree to come back to Moliston with us, I can guarantee your life. The choice is yours princess but, let me remind you, this is a onetime offer. Come next week, you will have one chance to decide, after that time has passed, you can't change your mind. So, I will let you think about it and when you have made your decision, let me know."

"You can guarantee that I survive? What will my life be like there?" She asked mildly.

"Of course. I have great pull when it comes to Cynric. He will let me have what I want. As for your life there, I can promise you will have more freedoms. You can come and go as you please and you will never want for anything again. The brothers are quite fond of creatures who side with them; they will make you a queen of sorts."

Her lips pursed slightly as she considered his words. "I'll let you know on the night of the battle but, I ask that my sister be kept alive as well. You can destroy this island but, she gets to live. Do we have an agreement?"

His head bent slightly, place a gentle kiss on her hand. "You have my word. However, she will have to live as a mortal and will no longer have her wings."

"Fine. As long as she's alive I won't argue." She replied shortly, then, got up and left the room.

Harlem grinned widely for a few moments before returning to the party himself. *One thing down, one to go*, he thought.

Gemedes knew he shouldn't be nervous but, he really didn't want to mess this party up. So, Ananais had suggested he just stay up on the balcony that hovered over the entrance of the council room. The ball was in full swing, with the large pine, in the middle of the room. It was trimmed with gold, red, and green decorations, glistened with twinkling lights, and had a large red bow on top that cascaded down on all sides. Lighted garland covered every inch of railing on the steps, which lead from his balcony to the marble floor below, and large glittering balls hung from the ceiling in no particular pattern.

We pulled it off, he thought to himself, even with the battle looming over us, we're celebrating. Christmas was his favorite time. The season meant extra rations for his people, shorter working days, and a glimpse of happiness he never saw throughout the year. However, after they won the war, he was demanding better conditions for goblins. They deserved it just as much as anyone else.

Just then, he remembered the remaining fairy dust he had in his pocket. After turning Justahl into a goat, he was hurried out the door and didn't have time to put it back. So, he put it in his pants pocket. The same pants he was wearing now.

Grabbing the dust in his hands, he began thinking of ways to get rid of it safely. Coming up short, he decided to concentrate on something else. He had just pictured himself as a younger goblin, lying in a field of grass, while a flock of geese flew overhead, when he heard the laughs from below his feet.

Peering down, he noticed Harlem, his eyes glaring up at him. No, he was staring at the hand which held the dust. Suddenly, everything made sense. The black dust, trickled out from the cracks in between his fingers, making its way to the exact spot where Harlem stood. It landed in his snow white hair.

In the time it took him to come to his realization, Harlem was already standing beside him, furious.

"What are you doing with that?" He screeched, opening his hands as he spoke. "I was trying to make the sleigh outside fly, not change the reindeer into geese. Explain yourself."

Gemedes frowned, "I was just thinking about geese, honest. I never meant to interfere with your spell. Actually, I didn't even know the dust was leaking out until I saw you. I'm really sorry but at least the sleigh is flying now." He laughed dryly.

The warlock threw his arms in the air in defeat, then, disappeared. In his place stood the one person, Gemedes didn't want to see, Ananais.

"What is going on? Please tell me the geese stunt wasn't your fault." He asked.

"Not exactly. It depends on your definition of fault." Gemedes answered genuinely.

Ananais sighed, "Just give me the dust and I will pretend it was all a joke." His hand shot out to take the fairy dust.

"Harlem was the one who did the magic, I swear. I just thought about the geese." He added while slipping the remaining powder into the warlock's hand.

"Well, in that case, you may have saved those children from death. So, I guess I should be thanking you." Ananais said. "Just make sure he doesn't come back and I won't mention any of it to Aislinn. No need to alarm everyone." Then, he descended the stairs to change the geese back.

After Ananais was out of sight, Gemedes started doing his happy dance--consisting of several moves he'd witnessed while studying some street performers in Chicago-- and wasn't paying much attention to where his dance steps took him. Justahl fell down the stairs first, hit the table of food at the bottom, and sent the pig flying through the air into an un-expecting Harlem, before coming to a rolling stop in the middle of the council room. He knew he should just act like he hadn't seen what happened, it would have saved him more embarrassment, but instead, he ran down the stairs to help the fairy up.

"Sorry Justahl." He apologized over and over again as he helped lift him off the floor. All the eyes in the room stared at them so, he decided to direct the attention elsewhere. Noticing Harlem, still holding the pig, he spoke, "At least we didn't lose the pig. Look," He pointed to where the warlock stood, "Harlem caught it. That's a relief." It worked, everyone got back to what they were doing before the interruption, with the exception of Ananais. He just stood there, laughing about something, his gaze switching between Harlem and the pig. More than likely it was something less interesting than it appeared, so, he left the ballroom.

Gemedes knew Harlem wouldn't try anything else, at least not tonight. Whatever his plan had been, he had been outsmarted by a goblin. A goblin that now held his head a little higher, knowing he had finally shocked Harlem. Something was definitely changing inside of him and it was good change. He was a warrior now and for the first time since hearing about his ability, he felt like a true protector. Even if he had destroyed the food and any chances of patching up the transformation incident with Justahl; it was nice to feel needed.

Chapter 16

Beginnings End

"I realize that Justahl but, I can't help it. We no longer have that luxury. Putting anyone in the caverns now would only allow for a massive death trap. It's out of the question. Any other ideas?" Aislinn was bushed. She had done nothing but doze on and off for the last few days, and the effects were beginning to wear on her. The entire council was in an uproar and for good reason.

Years ago, before the Mazikeen castle was built, her father decided to have a series of caverns built one mile beneath the surface-just in case trouble ever presented itself and they needed to make a quick retreat. Complete with hidden passages, chambers, medical supplies, running water, and food, the place could hold thousands for at least a month if necessary. Now, this same safe zone, looked like it could cave at any moment. There was no way to fit five hundred children and elders in there without risking every last one of their lives.

She knew what her father would do; send them all through a portal to the safe house in Italy. The only problem was, she had no idea if it was still standing or not. One way to find out, she thought shortly, I'll call Elana and get more information.

Elana was her cousin from Rome, Italy. She was a fairy and an amazing protection knight; she served on the council there and had just been promoted to second in command a few years ago. Aislinn hoped she was still alive and knew about the safe house. If not, the children and elders would have to risk the caverns.

"Please continue to discuss ideas. I will return in a moment. Seth?" Her head turned to stare at her best friend. He plucked at his fingers in boredom. "Seth? Can you watch over the meeting until I return?" That got his attention and before she could even blink, she was in the hall calling Elana on her communication device.

Luckily, her cousin picked up after two rings. "Hello."

"Hello Elana?" Aislinn asked. "Is that you?"

"Yes this is Elana. May I ask who this is?" Elana asked mildly.

"Oh, I'm sorry, this is Aislinn Celthric from Roanke Island. I know it's a little inconvenient but do you happen to know anything about the safe house located there?" She crossed her fingers and hoped for the best.

In moments, Elana was discussing how the building had caught fire, burned to the ground one night last April but, she also told her about the rebuilding of a new safe house--one that was still standing and needed some life in it.

"What did you have in mind cousin?" Elana asked in a heavy European accent. "I do hope it involves that cutie of yours."

Aislinn had forgotten how obsessed with Seth she was. Ever since Elana had come to visit a few years ago, she hadn't talked about nothing but him every time they talked. Although Seth hadn't mentioned her at all since she left.

"Sorry, he has to stay here. He's going to become king soon. You should come watch his coronation next month. It should be interesting." She said with a smile. "Now, I will be sending five hundred children and elders to you in about five hours, ready the house for their stay, which should only be for a few nights, and make sure plenty of guards are standing by in case something goes wrong. Understand?"

Elana agreed but still asked, "What's going on Aislinn? You seem upset about something. Is it boy trouble?" She giggled.

"No. It's not boy trouble although I have met someone but, I'll tell you about him later. For now, I just need you to focus on the tasks I asked of you. Discussing the situation in further detail could put your entire colony in danger. I can't risk anymore lives at this time. Thanks Elana and I'll be seeing you soon. Chao." Her finger clamped down on the end button just before she re-entered the council room. Everyone else was still restless, now to put her plan to vote.

In the end everyone agreed except a select few, which didn't matter. Since the majority voted yes, the decision was final and the preparations were made. They had five hours to say their goodbyes and report back to the castle with all the elderly and children. To the elves, this was any creature unable to carry a weapon, they didn't rely on age. In the fairy race, the young were anyone under thirteen and the elderly were over two thousand. According to goblin history they were considered eligible to fight at age nine and no longer eligible after they received black spots on their skin--known as dying spots. All in all there were four hundred and seventy two creatures on the island that couldn't fight. The number who could was well over seven thousand.

At exactly eleven o'clock, the foyer was full of screaming kids, tears, and several tiresome faces. She knew how they all felt. Alone, betrayed, and heartbroken because for many of them, this would be the last time they saw each other. Glancing around, she noticed all the familiar faces, young and old. Creatures she had shared breakfast with at school, known since she was born, or just met in the countless trips she made to town. They all wore the same expression, fear. Every last fairy, elf, and goblin was scared to death for their neighbors, their spouses, and even their children. Some of them lashed out at one another because it was the only way to hide the pain they really felt.

Enough was enough and with a wave of her hand, the room fell silent. "I know this is a hard night for all of you but, let me assure you, this is the only way to ensure the survival of our people. All of us will not survive this battle but, at least we will live on forever through them." She pointed her finger at a few small children, huddled next to their mother, tears rolling from their swollen eyes. Turning to Ananais she added, "It's time my friend. Let us send out our future generations with love and comfort."

Ananais conjured up a portal and in seconds, children were stepping up and disappearing into the swirling purple and black smoke. It circled around them, spinning them to safety and pulling them farther from the battle and the past. It was hard to let go but, Aislinn knew it was the only way to be sure, so, without hesitation, she put on a smile and made her rounds, lending comfort to the creatures who would become her army in a matter of days.

Cynric paced around his tiny Chicago apartment. It wasn't yet dark outside, so, he had to wait a few more minutes before traveling to his demon camp on the other side of town. He couldn't believe it, the night he'd been planning for over a year now was about to be set in motion. In a matter of hours, he would be unleashing his army to invade Roanke Island. Their mission was simple, kill anything that moved, but their motive was much deeper. It was the hatred he felt for his father's death, channeled into each of their bloodstreams, then, intensified fifty times. That was the hatred those monsters felt for that pathetic island and Cynric's only request was to kill Galiron himself.

Donning on his favorite white leather coat and boots, he left the building that had been home for the past thirteen months. He sighed, taking in the magnificent building, then, he lit a match and touched the tip of it to the gasoline. The building was engulfed by a fire so large, he had to step back, just to admire his work.

Earlier that day, he'd surrounded the building in gasoline, leaving a trail that led around the entire bottom of the apartment complex. After this, he went upstairs and poured gasoline into the pipelines, making sure nothing would remain of this mortal residence after he was finished with it. Now that he was done, the flames flickering behind him as he walked away were a reminder that tonight was the start of a new world order. One he would be in control of for eternity. His father would be proud of him.

Everyone had dispersed back to their daily lives, leaving the castle eerily quiet. Aislinn, Seth, Justahl, and Dest sat around the dining room table, discussing possible defense strategies they could use during the battle. Since no one knew the exact time the demons would invade the island, the main issue was where Aislinn and Amara would be in the fight.

"I won't let the entire kingdom risk their lives for our safety, while I sit back and what? Twiddle my thumbs? I don't like that solution at all." Aislinn grumbled.

"Of course you don't." Seth rolled his eyes, then, looked at Dest, "Do you think she should fight?"

Dest cast a smile at her, taking her hand in his. "I'm sorry but, I agree with Seth. We can't risk having you out in the field, the demons will be trained to attack you first and Seth and I will be forced to protect you. Do you want us killed just so you can kill some demons?"

Well, he had her there. Cynric would have specified to kill her and Amara first, just so it would save him the trouble later. In fact, she was pretty sure all the demons that had showed up in the last few months, were after her. His eyes met hers and all at once, she forgot the argument all together. Shaking her head, Aislinn stammered out, "I don't want you all dead but, I can't sit here and do nothing either. Plus, I've been taking care of myself since I was five, which just goes to show you I don't need either of you to protect me. I'm strong, fast, and can hold a sword to anyone day or night."

Seth snorted, "I disagree. Dest here is pretty good with a sword. He proved it during that attack last week with the Ravark demon." He patted Dest on the back.

"Yeah. I bet I can take you anytime." Dest laughed slightly, the way he always did when she was the only one around. It made her smile just thinking about it. "However, I won't, especially since I know you'll want to remain in the castle that night. Cynric will expect you to be fighting, if you're in here, he won't be able to touch you. Besides, that's why Ananais trained Gemedes so hard. No one ever expected you to be in the battle, not even Ananais. With the exception of your father and the demons, everyone will want you here, in the castle, protected and ready to aid the wounded. I can't let you fight and you'll be more useful here. Alright?"

"Sure," She agreed reluctantly, "But, if anything goes wrong, I demand to know immediately." Pausing, she thought of other demands she should make. "Oh, I also demand a communication device to be with me at all times so, anyone who needs my help can reach me with one call. Is that clear?"

"Done." Seth spoke up first, although by this point she half expected Dest to tie her to a pillar if she didn't cooperate. "Now, I'm going to the training grounds to check in with Hunter. You know, see if the any of the new soldiers are worth sending into the fight. I'll return tomorrow with the list." He bowed and left the room in a near run.

Dest rose and pulled her into his arms. His warmth radiated through her body. She couldn't help it, when he held her this close, the entire world disappeared. Then his words brought everything back in focus.

"I'm going to keep close to the castle, just in case something goes wrong here. I won't be very far so, if you need me, just call. Please don't hate me for insisting you stay here. It's really for your own safety. You don't realize how dangerous he can be. The rest of us may die but, even if it's the last thing I do, you'll survive." He cupped his face in hers, "I promise you Aislinn, nothing or no one will hurt you."

His lips pressed down on hers, forcing her mind to shy away from the fact that he knew a little too much about the demons. Something that had struck her as odd before but, it took this new revelation to bring it all into focus. Now, it was clear in her mind. Dest wasn't who she thought he was but, that didn't answer the question of who he really was. Did she dare ask him? No, she would wait it out, see what else he knew about the demons, maybe he had met Cynric and Dimitri before. He had been on the council in Japan so, didn't that give him reason to know a lot about demons, especially the demon king and his brother?

He stopped kissing her and stared into her eyes. "What?"

"I was just thinking that's all."

"About what?" Dest lead her into the sitting room adjoining the dining hall and onto the red love seat. He sat, pulling her into his lap and cradling her in his arms. "Tell me what's troubling you; I swear I won't think badly of you for it."

She hesitated, which she knew only made him want to know more, but where did she begin? Certainly not with her true thoughts, although now would be the perfect time to ask him. They were completely alone and that never happened but, something told her to just keep quiet about the situation. Then, she knew what she needed more than anything. It was selfish but, she had to keep a close eye on him. Just in case he was a spy or something.

"I can't bear the thought of you fighting for me. It would literally kill me to watch you go out there and risk your life, knowing you may or may not come back." She sighed, leaning into him for support. "Ever since you arrived on the island we've been together. You're the only creature I've ever met who can calm me down when I'm upset. I laugh just because you laugh. You make me feel whole again, something I haven't felt in a very long time. I never believed in love but, then you show up and it's like my world shifted so you could be in it. You're the reason I'm even sane enough to talk to you right now. Without you, I would go insane. Please, just stay here with me. Gemedes can block us both if you want." She laid her hand on the side of his face, tracing the line of his jaw, down to the collar of his shirt; he shivered under her touch.

"I was hoping you would say that." Dest laughed. "And yes, I'll stay if that's what you need. Nothing could be the same without you. To be honest, I feel normal around you. Your world isn't the only one that shifted, mine did too. I fell so hard for you, the moment I saw those purple eyes I was lost forever but, it was a good kind of loss. No war could keep me away from you." He caressed her arms, then, spoke the words both of them wanted to say. "I love you."

Her lips widened into a full blown grin, flowing into her soul and leaving her breathless. It wasn't until he frowned that she noticed she hadn't said it back. "I love you too." She whispered. They spent the remaining hours of silence, kissing or just holding each other. It was wrong for her to act so loving when she was questioning his loyalty but, tipping him off that she suspected anything would only make things worse. Every move she made required planning and quick thinking. She couldn't help but feel like the battle had already begun; only this war was between her and the fairy she so desperately loved.

Walking across Michigan Avenue was easier in the dead of night, especially when every city official was on the other end of Chicago, tending to a building fire. Cynric smiled ruefully to himself as he thought about his earlier actions. It seemed so trivial to him but to humans a fire meant death, destruction, and crime, something had to be done and the person responsible would be caught. Right now they would be worried about it engrossing another building but soon, they would be on the hunt. Therefore, he had to release his army tonight, that way he would be long gone before the police started their investigation. No mortal could trace him to a supernatural island, especially one with blocking defenses and disguising spells cast over it. His plan was brilliant.

"It's about time you showed up." Harlem scolded. "I've only been out for oh, I don't know, TWENTY MINUTES!" His arms were folded across his chest which was covered in thick black leather. In fact, his entire outfit was made of tough leather, worked and encased by ancient warlocks long ago. The only reason Cynric knew this was because Harlem bragged about it every time he got to wear it.

"Just be quiet and get inside. I need to get everyone ready to leave in one hour. It will take us nearly five hours to get there and I expect the blocks to be down by then." He hollered back in a violent tone. One he only used when someone got on his nerves. "I assume you're going to travel by portal or something?" They walked into the head office where Frex was packing up the final boxes.

"Don't worry. It will be done by midnight like you asked. Any other demands?" Harlem asked, a hint of the sarcasm he was known for, dripping off his words.

Frex interrupted their bickering. "Er. I have some news from Japan. Galiron escaped this morning." He flinched as if awaiting a blow from Cynric's fist, when he just stood there, he continued. "Jamik and Arriann wanted me to tell you it wasn't their fault. They were in the room the entire time but, when they went to give him his breakfast. Well, the cuffs were there and he had vanished. They searched for hours but found no evidence of his escape. There wasn't even a trail to show where he'd gone."

Cynric sighed but deep down he knew this was all part of his plan. It had been his idea from the beginning to make it seem easy for the king to escape his kidnappers. If he thought he could give them the slip, he would return to the island confidently, making it easier for him to die. But, for now the plan was his own so, he had to at least act upset. "I don't see why it's so difficult to find good help these days. Where are they now?"

"Who? Jamik and Arriann?" Frex asked slowly.

"No. Bert and Ernie. Yes, I was referring to them two."

"Their plane should be landing in about," He looked at the Rolex watch on his arm, "Ten or fifteen minutes. Don't worry, they'll be here in time to leave for the island."

"For their sake, I hope so. Is everything else on schedule? Are the demons ready to shed their human forms and take to the sky?" Cynric asked casually.

"Yes, although some have already shed so to speak. I also coated everything in gasoline like you asked. There won't be a trace that we existed sir." Frex bowed, which infuriated him. He wanted power and respect but, the bowing would have to stop as soon as they returned to Moliston.

"Good. We leave in thirty minutes, so I suggest you get a team together to start the fire, preferably involving demons who can travel fast." He stalked out of the room, leaving Frex to his duties. Now to contact Jamik and Arriann, see if they might be able to go ahead and scope out the island with Harlem. It would get them out of his hair at least. Something he needed while making his final preparations for the king's destruction.

"Make sure to watch for aerial attacks, but all together I give you a seven. Yeah like that." Seth cautioned his younger brother. Quid had been in training for nearly three months now and improved drastically since then. Of course, he still wasn't good enough to be in the battle, even if it was still another week away, which it wasn't. Seth knew he had to get him prepared as well as he could, otherwise the demons would destroy him without blinking. "I need you to focus Quid. The real thing is nothing compared to these dummies, like for instance, right now you'd be dead if that grimalkin was real. They may be small but they're vicious if they get their teeth in you. One bite and you're dead." He stepped forward to demonstrate, "The only way to make sure they're dead," His sword came down into the dummies' throat, "Is to cut off their head. Now you try."

Quid slammed the blade of his sword into the dummy again and again but didn't slice off its head once. Finally, he stabbed it right in the throat before ripping it to shreds. Tiny wires splayed out of it all over and its head was jerking sporadically as if it were having a seizure. He stepped back to admire his work, panting from all the energy he used.

"Yes, that would kill them too but, not fast enough. During the battle, you won't have time to mutilate a demon because, at the same time more and more will come up and attack you from behind. Defensive maneuvers are the best techniques to learn during the next few days. I'll make sure you're ready to defend yourself well enough but, I still want Justahl with you at all times. It's just easier with an expert fighter. He'll watch your back."

"Alright but, I'm not a child so, I still get to learn offensive stuff too. Why not teach me that move dad was famous for?" Quid muttered out sharply. "I think it was called the jullar or something."

Seth lowered his head. He hadn't thought about that move in a while, and it had been even longer since he'd seen it. How did Quid even know what it was, or that it existed at all? Sighing, he lifted his sword, motioning for his brother to step back. "It's called the Velar and it requires your complete control over the weapon you're using.

Does your sword fit you good?"

"Does it what?" Quid held up his sword and examined it closely. "I don't know."

"Is it easy to move around and stuff?"

"Oh. Not really. I tried to find dad's old sword, since I used it a lot during our training sessions before he died, but no such luck. You wouldn't happen to know where it is do you? I could kill a fly with that thing." Quid joked, although his eyes held a feeling of despair and hurt within them.

"I put it away after his funeral. Couldn't bear to look at it anymore I guess. Stay here, I'll go get it for you." Seth turned and ran off, nearly disappearing with speed.

Quid had always wanted to be like his brother. He was strong, brave, loyal, and an excellent fighter. Seth didn't know it but, he was kind of his hero. No one would ever take his place and he never wanted to lose him but, he got this feeling like something bad was getting ready to happen. Rising to his feet, he glanced around for any immediate signs of danger. Nothing. Thinking about what Ananais had taught him, he reached out with his mind, trying to find Seth's thoughts. He found him, about a mile away from the Elventrale castle, he was still running pretty fast and they hadn't been but three miles away. His brother would be there in about a minute or so.

It was about five or ten minutes later, when Seth returned. He walked over to Quid and sat a long black case, trimmed in gold, on the rock beside him. "I think this is it, I just hope it isn't ruined or rusted." When he opened the flip top case, he found folds of fine black satin; the sword was encased inside them. "Isn't it beautiful? Not a scratch on it." He held it up to examine it closely.

The blade was engraved with an ancient Gaelic prophecy, surrounded by swirls of deep black metal. Its hilt seemed to grow off from the blade in a spiraling pattern, weaving into a net of metal and green jewels. At the very end was a dragon that seemed to come down and around the entire sword. It was almost as though an actual dragon had been turned to metal and formed into a weapon. Truly a magnificent piece of weaponry for anyone but, to him it was also a piece of his father.

Slowly bowing, he placed the sword into his brother's awaiting hands. "May our father watch over you during this battle and always be there even when I cannot." Seth spoke loudly.

Quid weighed it in his hands for a few moments, before returning back to his training. It was almost as if the sword made him a great fighter. Every demon dummy that jumped out, soon found itself in a tangled mess on the ground, and he even managed to slice off a few grimalkin heads in the process. Overall, it was turning out to be a good idea to let him train. He was almost better than Seth was and the velar came easy to him.

Our father would be proud, Seth thought silently, then, he turned his head towards the heavens and whispered a near silent prayer. "Father, please keep an eye on him. I don't know what to expect in the days or years to come and sometimes I'm lost without you. He's changing into a warrior, just like you always knew he would but, I'm afraid he won't need me anymore. To me, he's still that little child I cradled in my arms last year on the beach, when all our friends and family watched your body drift away. He needed me to protect him then, but now I feel unwanted and alone. I need some kind of guidance from you, show me what to do to help him. You always knew what to say, that's why you were such a great king but me, I'm nobody. Hell, I can't even keep my emotions under control, let along rule our colony of elves. If there's any way you can help us, I would greatly appreciate it but for now, just keep him alive during the battle. I need him more than he needs me."

Screams erupted from all around them. Cries of pain shot through Seth's chest like lighting, striking again and again. It was as if the war had already started. That's impossible, he thought, then, he looked at Quid.

By the time his brother's silhouette came into focus, it was already gone; shooting across the training field, straight for a group of swarming demons. For some reason, his body wouldn't move, it stayed glued in one place; struck with horror and surprise. Finally, his feet started cooperating and in a flash he was in the midst of a heavy battle.

Grimalkins swam around them in herds, revarks popped up in intervals almost like clockwork, and then there were these tiny insect-like creatures that stung his entire body, covering it in spots. They were going to die, if they didn't get back to the castle in Mazikeen City, but it was at least an hour journey on foot. Unless elves started sprouting wings or some miracle happened, they would be destroyed before they could even make it half way there.

Just when he was about to take out another grimalkin, he spotted wings flying overhead. Thousands of fairies were diving in to rescue them from the slaughter, each equipped with a bow and hundreds of arrows. The demons were all but disappearing when he and Quid were lifted into the sky. His brother was scowling in frustration.

"We could have taken them on. I was doing pretty well. How about you Seth? Did you kill any?" The fairy nearly dropped him a couple times, due to all his squirming around.

"Yeah and no, we would have died. That wasn't the only swarm out there; thousands will be coming to take their place. Even if we could have killed all those, and I'm not sure we could have, more would appear. The only option was to retreat back to the castle and head out from there. Aislinn, I'm sure is expecting us. Now quit fidgeting before Edroc drops you." Seth spoke harshly before closing his eyes to keep out the dust.

Back at the castle, things were in a disastrous mess. Aislinn and Dest were trying to get all the wounded sent down to the infirmary wing. Justahl was busy sharpening weapons and going over battle strategies with several hundred fairy soldiers, while Gemedes got the guests drinks and extra clothes if they needed it. He spotted Ananais leaning over a small elf girl; she looked like a rag doll, with deep, gaping cuts covering her entire body.

"What happened to her?" He asked calmly.

Ananais sighed, "I found her nearly crawling across the front lawn. That's how I found out the army had arrived. When I asked her what happened all she said was 'It's starting,' then she went out like a light. She hasn't regained consciousness but, I think if I can just get the bleeding to stop, I can save her. Want to fetch me some towels and warm water so I can clean her wounds?"

He obeyed, knowing the girl would survive at least through the night. That was long enough for her family to say their final goodbyes. Looking around, he noticed several other elves, fairies, and goblins that looked almost as bad. He had to admit, a surprise attack in the dead of night, wasn't a bad idea for Cynric. However, it was horrible for them. The war had begun and no one was safe. In a matter of hours, they could all be destroyed and demons would be allowed to roam the earth without consequence. It was going to be a really long night.

Chapter 17

Vengeance is Sweet

Aislinn paced the stone floor, her mind racing in all directions. Cynric's army was here, which meant the battle was starting whether her people were ready or not. There was no more time to plan or come to an agreement on what to do. The time to fight was rapidly approaching and her father still wasn't here. She thought for sure, that if he knew they were in trouble, some part of him would want to help, but she was wrong. Galiron was either dead or more than likely helping the demons to destroy them all. Either way, they were on their own, and she was their leader.

Dest walked over to her, taking her hand. "Justahl and I are going to fly out, see if anyone's still out there. Can you and Seth manage for a few minutes?" His other hand made tiny circles on her back, making her want to drift off into a deep sleep. He kissed her softly on the head while she mustered up the courage to answer his question.

"Yeah, just hurry back. Having you around keeps me calm." She whispered, then, placed a kiss on his lips. "Love you."

"I love you too and I'll be back in less than half an hour. If we need help, I'll call." He replied before returning to Justahl and setting out on their journey.

He is truly remarkable, Aislinn thought, I only wish he could stay here after the battle.

Seth interrupted her thoughts, "Ananais has healed everyone he can and is resting in his room. I'll send a guard to watch him. Is there anything else that needs to be done? Did Justahl and the others come up with a plan?"

"It's good that he is resting, he'll need it for the coming hours and yes, definitely send Edroc or someone up there to keep an eye on him. Also, send a few guards down to the infirmary; we don't need the wounded to be bothered right now." She thought about all that could be done but, decided it was best to do it herself. "And about the plan, we've decided to send you, Justahl, and Edroc out with an army each. You will be responsible for the outskirts of the island, pushing the demons towards the field just outside the castle. Justahl will take over from about five miles inward and drive them closer and Edroc will be here so, they can't infiltrate the castle. As soon as your army gets finished driving them to Justahl's soldiers, take to the skies and return to the field. Edroc's army will need all the help they can get. Justahl will return shortly after you all do."

Seth nodded as if the plan suited him well enough. "How many soldiers will each of us have?"

She thought for a moment, "Around five hundred all together, fairies, elves, and goblins. That reminds me, where do you want Quid?"

"I want him with Justahl at all times, no matter what. He will stand a better chance with him." He answered suddenly, as if he knew Justahl would make it out alive but he wasn't so sure about himself.

"Alright. Well, go gather your troops and make sure you're ready to leave when Justhal and Dest return." She looked at her father's pocket watch, which hung from a gold chain in her pocket. "You have about twenty minutes or so to prepare." Seth turned to walk away but she caught his arm. "Good luck and I'll see you soon. Please be careful."

He placed a kiss on her cheek, "Don't worry, those demons won't stand a chance against us. It's you I'm worried about; any word from your father?"

Aislinn shook her head, "Nothing. I tried contacting him earlier today but, all I got was static. I'll be alright though, Dest is going to stay in the castle with Amara, Gemedes, and I, so we should be safe. You better hurry and get your weapons ready." She watched him disappear into the crowd of creatures who filled the castle. Gemedes walked up to her.

"Hey princess, are you alright?" He asked.

"Er. Yeah. I'm fine just a little tired is all. Does everyone have enough food, water, and clothes?"

"Yes. Perdy fixed up a large bowl of potato soup and I offered it to everyone; along with water and fresh clothes. Most of them refused because of nerves but, a lot of them took the hospitality with gratitude. Do I need to do anything else right now?"

She patted him on the arm. "No my friend; you have done well so, rest for a bit. After everyone leaves we'll go to our safe room but until then, I just need to be alone for a while."

Gemedes looked at her for another minute or two, then, left to find a couch to lie on. He seemed to be remaining calm about the entire thing, something she hadn't expected but greatly appreciated. If they survived through the night, the goblins would receive an honorary council member and maybe even a Duke, but for now they just needed to wait for news. Aislinn returned to pacing the floor.

Dest and Justahl arrived a few minutes later, carrying five wounded elves; three dozen goblins trailed behind them, but they were in good condition. Gemedes ran to one of the shorter ones and grabbed it up into a tight squeeze.

"It's good to see you Rufus, where's Tawny and Malcolm." He asked, looking around for the goblins he'd just named.

The one he called Rufus bowed his head. "I tried to get to them in time but there was just so much smoke. I'm so sorry Gemedes." Rufus placed his hand on his shoulder, then, limped away-- his right leg had several long gashes on it.

Aislinn started to ask Gemedes who they were talking about but, he just waved her away for the moment. She decided it would be better to let him tell her when he was ready. Dest was already halfway to the infirmary by the time she reached him and Justahl.

"Hey, you all wait up." She called. "I want to go with you, you know see how everything's going down there."

Dest frowned, "Why? It will only make you feel worse. Most of them are going to die before dawn, especially if we are attacked again." He wrapped his free arm around her waist and pulled her along anyway though, which made her happy.

Justahl spoke up then, "Could you take this one Aislinn? He's not heavy at all and I think you might be a bit more gentle with him than I am." He pointed to the elf in his arms. It was a little boy, about the age of twelve, with blonde hair falling in waves around his bloody face. His entire body was covered in scratches and bruises, and his clothes were torn and dirty. She froze and immediately knew who it reminded her of, Seth at that age. It made her shiver just to think about.

Dropping away from Dest's grasp, she wrapped the child in her arms, cradling him like a baby. He looked like he was unconscious, which might have been a good thing if it wasn't for the knot on his head. She worried he might have a concussion, so, she made everyone pick up the pace, in order to get him to the doctor as soon as possible. It still took them about ten minutes to reach the guarded doors, and another two to convince the guards they weren't dangerous.

Inside, the smell of ammonia, vomit, and blood filled her nostrils. It made her gag and nearly drop the tiny elf in her arms, but she got him in a bed before throwing up. Dest just stared, the hint of a smile playing on his lips, while Justahl discussed patients with the doctor. She was about to go back into the hall and wait for them when a female fairy caught her eye. It was one of her friends from school, Gigi.

"Hello Gigi. Are you feeling alright? Can I get you anything?" Aislinn asked hesitantly. She knew the girl was probably thinking,

'No, I'm not alright and yes, you can get me out of here.' But all she said was.

"Aislinn, is that you? Is it really you? I've missed you," Gigi started coughing and blood spattered the stark white sheet laid over her body.

"Shhh. Don't talk. I'm here and I've missed you too." She answered sweetly. "What happened?"

"I...don't remember...exactly. My husband and I...were out in the backyard...working in the...garden...when it hit us." Her friend started coughing again and didn't stop for a few minutes. "The smell was awful and the smoke nearly choked us to death. Gabriel said he couldn't see what was going on, so, he ran off to find out. Did he make it here?"

Aislinn stared at the white floor tiles, trying to remember if she saw him or not. Then, she thought about a few of the bodies the others had drug in. She sighed and placed her hands on Gigi's. "I am so sorry Gigi, but no your husband didn't make it." The fairy only nodded, like she expected the news. She grasped her hand tighter and started to rise and leave but, Gigi stopped her.

"Please...don't go. I want to tell you something important. Don't trust him...he's no good...He has evil in him." With a final cough, blood poured out of her mouth, cutting off her air. She was dead.

"Who's evil?" Aislinn begged, shaking her friend like a rag doll. "Gigi? Gigi? Gigi?" She cried over and over again, as if her cries would make it better.

"Who's Gigi?" Dest whispered. He was standing behind her with an arm full of bandages and rubbing alcohol. "This is for the wounded who aren't bad enough to transport down here. The doctor says it's best for them not to come in. I assume some of the patients are oozing poison out of their wounds and he doesn't want anyone else to suffer from the infections."

Aislinn leaned against him. "I shouldn't have come with you." She asked pointing to the figure beside them. "This is...was Gigi and we were friends in school, I've practically known her my whole life." She paused, "She just died."

He put the supplies on the bed behind them and wrapped her in a hug. Leaning down, he whispered, "I'm sorry for your loss but, we must get back to the others. Seth's army is about to head out now."

Before they left, she unfolded the sheets and laid them over Gigi's face. "Le grá síoraí my friend." Then, she let Dest walk her down the hall, back to the rest of the world.

Soon, the only creatures left in the castle were Aislinn, Dest, Amara, and Gemedes, and they all just sat inside, waiting for news from the battle raging outside somewhere.

"I can't take this." Aislinn raged. "There is no way we can just sit here and wait for all our friends and family to die. They're out there, risking their lives for us and we're just sitting here twiddling our thumbs. I'm going to go crazy."

Amara giggled. "Going to go crazy. I think it's already started."

Dest couldn't help but smile, the two were more alike than they knew, which wasn't a bad thing. Watching them interact and argue was comical and completely entertaining. He turned to Gemedes and whispered, "All they're missing is some mud and bikinis."

Gemedes busted out laughing and ended up having to leave the room to regain his control.

Aislinn glared at him, "What were you two just talking about?"

"Mud." He answered coolly, while trying to stifle another laugh. "You two need to just sit and relax, because neither of you are going anywhere."

Just then a sound broke through on the communication device. It was Seth's voice.

"This is Seth. We've driven them to Justahl and are heading for the field. Meet you all there Edroc." His voice cut off, followed by two responses.

"Copy that. We're heading them toward the clearing. Man there sure are a lot of them and this smoke isn't helping anything at all." Justahl answered.

"I can see the smoke heading this way. Does anyone know what's causing it?" Edroc asked.

"No. I thought it might be some of the demons but, it lingers even after they're gone. Has either of you seen Ananais to ask him?" Seth replied calmly. The sounds of swords hitting flesh could be heard in the background. "Wait, I see him. He's up ahead of us...looks like he's fighting someone or something...is that? Yeah, it's Harlem. I think that might be where the smoke's coming from."

"Alright Edroc, Seth and I are driving the demons to you. Are your soldiers ready?" Justahl asked suddenly, cutting off the earlier conversation completely. Whatever Ananais was doing, it wasn't going to affect the main battle in the clearing.

Aislinn wondered if the smoke would clear before the demons reached the field outside. More than likely it wouldn't, but it was still looking pretty clear out there right now. She paced in front of the large bay window in her father's study. It was the safest room in all of Roanke Island, providing them with a good cover in case Cynric came into the castle.

"I can't see anything happening out there. Can you?" She motioned for Dest to come over and check it out but he just shook his head.

"Nope; I can only see darkness. Wait, I think I saw something go around the castle just now. Grab Amara and get down. I'll go check it out. Gemedes guard them, be right back." He called over his shoulder, then, disappeared out the door.

Minutes ticked away on the clock, but nothing came from Dest or the communicator. All at once, the light went out in their room. Amara scooted closer to her.

"Gemedes, go see if the lights in the hall are out too." She ordered. He did and nodded.

"Yeah. From the way it looks, the entire castle is out. Do you want me to go check on Dest?" He asked, his voice cracking on the end as if he didn't want to but would if she asked.

"That's not necessary goblin." Dest walked into the room and sat down beside her. "There wasn't anyone, just a tree I think."

Aislinn's stomach churned with fear, something was wrong and Dest knew what it was but wouldn't tell her. Maybe he was just scared to in front of the others. Either way it was weird. "Are the lights out everywhere?"

"Oh. Yeah, I doused them with a spell Ananais taught me last week. He said to when the demons get closer. It will make them think the castle is empty and they will be less likely to come inside. Guess I should have told you." He answered calmly.

"Yes, you should have." After everyone in the room calmed down, Aislinn told them to wake her if something happened, then, she drifted off to sleep.

Seth ran through the woods, his bow ready to fire at any sign of movement. The smoke made it nearly impossible to see anything and he had to duck down just to get some fresh air. Whatever this was, it was really causing a disadvantage for them. His army was just reaching the clearing when the screams started. When they stepped through the last bit of trees, it was as if hell itself had opened up right under their feet and Edroc's entire army was right smack in the middle of it.

It took nearly all his arrows just to reach Edroc, who was slicing off grimalkin heads left and right. "It's about time you all showed up. I thought you all were coming behind Justahl to make sure they followed you here."

Another hundred demons swarmed in to take the place of the fallen ones, making it harder to concentrate on anything else, but Seth managed to get out a few words. "We were but, he said to go ahead. It's a good thing too; otherwise you all would be dead." His sword crashed into a revark's skull, causing it to skitter backwards before disappearing altogether.

"Thanks. I guess I owe you, since you're helping me out." Edroc smiled as his dagger sunk into the side of a cresando--a demon with jagged scales all over its body and a wickedly sharp tongue. "Now enough with the chit chat, let's kill these monsters." He raised his sword in a sign of charge, just as Justahl's army filed into the clearing. The demons were trapped.

Seth looked around vigorously for his brother. "Quid? Where are you? Quid?" He cried out in frustration. It was just like him to be missing the best part of the entire fight.

The smell hit him before he saw it, the same demon that had attacked months ago in the woods. It reeked even more now and it's peeling white skin looked disgusting. All of these things came into focus after the main shock of seeing Quid fighting the thing alone, wore off. There he was, sword raised, arms bloody, and shaking, he looked close to death and the demon appeared unharmed. Seth knew he should help him, but what could he do. *That's your brother over there stupid*, he thought, then, he raced across the field, landing two feet behind it.

"Hey ugly," He called out, trying to deflect the attention off his brother. It worked because now the demon was coming straight toward him. Quickly, he took off into the forest, not thinking about what might lie ahead. All that mattered was getting that thing away from Quid. It followed of course and in a matter of seconds they were deep in Frost Forest.

Seth dashed behind a nearby oak tree, trying to buy some time before he had to face the thing again. It seemed eerily quiet out here. The birds didn't make a sound, the leaves were completely still, and the sound of rushing water was muffled by something louder. By the time he noticed all their piercing red eyes, Jamik already had him pinned against the tree, his hands wrapped around his throat.

Arriann stepped into view, clapping her hands together she smiled. "Well done Seth. I didn't think you'd fall for the trap but, I'm impressed. Your stupid brother wasn't so lucky."

"What did you do to him?" He spit out, his voice cracking from the lack of oxygen. Of course it had been one of her tricks. Transforming herself into that demon, knowing he would do anything to lure it away.

"Oh. Don't fret; I haven't done anything...yet." She laughed, grabbing his arms. Her touch sent a wave of electricity through his entire body. It made him want to scream but, he wouldn't let them have that luxury. He remained quiet and didn't dare speak anymore, it hurt too much. "Let him go Jamik. This really is pathetic. Come on, Cynric wants us at the castle."

Jamik growled but released him anyway. He sucked in the air, it burned at first but, eventually he could talk again. "Why is Cynric going to the castle?"

Arriann looked at him, the smile still lingering on her face. "For the king of course." Then, they both bounded off towards Mazikeen castle.

The only thing Seth could think of was his brother, so, he set off to find him.

Moments later, he arrived back in the heat of the battle. The bodies of his fellow soldiers were strewn everywhere and he kept waiting to find Quid's but he didn't. He saw a figure up ahead, only he couldn't make out who or what it was for the smoke. Raising his sword, he approached it slowly. "Who's there?" He called out but the figure didn't move, it only moaned in agony.

Getting closer, he could make out what it was saying. "Help me! Help me! Seth!" It was Quid; he would know the voice anywhere. He rushed to where his brother sat on the ground, kneeling beside him.

"Quid; what's going on? Are you hurt?" Seth's words jumbled together, making him sound like a madman, while his hands secured each place on his brother's body. He wasn't hurt any worse than before, so why was he not moving. "Quid, please answer me." He shook him hard a few times.

Quid turned to face him. "Seth? Is that you?" He threw his arms around him, then, he started sobbing. "I thought…you were dead. It wasn't the demon we fought before, it was Arriann. She made me trick you Seth. I'm sorry. Please don't be mad at me."

He started laughing, "I'm not mad at you and yeah I know who it was. I should have known before. Ughh, I swear when I get my hands on those two again I'm going to tear them to pieces." Seth got to his feet, dusting off his clothes. "Come on, we have to get back to the-"

All at once the world tilted, sending him to his knees, a searing white hot pain sliced through his body. Moments later it was gone and he was being carried away. He looked up but his vision was blurred. The last thing he heard was Quid telling Justahl to get back to the castle, then, everything went silent.

Chapter 18

The Demon Inside

"Aislinn?" Her father's voice called out for her. It was weird, this sense of reality even in the deepest of dreams. It was like he was standing right over her. Someone shook her awake. "Aislinn, wake up. We need to get out of here now. Where is Ananais?"

It was her father and this wasn't a dream. She opened her eyes and peered up at the man she had been longing to see for almost five months now. Here he was right in front of her and all she could think of was killing him. He deserved to die after what he'd done to her, to Amara, to Seth and Quid, and especially for what he'd done to this entire kingdom. She rose and backed away from him. "What are you doing here?"

He started after her but suddenly Dest was in his path, sword held at his throat. "She asked you a question. Now answer her." His voice sounded deadly and didn't shake like hers did.

"I was kidnapped by Cynric's goons but, I escaped this morning. Who are you anyway?" Galiron asked, his eyes not releasing their hold on hers, which was fine, she wasn't afraid anymore.

Dest smiled as if he was expecting this question. "My name is Dest," He extended his hand out in a sign of welcome. "I got here about three days after you disappeared in Japan. Queen Andorra sent me."

Galiron nodded, stepping around him to come face to face with her again. "I know everything. Ananais told me what happened with Seth's father. How could you do that to him? He was your friend and you betrayed him." She turned her face away from him then, making it clear she didn't want to see him right now.

"I was afraid he would tell you something like that. Honestly Aislinn, are you so desperate that you would turn to a warlock for answers. He's not an ally, he's the evil one not me." He spoke clear and precise, as if every word had to sink in before he could continue to the next.

"I don't buy that for a minute. He has been nothing but nice since we found him. Not to mention the fact that he was the only one who could help since you deserted us. Now if you would be so kind as to drop dead, it would really save me a lot of trouble." She shouted back at him. Holding down her anger was going to be harder than she thought. If this thing in front of her was a demon, one wrong move could make it angry, but if it was her father, she would really feel guilty if something happened. "Look, I'm sor-"

Her words were cut off, when the sound of the castle doors being slammed shut broke into the room. Dest grabbed her arm, "Come on. Your father or whoever is right we have to get out of here. Gemedes take Amara and find Ananais. Tell him to get back here immediately. You," He pointed to King Galiron, "Go ahead of us. If it's Cynric, he will want you and might leave everyone else alone."

Gemedes and Amara ran over to the window and climbed down the vines, which covered the entire wall of the castle. Galiron stood unyielding as Dest tried to convince him to move.

"I refuse to take orders from you, now silence." His staff came down, knocking Dest about ten feet back into a stone wall. "Aislinn as your father and your king, I command you to go see what happened down stairs." He must have noticed where her eyes lingered. An unconscious Dest lay crumpled on the floor. "Don't worry, I'll take care of him. Go!" He roared.

She was tired of being told what to do and quite frankly she wasn't sure what his plans were for her friend but, she knew they were bad. "NO! It's you he wants and you he will get." She began chanting the portal spell. "Goodbye father." Moments later, he was being sucked backwards into the swirling purple smoke, his eyes turning a deep crimson red as he disappeared inside. Quickly, she shut the portal and ran to get Dest.

He was just sitting up when she reached his side. "Where's your father?" His face was still beautiful, even if it was covered in cuts from the rough stone.

"I conjured a portal to send him into the foyer downstairs." She pulled him to his feet, making sure he was alright to travel. "Let's get out of here though, just in case Cynric changes his mind." Her hand found his and at once she felt safe, or at least until she saw his face.

He stared at her, his eyes flickering from black to dark blue and back to his natural color. Shaking his head to knock it off, he smiled, "I'm afraid that's out of the question. We have to get to the foyer. Let's go." He shoved her in front of him, causing her heart to race faster and faster. What was going on? Whatever it was, she was going to be a part of it and so was Dest.

Ananais dropped to the ground. His powers were diminishing rapidly and his opponent still seemed to be in peak magical fitness. Harlem towered over him, his hands sparking with golden bolts of light.

"Give up old friend?" He mocked. "Or do I have to finish you off?"

"You will never win Harlem, no matter if I die, others will destroy you in time. This world is filled with more magic than you or I can possibly dream of. Just look down there," His fingers pointed to the clearing below them, where the final batch of demons was being slaughtered by the citizens of Roanke Island. "Good always triumphs over evil; remember that." He could feel the last of his magical energy draining out of him, receding back into the earth where it originated.

Harlem started laughing, "I could care less about Cynric's stupid

213

army of demons. To be honest, he had it coming. Going around for a year and a half, waiting for the perfect moment to unleash his army and get revenge for his father's death. He is just as stupid as his father and deserves the same fate as far as I'm concerned."

Now that was a surprise, Ananais thought the two of them were close. "Then why the war? Why side with him if you're just going to kill him later?"

"Oh no. I'm not going to kill him; someone else will take care of that after he takes care of your precious king. No, I will get out of here alive, after I kill you of course, and start a new race of humans. I will train them to be sorcerers and witches. They will have part demon blood, so they can run fast and fight, and train in magic like you and I. In a few decades, they'll be unstoppable and I'll be their ruler. Can't you see it now? A new world, filled with magic and power. It will be magnificent." Harlem looked up to the sky. "I just wish you were going to be around to see it. Oh well. Goodbye Ananais. I would say it's been fun but, actually it hasn't. You've been like a pebble in my shoe since the day you were born but, that ends tonight." He spun and was just about to stab his cane-which doubled as a sword-into him, when the feeling took over.

It was like a new wave of power rushed over him and he was suddenly stronger than ever. He didn't know how but, he rose from the grass and stood to face Harlem, his fingers sparking back up again. "Now that the emotional, sappy talk is over, perhaps we can return to the rest of this evening's events." Ananais started chanting a counter spell, driving the demons back and lifting the smoke all in one. It was the most powerful spell he had ever accomplished and it didn't take away any of his energy. When the smoke had cleared, Harlem was gone and so were all the demons. The valley below erupted into a single sound of victory, as the wave of power left him. He didn't know where it had come from, but he had a good idea. "Thank you Evangeles."

Just as he was about to descend to gather the wounded, Gemedes raced to where he stood, Amara not far behind. He panted wildly, "Dest...trouble...King Galiron...back...trouble." Then he fainted from exhaustion, leaving Amara to carry him back to the castle. Apparently the battle he thought was over, had just begun.

"Hold on Seth," Justahl begged. "We'll be there in a moment. You can't die on me now, not before I wipe the floor with you at Guitar Hero. Remember, you promised you'd play next week."

It was funny, he could hear him talking but couldn't move his mouth to reply. He slipped back into unconsciousness and when he woke up, he was in the infirmary. Justahl and Quid stood over him expectantly.

"Oh, you're awake." Quid jumped, nearly knocking over the curtains around his bed. "Don't scare me like that ever again."

Justahl patted him on the shoulder as he sat up in bed. "Doctor says you can leave as soon as you want to. It was only a mild concussion."

Seth felt the knot on the back of his head, then, remembered the woods. He leaped out of bed and started gathering his weapons. "Where're Aislinn and Dest?"

Justahl looked at Quid and shrugged. "We don't know. I guess still in Galiron's study. Why?"

He didn't have time to answer questions. If Arriann was right, Cynric was either here or would be in a few minutes. He had to find Aislinn but, he also had to do it alone. "Is the battle over?"

"Yeah; seriously man, are you alright? Maybe you should lie back down." Justahl pushed him back towards the hospital bed. "Quid and I can go check on the others in the field. Come on," He grabbed his brother's shirt and shoved him gently toward the door, which led outside. "Your brother needs his rest."

As soon as the two of them were outside, he got dressed, loaded his bow, and raced off towards the other end of the castle.

"Well, well, well, if it isn't our little hostage. I see you escaped. Good, it saved me from having to kill you unarmed." Cynric was leaning against the fireplace, poking at the ashes with his black leather boot. "I feel as though we should be in black and white. It would make this more dramatic. Oh well, you'll die just the same."

Dest pushed her around the corner, forcing her to look straight

215

ahead. "I have her. Where do you want me to put her?" He asked, his eyes trained directly on the demon in front of them.

"Aislinn, how good for you to be here to witness this. I understand you took over the kingdom in daddy's absence. Let me say, I'm impressed with the strategy the council came up with under your command. Much more effective than those your father used." Cynric clapped his hands together, which were also covered in black leather. "I find you fascinating." He slithered to where she stood, clasped in Dest's arms like a trapped animal. His hand scraped the side of her face slightly, making the hairs on her neck stand up in response. It was a natural born tendency, brought on by thousands of years of hatred toward demonic creatures.

"You're despicable." She spit in his face, hoping it would land in his sick emerald green eyes. "Nothing you say will make me like you, so, why don't you go to hell?!"

He slapped her clean across the face, causing a searing hot pain to spread through her body. "Been there sweetheart and let me just say, it's a lot better than the dump of a town I've been staying in for the past year. Humans are disgusting creatures and really dimwitted. Although the later part of their being comes in handy quite often, especially if I want to trap them to eat."

Her stomach churned at the thought of eating humans. Dest's arms relaxed around her and while Damien walked back over to her father he leaned down to whisper in her ear. "I'm sorry. Please don't hate me for this. I had to do it; it was the only way to keep you safe."

"By bringing me to him? Any safer and I'd be in his arms instead of yours, or better yet why don't you just kill me so, you can say that was for my own good too." She snapped back at him. Cynric was still circling Galiron.

"You have every reason to be mad at me and I understand if you want me to kill you. Trust me, I would be doing you a favor if I did but, that wouldn't solve anything now would it?" He lowered his voice, reminding her to be quiet.

Enough was enough. First, her father shows up and tries to offer her as bait, now, this. It was all too much and she was losing control.

Wriggling free she started to scream at him, "Kill me! If you want me dead, then kill me but let me tell you something," She shoved her finger into his chest. "No matter if I die or not, you will never take this kingdom."

Dest's eyes flashed to Cynric, who had stopped circling her father and was now heading straight toward her. The minutes that passed after that were a blur, one minute she was standing there, her sword drawn to fight the demon who wanted her dead, and the next she was across the room, her sword thrown from her grasp.

"I told you they weren't worth your time. Now look at her, she thinks she has a chance against us." Cynric shook his head as if this bothered him. "I don't see why you just didn't tell her in the first place. It would have saved you both a lot of regret."

Aislinn was confused, "Tell me what?" Her mind reeled at the word 'us,' like Dest had something in common with him.

"That he's a demon sweetie. How did you not notice him? I mean hello, his body feels like an open flame for goodness sakes. Did it never occur to you that he was a little too nice, a little too convincing with his story?"

His words hurt her worse than if he had tortured her to death; each one ripping her in two and driving a knife through her heart. Dest was a demon and she had fallen for him. Was this what the ancients had meant before? This was worse than any pain either of them could inflict on her, actually she would welcome it gladly, just to escape this world where everyone she loved was slipping away. She could feel herself sinking lower to the ground and the feelings she'd been keeping locked down for so long, threatened to surface.

Cynric's clapping startled her, making her flush with rage all over again. "Bravo. I see he wasn't exaggerating when he said you two were in love. Well, I guess this revelation shoots that all to pieces." He turned to Galiron, "Did you know she loved the one thing you hate? The one thing that is killing you from the inside out?"

Her father looked at him, his eyes returning back to their normal purple blue hue--a sign that her real father had overcome the demon long enough to face Cynric head on. "I feel sorry for you."

"What?" That caught him off guard. "You what?"

"I said I feel sorry for you. You will never know what love is. All you'll know is hate, destruction, and fear, and I think that really sucks. I couldn't imagine living without at least a little love in my life. Doesn't it get lonely? Spending all that time by yourself, one of the two people you've ever cared for is dead and the other loves the one creature YOU can't stand. Don't tell me what I feel because it sure isn't hate. I don't hate my daughter for loving him and I don't hate her for hating me. She has every right to despise me after what I've done, but I want you to know Aislinn, it was him not me. This demon inside me is the one who made me kill Seth's father. He was like a brother to me and I let him down. I was too weak to overpower the demon long enough to save him and for that I am sorry. But I'm not sorry for abandoning you while this war was being created. You've grown into such a brave young woman and I want you to know I'm proud of you. You will be a great queen when I am gone and someday you'll probably be greater than I was. You have the one thing I didn't have; true friends who will help you. Don't be afraid of what the future holds because no matter what happens it will always get better. Goodbye Aislinn. I will always love you and tell your sister the same." Galiron's eyes flashed as he tried to fight the demon inside him.

"Oh good. Now that that's over, I can send you back to where you belong." Cynric yawned as if this situation bored him. He swung his sword and sliced through her father's chest, sending a rush of blood and the black blood of the demon, oozing across the floor. He began cleaning his sword, using one of the tapestries as a cloth, then, he was about to leave when he caught her eye. His eyes turned a sick acid green as he walked toward the door, "Take care of that would you." He commanded Dest, who pulled a sword from his belt.

She knew she should fight back but her body wouldn't respond. Her father was gone and the demon was either back in hell or possessing someone else. The sword came closer, held in the hands of her string of sanity.

How could she have ever loved this monster? Was it all a part of his demonic mind tricks? Others had told her about what the demons could do but, part of her wanted to kiss him, while the other wanted to slice his head off. It was like all her emotions, feelings, and fears were being conjured up into this final moment. What happened in the war outside? Did the demons win that one too or was Ananais going to pull through? Amara could take over, that was no problem. Seth would be hurt at first but, he would get over it eventually. He was strong, like his father. He would protect the kingdom and help her sister be a good ruler as well.

Suddenly, instead of the pain of death entering her body, all she heard was a scream.

"GET AWAY FROM HER!"

Seth, she thought, *when did he get here?* She opened her eyes and saw her best friend in one on one combat with Dest, the fairy she thought was from Japan but turned out to be just a spy for Cynric. Speaking of which, where was he? She glanced around, trying to find him but her attention kept being drawn back to the fight a mere two feet away from where she still sat on the stone floor.

"Seth. I don't want to fight you, just leave and no one has to die." Dest argued, his sword coming down and hitting the hilt of Seth's, inches from his shaking hands. Was he injured already or was she just imagining the scars on his arms and face?

"Wrong again. You do!"

Their swords clanked again for what seemed like hours, although she knew that couldn't be true. Sword fights never lasted more than ten minutes, and that was very rare. Then, it happened. Seth's arm faltered, allowing a tiny opening in his defense, and Dest stabbed him in the chest.

Her best friend dropped to the ground with a thump, his eyes opening wide with fear. She raced to his side, cradling his head in her arms as the life drained out of him. His eyes flittered open for a moment, staring straight into hers.

"Aislinn?" He began coughing, blood splattering his shirt as he spoke. "I'm sorry I didn't get here sooner…please forgive me."

She was on the verge of tears but she didn't let it show. "There's nothing to forgive Seth. You've done well soldier." Her words faltered on the last word because soldier was so formal, he deserved something better like brother, or friend, but it took all her strength to say what she did.

"Promise me…you'll keep Quid safe. Make sure he knows how much I love him…and that none of this is his fault." Seth's eyes began to close slightly.

Tears streamed down her cheeks, the little bit of strength she had left vanished. "I promise. I love you Seth and I'm sorry that I failed you. Le grá síoraí. May you rest with the heroes who have died before you." She began whispering the funeral song her father sung at her mother's funeral years ago. They hadn't sung it in years but if anyone deserved it, Seth did. "Goodbye my loved one, my hero, my friend; your time on this earth has come to an end. Hang up your weapons, forget all your pain. Rest in sleep; peaceful sleep."

He grasped her hand, his heart slamming against her chest as she held him closer. Her best friend was dying and there was nothing to do now but watch his life dwindle into nothing. All those years of promising to protect each other were gone, destroyed by the one creature she vowed to kill no matter what. But could she kill him? Seth's heartbeat began to slow and his eyes closed. It was over, he was dead, but instead of sadness, rage filled her entire body; burning her from the inside, out. Yes she could.

She looked up in time to see Dest backing away, dropping the sword to his feet. Her mouth opened to say something when Cynric walked through the door.

He glanced around, noticing the three of them. "Well done. Not the one I was expecting to see dead but outstanding just the same. I would say go ahead and just finish her off but we haven't got the time." Cynric's eyes trained on her, "Don't worry, this war is far from over." He turned to leave, "Come along brother, Harlem is readying the portal to take us back to Moliston." His leather boots glided past her, and out the door.

Brother? She looked up to see, the creature she believed to be Dest, change back into Dimitri. First his eyes changed from their normal sky blue to the color of sapphires. His hair changed became golden with brown highlights and finally his wings dissolved into nothing. He was gorgeous but, it didn't matter, he would never be her Dest again. The trusting, loving, and beautiful creature she'd fallen in love with was not only a demon but a demon prince. Her thoughts screamed in her head as she watched him disappear after Cynric; she hoped he could still hear her, and some part of him would actually care. "I'll never forgive you for this."

He returned for a moment, his dark eyes catching in the fairy light. It made him look wicked and unnatural. Then he spoke, "I never meant for you to love me." Dimitri turned and walked out the door, leaving her completely alone.

Aislinn looked around the room, her father was dead, her best friend was dead, and now the one person who could have saved her was gone too. She felt herself slip off the edge as waves of black oblivion took over and consumed her in darkness.

ABOUT THE AUTHOR

Emily McCombs was born and raised in a small town in Kentucky at Twin Lakes Regional Medical Center on July 29, 1990. As a child she enjoyed drawing and playing dolls with her younger sister. She first learned of her hidden writing talents when she read the Harry Potter series in middle school, but didn't uncover the idea for this novel until she was in her late teens and out of high school. Emily now lives with her loving husband, James McCombs Jr, in an apartment in Sevierville, Tennessee, with their fish and tons of fantasy novels. Although a lot has changed in her life, one thing will always remain; friends, family and God come first, and no matter where life takes her she will always be true to herself and her roots in a small town.

www.ingramcontent.com/pod-product-compliance
Lightning Source LLC
Chambersburg PA
CBHW070454260626
47161CB00004B/1301